"Please allow me to give you a small gift."

The baron's wife smiled and slid a worn plastic bracelet off her wrist.

"Thank you, my lady," Mildred replied with a forced grin, trying to appease the woman. In her time, the garish trinket had been the kind of thing you could buy from a vending machine for a quarter. Nowadays, it was the jewelry of the high and mighty.

However, as the physician reached out to accept the bracelet, the woman roughly grabbed her hand and pulled Mildred closer, staring intently at her face. Then she nodded in grim satisfaction.

"Yes, I thought so!" she shouted in triumph. "Look there—metal! The outlander bitch has steel in her mouth!"

Jerking free from the grip, Mildred stared at the woman as if she was insane. Then the truth of the matter hit her like an express train. Her fillings! Mildred had completely forgotten about the silver fillings in her back molars!

"Close the gate! Protect the baron!" Donovan roared.

But as fast as the sec chief was, Ryan matched his speed, whipping out the SIG-Sauer in a blur of motion, and the two men fired simultaneously at point-blank range.

Other titles in the Deathlands saga:

JAMES AXLER

DEATHLANDS®

Time Castaways

A GOLD EAGLE BOOK FROM
WORLDWIDE®

TORONTO • NEW YORK • LONDON
AMSTERDAM • PARIS • SYDNEY • HAMBURG
STOCKHOLM • ATHENS • TOKYO • MILAN
MADRID • WARSAW • BUDAPEST • AUCKLAND

Recycling programs
for this product may
not exist in your area.

First edition December 2009

ISBN-13: 978-0-373-62599-4

TIME CASTAWAYS

Printed in U.S.A.

I come to do the deed that must be done—
Nor thou, nor sheltering angels, could prevent me.
—C. R. Maturin, 1780-1824

THE DEATHLANDS SAGA

This world is their legacy, a world born in the violent nuclear spasm of 2001 that was the bitter outcome of a struggle for global dominance.

There is no real escape from this shockscape where life always hangs in the balance, vulnerable to newly demonic nature, barbarism, lawlessness.

But they are the warrior survivalists, and they endure—in the way of the lion, the hawk and the tiger, true to nature's heart despite its ruination.

Ryan Cawdor: The privileged son of an East Coast baron. Acquainted with betrayal from a tender age, he is a master of the hard realities.

Krysty Wroth: Harmony ville's own Titian-haired beauty, a woman with the strength of tempered steel. Her premonitions and Gaia powers have been fostered by her Mother Sonja.

J. B. Dix, the Armorer: Weapons master and Ryan's close ally, he, too, honed his skills traversing the Deathlands with the legendary Trader.

Doctor Theophilus Tanner: Torn from his family and a gentler life in 1896, Doc has been thrown into a future he couldn't have imagined.

Dr. Mildred Wyeth: Her father was killed by the Ku Klux Klan, but her fate is not much lighter. Restored from predark cryogenic suspension, she brings twentieth-century healing skills to a nightmare.

Jak Lauren: A true child of the wastelands, reared on adversity, loss and danger, the albino teenager is a fierce fighter and loyal friend.

Dean Cawdor: Ryan's young son by Sharona accepts the only world he knows, and yet he is the seedling bearing the promise of tomorrow.

In a world where all was lost, they are humanity's last hope....

Prologue

The creature exploded out of the laurel bushes and charged across the dirt road, its four arms raised for a fast chill, the black talons dripping green venom.

"Ambush!" sec chief Charles Donovan cried, flicking off the safety on his massive crossbow. "Gene and Rosemary, stay with the cart! Everybody else, form a firing line!"

As the team of horses whinnied in fear, the sec man in the buckboard wagon holding the reins tried to control the animals while his partner lifted a balanced pair of throwing axes into view. Meanwhile the rest of the platoon brandished their crossbows and formed a defensive line between the charging monster and the imperial treasure cart. Assuming a marksman stance, Donovan aimed his heavy crossbow and fired. A split second later the other sec men did the same with their smaller version, unleashing a maelstrom of wooden shafts.

Bristling with arrows, the creature recoiled from the staggering impacts, but the heavy wooden slats covering the giant man were not penetrated. Bellowing loudly, the armored coldheart shook his two arms in rage, the fake arms suspended underneath them duplicating the motion precisely. Then a second armored man came out of the bushes, closely followed by two more.

"Keep firing!" Donovan bellowed, reaching over a shoulder to pull a stone quarrel from the quiver on his back.

At the sight of the additional coldhearts, the Anchor ville sec men needed no prompting to work the levers on their complex crossbows, the wooden machinery automatically drawing back the bow string and feeding another half-size arrow into the firing notch from the box magazine mounted on top. They fired in unison, and one of the attackers dropped to a knee, blood pouring from a small gap between his leg and belly.

Stepping protectively in front of their wounded brother, the other coldhearts coughed inside their misshapen headmasks, and something flashed across the dirt road too fast to see clearly.

Dropping their weapons, two of the sec men staggered backward. Gurgling horribly, they raked fingernails along their throats, desperately clawing at the tiny feathered darts buried in their skin. Already their flesh was turning a bilious green, and flecks of foam began to appear on their deathly pale lips.

Pausing for only a moment, Donovan mercifully shot an arrow through the head of the nearest sec man, while the rest of the platoon did the same for the second man. There was no antidote for kraken poison.

Reloading quickly, the sec men fired again, wounding another of what they called Hillies. Retreating slightly, the coldhearts coughed again, but ready this time, the sec men managed to dodge the incoming darts successfully. However, that was when Donovan suddenly noticed a dozen figures moving among the trees edging the road. Shitfire, he thought, the rad-suckers had to have brought along the whole tribe for this attack! The grim man had no idea how the bastards knew about the cargo in the treasure wag, but there was no way he was going to let his baron's prize fall into the dirty hands of these stinking inbreed throwbacks.

Tossing aside his loaded crossbow, Donovan clawed open the sealed holster at his side and hauled a predark blaster into view. Lovingly polished every day, the revolver shone rainbow bright with the reflected lights of the aurora borealis filling the sky.

"Akhmed, Hannigan, watch the trees," Donovan shouted, sliding a single brass round into the blaster and closing the cylinder with a jerk of his wrist. "Everybody else, flanking positions."

Launching another volley, the sec men hastily reloaded and quickly formed a wing formation behind their chief. Coughing out more darts, the Hillies bellowed angrily, then charged, concentrating on a young sec man struggling to clear an arrow jammed in the loading mechanism of his crossbow.

Hastily taking aim, Donovan fired, and a Hilly stopped running, blood pouring from the mouth of his carved wooden mask. But even as the dying coldheart sank to his knees, the rest of the Hillies converged on the teenager just as the jam came free. The sec man raised his weapon and fired, but the half-arrow only dully thudded into the thick chest armor of the lead coldheart. Then the others struck, the bear talons on their four arms raking the youth, slicing him open and ripping out bloody gobbets of flesh.

Horribly shrieking, the sec man went backward, his uniform slashed apart and soaked with blood. Feebly, the youth clutched the ruin of his face, an eyeball dangling between his bloody fingers on the end of some white ganglia, then his belly opened wide and ropy intestines slithered out, steaming from the cold air as they fell onto the cold ground.

Without hesitation, the sec men aced their friend, then savagely hammered the hated mountain men with flight after flight of half-arrows, focusing on the narrow opening of the mouth in their grotesque masks. Waving their double set of arms as a distraction did nothing this time, and two of the Hillies slowed, red fluids trickling out of their wooden collars.

Unexpectedly, a boomerang flashed over the sec men to brutally hit the mask of an undamaged Hilly. The deadly 'rang did no damage to the stout oak armor, but the attack distracted the coldhearts for a moment, just enough time for Donovan to finish unearthing a second bullet.

Hastily firing, the sec chief carefully took out the knee of a Hilly, gore and splinters spraying into the trees. In a strangled cry, the coldheart feebly grabbed the wounded leg with his gigantic wooden gloves, trying to staunch the flow of life. However, designed to be frightening, the gloves were useless for the simple task and the blood continued to flow unchecked.

At the sight, the lead Hilly paused for a long moment, arrows hitting his armor in a steady patter. But he yanked something from around his waist and threw it down hard. Instantly there was an explosion of dark smoke, the roiling cloud rapidly swelling to fill the road for yards.

Quickly backing away from the mysterious fumes, the Anchor sec men shot half-arrows blindly into the smoke, but there were no answering thunks of a hit. Only the sound of heavy footsteps heading away, down the roadway toward the nearby shore.

With a start, Donovan realized that the mountain men had to be trying to reach a boat, which could only mean reinforcements, more weapons or, worse, escape. Nuke that drek! the sec chief mentally snarled. Nobody aced one of his sec men and lived to tell the fragging tale.

Donovan pulled in a deep breath and charged into the fumes, braced for a wave of searing pain. But nothing occurred, and when he finally had to breathe, there was only a sweet smell of flowers and kelp. Shitfire, it was only smoke, not poison.

"Stay with the wag," the chief sec man bellowed, redoubling his speed into the murky cloud. "These gleebs are mine!"

"But, sir…" a sec woman began, taking a step forward.

"This could be a diversion," Donovan shouted, pulling out an obsidian ax. "Stay with the wag."

Just then something flew through the smoke, leaving spiraling contrails behind. So they had more darts, eh? Donovan grimaced, and tightened his grip on the ax and blaster.

Shouting a rally cry, the sec chief dodged to the side, and, as expected, more darts flashed by, missing him by only a few inches. Pausing to listen for their footsteps, Donovan heard only the rustle of the leaves in the trees, then there came the soft sound of waves cresting on the beach. Zigzagging through the smoke, the sec chief ran as fast as he could and as the fumes began to thin, there were the Hillies, both brandishing axes and coming his way. Another damn trap.

Diving forward, the man rolled under the swing of the double blades and came up standing behind the coldhearts. Shoving his blaster against the neck of the closest one, he fired, and the wooden helmet was blown off the man's head, his face exploding outward in a horrible geyser of teeth and eyes.

As the last Hilly spun around, Donovan saw that it was their leader, the elaborate designs on the armor proclaiming his exalted rank. The two men locked gazes for a full heartbeat, each testing for any sign of fear, then they swung their war axes in unison. The heavy obsidian blades met in a strident crash and each ax shattered, razor-sharp shards of green volcanic glass flying everywhere.

Cursing vehemently, Donovan backed away, wiping at his stinging eyes, while the Hilly chuckled and pulled out a granite knife, the feathered edge gleaming bright as steel.

Swinging up his blaster, Donovan expertly met the thrust and stone clanged off metal, the sound loud in the thinning smoke.

"Shoulda stayed with your ville boys," the coldheart said, a narrow slit displaying rows of rotten teeth.

Caught by surprise, Donovan almost flinched from the wave of fetid breath. It was worse than a burning dung pit. But the sec chief forced himself to stay close, and slam the wooden shaft of the broken ax against the side of the Hilly's head. The wooden helmet thumped and shifted slightly, covering the coldheart's eyes.

Snarling curses, the Hilly pulled back, one gloved hand fumbling with his helmet while the other waved the granite blade around wildly.

Accidentally the blade scored a blood slash across Donovan's chest, and he cried out in pain. Then he changed targets and with his ax handle started battering at the arm holding the blade. Spitting in rage, the Hilly clawed for a lumpy globe hanging from around his waist, but Donovan smacked the hand aside and went on hammering the wooden glove. Splinters came free and the coldheart tried to shift the blade to his other glove, but Donovan managed to smack it away and the blade went spinning into the forest and disappeared among the bushes. The Hilly dropped his gloves and grabbed the sec chief by the throat.

Fighting to draw a breath, Donovan slammed his fists into the belly of the coldheart, but only managed to skin his knuckles against the battered armor. Thrusting upward, he then attempted to jam his fingers into an eye, but the slits were too narrow.

Chuckling, the Hilly tightened his hold, his thumbs crushing deep into the neck of the struggling man. "Time to die, ville boy," the coldheart whispered.

Refusing to surrender, Donovan kept punching away even as his lungs began to ache then burn with their need for air. His heart was pounding in his chest and there was a growing ringing in his ears. Suddenly the world began to blur then spin out of control, black spots swimming in his sight, when the Hilly jerked and bizarrely released his grip.

Gasping for air, Donovan backed away and saw that an arrow was embedded in the Hilly's helmet, blood trickling along the shaft.

Massaging his sore throat, Donovan looked up just as the treasure wag rolled into view out of the smoke, every sec man steadily firing flight after flight of half-arrows at the Hilly, the sec woman, Rosemary, triggering Donovan's big crossbow.

Snarling in rage, the Hilly reached for a smoke bomb on his belt, and Rosemary fired, the heavy shaft pinning his bare hand to the wooden armor. The coldheart shrieked at the pain, then half-arrows slammed into his other hand, slicing off fingers.

Gibbering from the agony, the coldheart attempted to flee, clearly planning to simply throw himself off the cliff to escape his tormentors. But as he turned, a bald sec man threw a bolo. The stones tied to lengths of stout rawhide neatly spun across the intervening space and wrapped themselves tightly around the Hilly's armored legs, trapping him in place.

Stopping the treasure wag, the sec men poured onto the road and swarmed the helpless coldheart, concentrating their half-arrows for the narrow eye slits in the wooden mask. The terrified mountain man raised his wounded arm as protection, and a flurry of half-arrows nailed it permanently in place.

"Pax! Pax!" the Hilly cried. "I surrender!"

"Tough," Donovan croaked in a barely recognizable voice. He held out an empty hand, and somebody slapped an ax into his palm.

Tightening a fist around the fish-hide grip, the sec chief swung the weapon with all of his might and buried the polished granite blade deep into the back of the weeping coldheart. Then shouting curses, Donovan began hacking at the Hilly as if chopping down a tree. Chips flew off under the brutal impacts of the granite blade, then leather padding came into view and finally human skin….

When he was finished, Donovan wiped the cracked blade clean on his pants and returned the borrowed weapon to the bald sec man.

"Thanks," Donovan whispered.

"Always got your back," Hannigan said proudly, slinging the weapon over a shoulder. "Now we go after those others in the forest?"

In a rush of anger Donovan tried to speak, but could only cough for a few minutes. Akhmed passed over a gourd, and the sec chief pulled out the cork to pour the contents down his aching throat. The shine burned like fire, then the tenderness eased and he took his first deep breath for what seemed like an eternity.

"No," the sec chief said, speaking almost normally. "There could be more tricks, more traps. We're heading for home, and not stopping for anything until we have a wall around our asses again. Savvy?"

"No need to rush, Chief," Gene said, both hands on the reins controlling the horses. "Whatever those things were in the forest, they skedaddled the minute that Hilly started eating dirt."

"Hillies," Rosemary snorted in contempt, resting a throwing ax on a shoulder. In spite of wearing the largest size of body armor available, her ample breasts were simply much too big, and deliciously muffined over the top. Every man privately enjoyed the delightful sight, but the sec woman's dire expertise with a throwing ax kept them all respectful and courteous even when far away from the ville on patrol. "Think they knew what we're carrying?" The woman glanced into the cart. Set among their piles of supplies, barrels of water and such was a wooden strongbox bolted to the floorboards. Without explosives, it would take a day to chop into the box, and the only way to steal it was to take the whole cart. This was the best the ville had, but what it contained was more valuable than black powder.

Making a face, Hannigan grunted. "Shitfire, if they knew what was in that box, the bastards would have sent a dozen coldhearts after us."

"Can the chatter, and go collect your arrows," Donovan ordered, passing the gourd back to Akhmed. "The damn things don't grow on trees, ya know."

Chuckling at the very old joke, the sec men dutifully retrieved the spent arrows, carefully pocketing the fletching and stone heads found with broken shafts. Sadly, quite a few of the half-arrows were gone, lost in the forest.

Reclaiming his crossbow, Donovan slung it over a shoulder, then hunted for the blaster. He found it in the bushes, undamaged, just smeared with blood and dirt.

"Here, I got the lead back for you, Chief," MacDouglas said, proffering a small disfigured blob of gray metal.

"Thanks, Mack," Donavan said, tucking the slug in a shirt pocket along with the spent brass.

"Excuse me, sir?" a bald sec man asked respectfully.

"What is it, Carson?"

"What should we do about the others?" the man asked, looking forlornly up the roadway. The herbal smoke was almost completely gone now, and the bodies of the fallen sec men could be clearly seen.

"We're short on time," the sec chief began, but then relented. "But we'll wait. Take a shovel and bury your kin. Save their crossbows for the baron, but you can have everything else for their kin."

"You want a hand?" Akhmed asked, tucking some loose fletching into a pocket.

Shaking his head, Carson got a shovel from the cart, then trundled off to drag a tattered corpse into the bushes and perform the odious task in private.

Shrugging his crossbow into a more comfortable position, Hannigan scowled at the aced Hilly lying mutilated in the churned dirt. "That was a hell of a scary mask," he said, speaking as if the words had a bad taste. "Ya think the bastard based it upon a real mutie? Something from one of the outer islands? Those got hit a lot worse than us in the endwar."

"Makes sense," Akhmed replied, clearly unconvinced. "Unless the ocean currents have changed again. Remember when that mutie that looked like a man but was covered with suckers washed ashore from the mainland?"

"Oh, don't be a feeb," Gene snapped impatiently. "There ain't no mainland anymore. The whole damn world got nuked during the Big Heat. There's only this chain of islands, nothing more. Baron Griffin says so."

The unflappable sec man shrugged in dismissal. "If you say so, cousin." Thunder rumbled above and Donavan climbed into the back of the cart to drape a tarpaulin over the strongbox. It didn't really need the additional protection, even if it was acid rain coming, but he felt it wise to be cautious with this cargo. A slave had found the treasure on the shore, of all places, and immediately turned it over to Baron Griffin for the promised reward of freedom. It was granted, the baron always kept his word. However, once the former slave was outside the ville where none of the civies could see, the sec men on the walls had shot him down in cold blood. Slaves were not allowed on the beach under any circumstances, and the punishment was death. The ancient laws ruled supreme on Royal Island, even when their transgression yielded the greatest treasure in the world.

Metal. A big jagged chunk of rusty, corroded, glorious metal. Almost a full ten pounds. None of the sec men had any idea what the irregular lump had once been, but soon the ville blacksmith would convert it into a new hinge for the front gate, edging for a dozen knives and deadly tips for a hundred war arrows, vital protection needed by the ville against the hairy-ass barbs in the west, and that tricky bitch Wainwright to the far east. Anchor ville sat smack between the two, cursed with a baron more interested in dance and song than chilling. They were thankful for his wife. Lady Griffin was more of a warrior than any ten sec men in the ville.

Including me, Donovan grudgingly admitted in private. Plus, the busty woman was also a lusty sex partner. The woman fought like a sec man and fucked like a gaudy slut. Now, that was a real woman! A proper ruler for any ville. It was just bad luck that the Book of Blood had decreed she had to marry that smiling feeb from Northpoint ville. But then, the Book had to be obeyed. End of discussion. Only the throwbacks, barbs and Hillies screwed whomever they wished, which was why so many of them were born…different.

Dragging the dirty shovel behind, Carson returned from the bushes, looking years older. Shoving the wooden tool into a leather boot set alongside the cart, the sec man wordlessly assumed his position alongside Gene on the front seat. His shoulders were slumped, but his rapidfire crossbow was primed, and Carson looked hard at the foggy bushes and trees, as if eager for an attack on the group so that he would have an excuse to chill something, anything at all.

"All right, mount up," Donovan commanded, sitting on the treasure box and placing the loaded crossbow across his lap. "Let's go home."

High over, the cloudy sky was alive with the multicolored radiance of the daily aurora borealis. Softly in the distance, thunder rumbled, warning of an approaching storm.

Chapter One

The thud of a heavy bolt disengaging echoed in the Stygian gloom. Then with squealing hinges, the oval portal in the rusty wall ponderously swung aside, resisting every inch of the way.

Holding road flares and blasters, two men stepped through the opening and warily looked around the darkness, ready for any possible danger. The sputtering flares gave off a wellspring of light, but there was nothing in sight but some old-fashioned gym lockers attached to the riveted steel walls and a couple of plastic benches thick with dust.

"Fireblast, where the fuck are we?" Ryan Cawdor muttered uneasily, tightening his grip on a SIG-Sauer 9 mm blaster. A Steyr longblaster was hung across the broad back of the one-eyed man, and a panga was sheathed at his side.

"Beats the hell out of me," J. B. Dix muttered uneasily, the harsh light of the road flare reflecting off his wire-rimmed glasses. "But it doesn't resemble any redoubt I've ever seen before."

Dressed in a worn jacket and battered fedora, the wiry man was cradling a Smith&Wesson M-4000 shotgun in both hands, and an Uzi machine blaster hung across his back. At his side was a lumpy munitions bag packed with high-explosive ordnance, a homemade pipe bomb jutting out slightly for easy access.

"Agreed," Ryan growled, straining to hear any movement in the murky shadows. But the silence seemed absolute, as if they were the last two people in the world.

This room should have been the control room for the redoubt, jammed full of humming machinery, winking lights and scrolling monitors. Instead, it seemed to be inside some kind of abandoned gymnasium. Even stranger, there was a strong smell of living green plants in the dusty atmosphere, which should have been flat-out impossible.

Built by the U.S. government before the last nuke war, the redoubts, massive military fortifications controlled by banks of advanced computers, were hidden underground, safely sealed away from the outside world. Powered by the limitless energy of nuclear reactors, the subterranean forts were safe havens of clean air and purified water, a tiny oasis of life secretly buried deep within the radioactive hellzone of North America.

When the companions had arrived at this location, the mat-trans unit promptly blew and everything had gone dark. Patiently, they'd waited for the system to automatically reboot. But when that didn't happen, they were left with no other option than to proceed deeper into the strange redoubt and hope that they could find an exit to the surface. The possibility that the redoubt was located at the bottom of a glowing nuke crater or covered by the wreckage of a fallen skyscraper was something they tried very hard not to think about. If this was the end of the trail, so be it. Everybody died, that was just the price you paid for the gift of life.

Reaching the middle of the metal room, Ryan and J.B. exhaled in relief as they spotted a way out of the gymnasium, a circular metal door closed with an old-fashioned wheel lock, as if it were a bank vault. However, this door was heavily encrusted with corrosion, big flakes of rust fallen to the floor like autumn leaves. It was an unnerving sight.

After whistling sharply, Ryan waited expectantly. A few moments later four more people stepped from the gateway in combat formation, each of them carrying heavy backpacks, a softly hissing butane cigarette lighter and a loaded blaster.

"How peculiar, do…do I smell ivy?" Doc Tanner rumbled in a deep bass voice, brandishing a weapon in each fist.

Tall and slim, Theophilus Algernon Tanner seemed to have stepped out of another age with his frilly shirt and long frock coat. But the silver-haired scholar also sported a strictly utilitarian LeMat handcannon, along with a slim sword of Spanish steel, the edge gleaming razor-bright in the fiery light of the road flares.

"Ivy? Sure as hell hope not," Krysty Wroth muttered.

The woman breathed in deeply, then let it out slow. Okay, she could smell plants nearby, but there was no trace of the hated ivy. Relaxing slightly, the woman eased her grip on the S&W Model 640 revolver.

A natural beauty, the redhead's ample curves were barely contained by her Air Force duty fatigues. A bearskin coat was draped over her shapely shoulders. A lumpy backpack hung off a shoulder, and a gunbelt was strapped low around her hips.

"Weird place, what is?" Jak Lauren drawled, arching a snow-colored eyebrow. A big-bore .357 Magnum Colt Python was balanced in the pale hand of the albino teenager, the hammer already cocked into the firing position in case of trouble. A large Bowie knife was sheathed on his gunbelt, and the handle of another blade could be seen tucked into his combat boot.

"My guess would be some kind of a ready room," Dr. Mildred Weyth countered, easing her grip on a Czech ZKR .38 target revolver. The stocky woman was dressed entirely in Army fatigues, and a small canvas medical bag hung at her side.

Before the maelstrom that ended civilization, Mildred had been a physician, but a medical accident had landed her in an experimental cryogenic freezing unit. A hundred years later, Mildred awoke to the living nightmare of the Deathlands, and soon joined the companions, both her vaunted medical skills and sharpshooting ability earning her a place among their ranks.

"A ready room, yeah, that makes sense," J.B. said hesitantly, tilting back his fedora. "Someplace where the predark soldiers arriving via the mat-trans unit could change into their uniforms."

"Or out of them," Ryan said, warily using the barrel of the SIG-Sauer to tease open the latch on a locker. As he gently pushed aside the thin metal door, the hinges squealed in protest and a small rain of reddish flecks sprinkled to the riveted floor.

Inside the locker Ryan found the moldy remains of what looked like civilian clothing hung neatly on hangers: sneakers on the floor, a Mets baseball cap on a small shelf, along with a small mirror and a few personal items covered with a thick layer of dust. Checking the door, the man found the expected picture of a smiling young woman cradling a newborn in her arms, the faint residue of a lipstick kiss still on the faded photograph. She was very pretty and wearing an incredibly skimpy bikini. Moving the flare closer for a better look, the Deathlands warrior then blinked at the sight of a gray plastic box on the shelf.

Balancing the flare on the edge of a bench, Ryan took down the box and slid the plastic lock to the side. The lid came free with a faint crack to expose a spotlessly clean .44 Ruger revolver, along with a cardboard box of ammunition. There was a brass brush for cleaning the cylinders, and even a small plastic bottle of homogenized gun oil.

Opening the box, Ryan half expected it to only contain some wad-cutters, cheap bullets used for target practice. They were virtually useless in a fight these days, except at point-blank range.

However, to his surprise, the box was nearly full of regulation U.S. Army combat cartridges, semijacketed hollowpoints, as deadly as brass came, and the ammo was in perfect condition. The man could not believe his luck. Thirty-four live rounds.

"Ready room, my ass. This is a ward room," J.B. exclaimed, eagerly going to the next locker and pushing open the corroded door. Hanging inside was more decaying clothing, a three-piece suit this time covered with tiny mushrooms, and on the shelf was an open gun case. The 9 mm Beretta pistol had been reduced to an irregular lump from the pervasive damp, the deadly weapon now as harmless as a roll of toilet paper.

Checking a locker in another row, Mildred discovered the sad remains of a flower-print dress, along with a matching half-jacket, and scarf. On the shelf were a few containers that the physician recognized as pricey cosmetics: organic foundation, dusting powder, mascara, a small tube of lipstick and a fancy glass perfume bottle. At the sight, the woman felt a rush of bittersweet memories from ancient high-school proms and dating medical students at college.

Reaching out to tenderly stroke the dress, Mildred frowned as the flimsy material crumbled away at her touch, the past returning to the past. However, hanging behind the rotting strips of cloth was a small shoulder holster containing a slim Beretta Belle. The 9 mm weapon was exactly what a woman would carry to not disturb the flowing lines of a formal ballgown or lightweight summer jacket. Interesting.

Gingerly extracting the blaster, Mildred saw that it was only streaked with surface corrosion. The Beretta could probably be salvaged with a thorough cleaning. Dropping the clip, Mildred found it fully loaded with oily cartridges that looked in fairly decent condition. Then she blinked. Those weren't standard lead bullets, but Black Talons, armor-piercing rounds, extremely illegal for anybody to carry except special government agents.

Returning the blaster to the holster, Mildred rummaged about to locate a tiny decorative purse. As expected, she found only a plastic-coated driver's license, some folded bills now thick with gray fuzz, an expired credit card, a lump of crud that might have once been some candy breath mints and a folded leather wallet. Opening it carefully, Mildred saw a faded picture of the owner, a slim blonde with a lot of freckles, and a laminated government-issue identification card bearing the Great Seal of the United States, and the embossed seal of the United States Navy, Special Operations.

"Well, I'll be damned, this woman was Navy Intelligence," Mildred said.

"A sec man?" Jak asked.

"An extremely good sec person," Mildred corrected, with an odd sense of pride.

"Indeed, madam," Doc said thoughtfully, easing down the hammer on his LeMat. "But more important, if she was a member of the United States Navy, then mayhap we are currently on a ship of some kind." While the rest of the companions used modern-day weaponry, the Vermont scholar preferred his antique Civil War handcannon, primarily because it came from his own century. The black powder revolver was a deadly piece of home that the time traveler carried in his gunbelt as a constant reminder of better times, and better days, in a much more civilized world.

"A ship? That would explain the riveted walls and floors," Krysty muttered, quickly checking the ceiling for vid cams or traps.

"Don't feel waves," Jak said carefully, trying to get

any subtle sense of motion. "Not drifting at sea. Maybe in dock?"

"Not necessarily. If this is a ship, it would have to be enormous to hold a mat-trans unit," J.B. theorized, adjusting his glasses. "Anything that huge and we'd never feel the waves unless trapped in the middle of a hurricane, and maybe not even then."

"An aircraft carrier was certainly large enough to carry a mat-trans unit," Mildred said, folding shut the Navy commission booklet. "The vessels were often called oceangoing cities, they were so huge. A carrier held a hundred jetfighters and a crew of over a thousand. More important, they were powered by nuclear reactors."

"Tumbledown," Jak said, as if that explained the matter.

Everybody present understood the cryptic reference. When skydark scorched the world, radioactive debris from the nuked cities rained down across the world. Houses had been found on mountaintops, toilet seats in the middle of a desert. Anything close to an atomic blast was vaporized, and after that objects melted and burned, but then they simply went airborne, including office buildings, suspension bridges and sometimes even warships.

"Buried alive," J.B. whispered, his throat going tight.

"I consider that highly unlikely, my friend," Doc rumbled pleasantly, recalling the brief smell of fresh greenery. "Plants need sunshine to live, even that accursed mutant ivy. So, whatever type of vessel this is, there must be a breach in the hull, and thus direct egress to the outside world."

"Sounds reasonable," J.B. said uneasily. "But the sooner we see daylight, the better."

"Agreed," Ryan stated roughly. "But we're not leaving all of this live brass behind. Everybody grab a partner and do a fast recce of the lockers. Take only the brass, leave the blasters behind for a scav later."

Nodding their agreement, the companions got busy. Moving steadily through the array of lockers, they soon amassed a staggering collection of clips, magazines, speed loaders and loose brass in a wide assortment of calibers, along with a couple of blasters in reasonably good condition. If there were any villes nearby, a functioning weapon could buy them a week of hot meals and clean beds, as well as other items in trade. There had even been a few grens, but the military spheres were so thick with layers of corrosion, any attempt to use the deadly explosive charges would be tantamount to suicide.

Naturally, there had not been anything usable for Doc's black powder LeMat amid the civilian arsenal, but the scholar had discovered a .44 Ruger revolver, a sturdy weapon of devastating power, along with a full box of fifty hollowpoint Magnum cartridges.

Sheathing his sword into an ebony walking stick, Doc twisted the lion's-head newel on top to lock it tight, then tucked the stick into his gunbelt. Testing the balance of the two monstrous handcannons, the old man decided that the combination was too much for him to easily handle, and wisely slipped the Ruger into one of his deep empty pockets.

Finished with their scavenging, the companions

tucked away their various finds, then, assuming a combat formation, approached the circular door. The formidable barrier was veined with heavy bolt, the locking wheel situated in the middle. Ryan illuminated the door with a road flare and saw that it was firmly locked. But rust had eaten away the metal along the edge of the jamb, and there was a definite breeze blowing into the ready room, carrying a faint trace of plantlife and something else.

Pointing at the others, Ryan directed them to flanking positions on either side of the door while J.B. knelt on the floor and checked for traps. Angling his flare to give his friend some light, Ryan watched the man run fingertips along the rough surface of the door. Then he pressed an ear to the metal to try to detect any mechanical movements, and finally passed a compass along the material to check for any magnetic sensors or proximity triggers. After a few moments the Armorer tucked the compass away and smiled, proclaiming it was clean. At least, as far as he could tell.

Holstering his blaster, Ryan passed the flare to J.B. and exchanged positions with the man. Taking hold of the locking wheel, Ryan tried to turn the handle, but it stubbornly refused to move. Reaching into a pocket, he pulled out a small bottle of gun oil and squirted a few drops on the spindle and hinges, then tried again. Still nothing.

Brushing off some loose flakes of rust from the wheel, Ryan spit on his hands and got a firm grip. Bracing his boots for a better stance, the big man tried once more, this time putting his whole body into the effort, but very carefully increasing the pressure slowly to make sure the corroded metal didn't shatter, sealing them inside the room forever. They had explosives, but sealed into a steel box, those would only be used as the very last resort.

Long moments passed with nothing happening. Then there came an audible crack and Ryan nearly fell over as the wheel came free and began to turn easily. As the bolts disengaged, he started to walk backward, slowly hauling the door open against the loudly protesting hinges.

Sharing glances, the companions said nothing, but it was painfully obvious that any hope they had of staying covert was now completely gone. If there was anybody else in the vicinity, they knew that somebody was coming out of the ready room.

As the thick door cleared the jamb, J.B. squinted into the darkness on the other side. "Okay, looks clear…son of a bitch!" he shouted, and the shotgun boomed.

In the bright muzzle-flash, something large was briefly seen in the outside corridor. Then a metal arm extended through the doorway and mechanical pinchers brushed aside the shotgun to close around the man's throat with a hard clang.

THICK FOG MOVED OVER the walls of Northpoint ville like a misty river flowing steady across the high stone walls. Somewhere in the distance, low thunder rumbled, and from the nearby ocean came the sound of rough waves crashing upon a rocky shore.

Crackling torches were set at regular intervals along

the wall, giving the sec men walking patrol on the top plenty of light, and every structure inside the ville was brightly illuminated by the yellowish glow of fish-oil lanterns or the cheery blaze of a fireplace. A hundred stoves blazed bright and hot inside the ramshackle huts of the ville like imprisoned stars, the delicious waves of fragrant heat banishing the eternal fog and affording the inhabitants a small zone of clear air within the confines of the ville. Winter had never been a problem in Northpoint. A nearly limitless forest of pine trees grew on the outer islands, so wood was always in abundant supply, and the freshwater bay teemed with fish, most of them not muties, so there was more than sufficient food for all. Only salt, precious, life-giving salt, was in desperately short supply.

But with any luck that problem would soon be solved forever, Baron Wainwright thought privately, taking another sip of the mulled wine.

Set in the center of the log cabins, smokehouses, barracks, patched leather tents and stone fishing shacks was a pristine field of neatly tended grass, as smooth as a piece of predark glass. Standing tightly packed on the field was a large crowd of civies gathered around an old whipping post where a naked man stood, his wrists bound with rope to the crossbar of the infamous learning tree. Tiny rivulets of blood trickled down his skinny shanks, oozing steadily from the crisscross of open wounds covering his back. The tattered remains of a uniform lay on the grass around his trembling feet, and both arms were marred with glassy patches of freshly burned skin.

"Twenty-seven!" the executioner announced, and lashed out once more with a coiled whip. The smooth length of green leather cracked across the raw flesh of the prisoner, but he only shook and groaned in response.

"Burn the bastard!" a young woman yelled, spittle flying from her mouth. "Slit open his belly and feed his guts to the river snakes!"

"No, make it last! Whip him harder!" an old woman snarled from the crowd, the face of the wrinklie contorted into a feral mask of raw hatred.

"Blind him!"

"Cut off his balls!"

The furious civilians roared their approval at that idea, and after a moment the executioner nodded in agreement. Tossing aside the lightweight horsewhip, he extracted a much heavier, knotted bullwhip from the canvas bag hanging at his side. The muscular man uncoiled the full length onto the dewy grass, creating a brief rainbow effect from the reflected light of the nearby torches. A touch of beauty amid the field of pain. Then he expertly flicked the bullwhip a few times, making the stout leather strips crack louder than a blaster to test the action. Hearing the noise, the prisoner bowed his head and wept openly, knowing the hell that was to come.

Sitting on a rosewood throne on a fieldstone dais, Baron Brenda Wainwright refilled her bone chalice with a wooden flask, waiting for the torture to continue. She disliked watching punishment details, but her presence here was necessary as the absolute ruler of the ville. She had blasters in her private arsenal, lots of them, but the sec men obeyed her commands primarily because the baron was smart. She constantly outwitted their enemies and always found some clever new way to put food on the table and, more important, salt. Without that precious commodity, everybody in the ville would have been aced decades ago. No matter what herbs or potions the healers tried, people needed salt the way a candle needed a wick, without it, they simply got weaker and weaker then just stopped working entirely. Even the dead were boiled down in the smokehouse, reduced to their very essence to reclaim every single grain. Salt was life.

Which was why we're having a public execution, the baron reminded herself. That old doomie had better have been right about this. The ville was down to less than a hundredweight of salt in the armory, barely enough to last them until spring. If this plan didn't work, then there would be no choice but to declare war on Anchor ville. Brother fighting brother, a civil war. The thought was intolerable. Not new, just intolerable.

Dressed for combat on this special day, the woman was wearing a heavy blue gown cut high in the front to show off her new snakeskin boots. A gift from a secret lover. An ebony cascade of long hair hung loose around her stern face, artfully disguising the fact that she was missing an ear from a mutie attack when she was a small child. A necklace of the creature's polished teeth was draped around her badly scarred throat as a grim remembrance of that dark day, and a black leather bodice supported her full breasts. A wide gunbelt circled her trim waist, embroidered

gloves tucked into the front, a sheathed knife and holstered blaster riding at her hips. Ancient plastic rings
of outlandish design adorned both thumbs, and an in-
tricately carved wooden bracelet studded with tiny
bits of sparkling car window glass flashed from her
left wrist.

Finished testing his deadly tool, the executioner adjusted his fish-leather mask and looked at the baron.
Everybody knew it was the blacksmith, but the social
custom of pretending that the executioner was from
another ville still held.

The baron waved a hand in authorization. Grinning
fiercely, the executioner lashed out with the bullwhip,
and the prisoner violently shook all over from the brutal strike, a wellspring of fresh blood gushing from the
deep cut across his shoulders. Laughing and cheering,
the crowd voiced its hearty approval.

Trying not to scowl, the baron refilled her mug from
the flask and took a small sip of the dark brew. Death
was part of life, as unstoppable as the morning fog.
However, the old doomie known as Mad Pete had
deemed that this particular demise was absolutely necessary to the welfare of the ville. Even then, she disliked casual chilling so much that the baron had waited
patiently, and then impatiently, until some triple-stupe
fool broke a major law and could honestly and fairly
be executed. If he had been drunk on duty, or stolen a
lick of salt, the bastard would have simply been beaten
to death and sent to the boiling pot in the smokehouse.
But he had done much worse by forcing himself upon
the wife of another sec man. No matter who you were,

rape was a capital offense in every ville along Royal Island. End of discussion. Her hands were clean.

At that, Wainwright almost smiled. Well, at least on this particular death, she internally chuckled. Nobody ruled a ville without knowing how to chill. She had been planning to remove her fat brother from the Oak Throne when he'd greedily eaten an unknown type of fish and died of food poisoning. As father had always said, stupidity was its own reward. True words.

"It's almost time, Baron," sec chief Emile LeFontaine muttered, flexing his monstrous hands. Standing at the Maple Throne, the hulking giant held a perfectly balanced obsidian throwing ax in a gloved hand, and there was a longblaster strapped across his wide back, protected from the harsh elements by a thick wolfskin sheath, the snarling head of the beast peeking over his shoulder in a most disturbing manner.

Nodding in understanding, the baron checked the blaster at her hip, making sure the weapon was fully loaded with six live rounds. Mad Pete had predicted this day would come, and she had immediately started preparations.

Suddenly the weakening prisoner cried out for the first time, and the townsfolk joyously voiced their full approval. Their desire to see him punished was almost palpable, like waves of heat radiating from the stove.

Tossing aside the blood-soaked bullwhip, the executioner pulled a fresh one from the green leather bag at his side. But just then the prisoner howled again, louder this time, even though he was standing limply at the learning tree.

"Silence!" the baron commanded, rising from her throne.

In ragged stages, the mob stopped making noise, and this time everybody heard the low ghostly moan, echoing over the ville as if coming down from the cloudy sky.

"Sweet nuking hell, that came from the sea," the sec chief whispered, his scarred face going pale. "The screams of the prisoner must have caught the attention of…of…."

Slowly a dark mountain of flesh rose from the other side of the ville wall, six huge, inhuman eyes glaring down at the scene of torture even as a hundred tentacles began to crawl over the granite block wall.

"Kraken!" a sec man on the wall shouted, firing his crossbow.

Then a tentacle wrapped around his waist and the cursing man was hauled out of view.

As the alarm bell began to sound, the civies started screaming and racing around in a blind panic. Trying to control her breathing, Baron Wainwright could only stare in wonder at the mountain of flesh looming over the wall. So the old doomie had been right! The death screams of the condemned man had summoned a kraken. Now, the colossal mutie would level the ville, unless the defenses held. However, the sec men had been preparing for this battle for a year. Hopefully it would be enough.

"Defend the ville," the baron yelled, pulling a Navy flare gun from her gunbelt and firing the charge straight up into the fog. The explosion of colored lights distracted the mutie, several long tentacles reaching upward for the sizzling charge slowly drifting downward on a tiny parachute.

As the kraken rose behind the ville wall, ropy tentacles extended into the streets searching among the stone houses for anything edible. A stray dog sniffing at the barrels of fish offal was caught and hauled bodily into the gaping maw of the horrendous creature.

By now, the sec men were launching swarms of arrows into the goliath. But if they did any damage it was not readily apparent, and the mutie continued feeding upon the population.

Scampering out of an alley, a gaudy slut tried to get back into the tavern when ropy death came wiggling out of the sky and grabbed her around the neck. Shrieking in terror, the slut pulled a bone knife from her bodice and started wildly stabbing at the tentacle. But the resilient hide was too tough for the blade, and she was hauled upward, going over the wall, cursing and fighting until the very end.

Meanwhile teams of sec men in the guard towers feverishly operated the hand cranks to pull back the mighty arbalests. The giant crossbows were thirty feet long, and used three bows working in conjunction. Each arrow was twice the size of a man, and the barbed head was edged with thin strips of genuine predark steel.

"Pull, you lazy bastards!" a sergeant bellowed. "Pull or die!"

Attracted by the shout, the kraken headed toward the guard tower, and Baron Wainwright quickly fired another flare. Once more, the beast turned to try to catch the descending flare, giving the team of sec men just enough time to load the arrow into the arbalest, the catch engaging with a hard thunk.

Grabbing the aiming yoke, the burly sergeant swung the colossal weapon around toward the mutie, aimed and yanked hard on the release lever. There came a groan of wooden gears, then the triple bows let fly and the giant arrow went straight into the kraken's throat.

Bellowing in rage and pain, the mutie turned toward the source of the agony, its tentacles lashing out wildly.

But more giant arrows were launched from the other guard towers, and the kraken twisted madly in the deadly cross fire, roaring defiantly.

A catapult snapped upward from the roof of the barracks, and a wooden barrel arched gracefully upward. It sailed over the guard towers and ignited a split second before crashing on top of the kraken. Covered with burning shine, the mutie went insane, lashing its tentacles around and knocking a dozen sec men off the walls. A flurry of crossbow arrows slammed into the beast, as additional firebombs hammered the creature. However, the attacks were only enraging the beast, and it sent several long tentacles snaking into the ville to snatch away the bloody corpse of the prisoner, leaving behind the ragged stumps of his arms still tied to the learning tree.

Inside their ramshackle homes, the civies were quaking with fear, muttering prayers to forgotten deities.

In a crash of splinters, the gate leading to the dockyard slammed open and a host of writhing tentacles entered the ville. But forewarned of the attack by the baron, the fishermen had a double line of crackling bonfires already burning between the gate and the rows of homes. Hesitating in front of the wall of flames, the kraken tried to find a way around the painful barrier, then it attempted to go underneath, and finally withdrew. It reappeared a few moments later, the tentacles shoving several fishing boats taken from the docks to crash a path through the fiery obstruction.

"Baron…" sec chief LeFontaine said as a question, his face tense, a throwing ax in his hand.

"Not yet, my friend," the baron muttered, loading the last flare.

More firebombs and arbalest arrows slammed into the monster, along with a score of spears, boomerangs and a fishing harpoon that just missed going into one of the huge, inhuman eyes.

Dodging a tentacle, a sec woman fell off the wall and crashed onto the roof of a shed. The distance was not very great, but she did not rise again, and after a few seconds something red began to trickle down the side of the building.

"Milady, please…" the sec chief begged, taking a half step toward the tumultuous combat. His face was flushed and he was breathing heavily from the strain of not joining his troops in combat.

"Just a few ticks more, Sergeant," Wainwright said gently, cradling the flare gun protectively in both hands.

Unexpectedly, the body rolled off the little shed as the roof slid aside, exposing a honeycomb of bamboo tubes. A nest of fuses dangled from the rear of each and as the baron watched in growing horror, a torch was touched to the group fuse, setting them aflame.

"No! Too soon!" Wainwright cried.

"Too late," LeFontaine replied curtly.

With no other choice, the baron jumped off the dais and raced into the middle of the ville square. Raising both hands, she carefully aimed the flare gun and fired. The charge thumped from the wide barrel and streaked away to hit the kraken in the face. Snapping around with surprising speed, the colossus stared down at the tiny norm in open hatred and moved along the wall, its tentacles reaching out for the fresh meat.

In a stuttering series of smoky explosions, the top row of bamboo tubes unleashed a dozen homie rockets, closely followed by the second row, then the rest.

The rockets flashed upward and slammed into the kraken, disappearing into the mottled hide. Howling in anger, the mutie probed the tiny wounds with some tentacles just as the next wave of rockets struck, and then the first salvo detonated.

Gobbets of raw flesh exploded like a geyser from the monster, sending out a ghastly spray of piss-yellow blood. That was when the next shed lost its roof and more black-powder rockets launched, peppering the monstrosity with high-explosive death.

Bawing in agony, the kraken lashed out mindlessly as the new rockets detonated inside the beast. Literally torn apart from within, a tentacle went limp, an eye turned dead-white and torrents of yellow blood gushed from the hideous wounds.

Enthusiastically cheering, the sec men redoubled their assault on the mutie, the arbalests now targeting the open wounds.

Turning to flee, the weakening mutie discovered there were iron chains attached to the arrows, the barbed heads caught deep within the belly of the beast in exactly the same way its own tentacles dragged a victim to their death in its cavernous maw.

Its inhuman brain sluggishly comprehending that death was coming, the kraken threw itself at the ville wall, hammering the stone ramparts with its full weight. The entire shoreside wall trembled from the impacts, and several sec men lost their grips and fell screaming onto the cobblestone streets below with grisly results. But even as the baron watched, the struggles of the creature became noticeably weaker, the rush of blood increasing.

"More rockets!" Wainwright yelled, running toward the thrashing kraken. "Fire them all!"

A grip of iron grabbed her arm, stopping the woman in her tracks.

"No closer, Baron," sec chief LeFontaine commanded. "I won't allow it."

Contorting her face into a sneer, the baron started to reach for her blaster, then grudgingly relented, realizing the wisdom of the caution. Any animal was at its most dangerous when it was wounded and dying.

Chewing on the chains to try to get free, the kraken was hit with a third wave of rockets and then a fourth, the last few of them going completely through the mutie and coming out the other side to arch away over the bay. Yellow blood was everywhere, flowing down the sides of the stone wall and forming deep puddles in the street.

In a final rush of hatred, the dying kraken reached out with every working tentacle and wrapped each around the nearest guard tower and squeezed hard. Astonishingly, the support timbers audibly creaked from the titanic strain, and a wealth of crossbeams fell away like dry autumn leaves. As the tower began to tilt, the sec men inside cursed at the unexpected tactic and tried to hold on to the railing for dear life.

That was when there came a high-pitched keen of a steam whistle from the other side of the wall, and more rockets slammed into the back of the beast, widening the exit holes of the arrows.

Shuddering all over, the kraken released the guard tower and sluggishly tried for the bay once more, but again it was stopped by the iron chains. Mewling weakly, the creature reached out with a gory tentacle, the tip just managing to reach the cold, clear water of the bay. Then it sagged and went still, the flood of blood quickly slowing to a trickle, and then stopping entirely.

Instantly a new bell began to clang. Minutes later every man, woman and child in the ville stormed out of the dockyard gates, each equipped with a wicker basket and a sharp obsidian knife. Resembling an army of ants, the people crawled over the chilled mutie and started to slice off pieces. Meanwhile, sec men armed with torches and axes began to hack apart the corpse, chopping a tunnel into the thing, and soon disappeared inside.

"It worked! We aced a kraken!" The baron chortled, slapping her sec chief on the back. "What a glorious day!"

"You can load that into a damn crossbow and fire it,"

LeFontaine agreed wholeheartedly, rubbing his hands together. "We'll get enough salt from the gizzard to last the ville for months, for years."

"Plus, there's enough good leather for everybody to get new boots, belts and winter jackets," she agreed with a smile, watching the harvest progress. "Sinew for a thousand crossbows, enough bones to…well, for any damn thing we need until further notice." Plus, that bitch at Anchor ville would pay a baron's ransom in metal for a single pint of kraken blood. But Wainwright kept that observation to herself. In the right circumstances, the blood of a kraken was the most valuable thing in the world.

"Sadly, we lost the dockyard gate, a horse and at least a dozen sec men," LeFontaine muttered unhappily. The dogs and the gaudy slut were of no real importance.

"Yes, a pity," Wainwright agreed. "But still, a price that I would be willing to pay anytime for the death of a kraken. The bay belongs to us now. No more will our fishing boats be pulled underwater, the crew drowned, the catch destroyed."

"Aye, that's good news. Too bad we can't eat the meat," LeFontaine said. "I hear it tastes fine, but soon afterward…" He gave a shiver. Any further embellishment was unnecessary.

"Leave some outside the wall for the Hillies to steal," the baron ordered. "Maybe we can ace two birds with one stone, eh?"

"By your command, Baron," the sec chief agreed, giving a small bow. "I live to serve."

Trying not to smile, the baron acknowledged the

formal action with a prim nod of her head, mentally deciding to reward the man for his action later in her private bedchamber.

As for the ville, both the civies and sec men would spend the rest of the day and most of the night dissecting the mountainous mutie, scavenging everything of value. Even the fat of the monster could be boiled down into a crude form of tallow for candles. When that odious task was accomplished, the crew of the *Wendigo* would haul what remained of the bedraggled corpse out into the deep water near Liar's Gate, so that the smell of the decaying corpse would scare away any other kraken for years.

The baron ruefully smiled. Then she would open the royal wine cellar and authorize a shore party the likes of which had never been seen before! It would be a day of rest for the slaves and roasted meat for the civies, while the sec men would revel in enough shine, sluts and song to satisfy even their warrior appetites.

Feeling exhausted, and exhilarated, the baron started back for the stone dais to watch over the rest of the harvesting. In the back of her mind, the woman tried desperately to ignore the rest of the doomie's prophesy, that soon after this day-of-days the ville would be destroyed, and she would be forced into the ultimate act of depravity—marriage to a blood kin.

Chapter Two

As the robotic arm started dragging the struggling J.B. out of the ready room, the companions saw a hulking machine of some kind filling the outside corridor.

There was a domed head and a cylindrical body with treads on the bottom like an army tank. More important, the machine possessed six arms, each of them brandishing spinning buzzsaws, pinchers or pneumatic hammers. The terrible sight fueled them with cold adrenaline. This wasn't a sec hunter droid, but it was clearly built for the same purpose—to ruthlessly chill invaders.

As Ryan scrambled from behind the heavy door, Doc assumed a firing stance and grimly triggered the LeMat. The weapon boomed and the huge .44 miniball of the Civil War handcannon slammed into the joint of the pinchers, cracking the seal, and amber hydraulic fluid gushed out like opening a vein. As the pressure dropped, J.B. forced the pinchers apart and wiggled free to drop flat and get out of the way of the others. Quickly withdrawing the damaged limb, the robot extended two more arms, each tipped with a spinning buzzsaw.

Now unencumbered by the presence of their friend, the rest of the companions cut loose with a fusillade of destruction, the volley of rounds hammering the big machine. Scrambling to his feet, J.B. swung around the Uzi and raked the droid with a long spray of 9 mm Parabellum rounds.

Stabbing out with a ferruled arm, the droid sent a buzzsaw straight toward the closest companion. Jerking aside, Jak felt a tug on his hair and saw some loose strands float away.

Raking the big droid with their combined weaponry, the companions pulled back to gain valuable combat room. However, the machine was too large to get through the hatchway, and all it could do was reach out with ferruled limbs, the buzzsaw jabbing for their faces and hands. Unlike a sec hunter, there were no visible eyes on this droid. Aiming for the silvery dome on top, Ryan pumped several 9 mm rounds into the shiny head of the machine. The hollowpoint rounds ricocheted off the shiny material, but the dome bent and the droid began to wildly jerk, the metal arms flailing uncontrollably.

Focusing all of their blasters on the head, the companions mercilessly hammered the droid until it began to turn randomly, the armored treads going in different directions. Suddenly smoke began to rise from the joints, fat electrical sparks crawled over the machine, and then it went stock-still, a low hum rapidly building in volume and in power.

Biting back a curse, Ryan and Krysty both rushed for the door and together slammed it shut. They only turned the locking wheel an inch before there came a deafening explosion from the other side. The entire ready room shook, the locker doors flopping open, miscellaneous items tumbling to the riveted floor as a crimson snowstorm of rust sprinkled down from the ceiling.

Waiting a few minutes for the reverberations to die away, Ryan gingerly probed the wheel to find it extremely warm, but not too hot to touch. Pausing to reload his blaster, he boldly cracked open the circular door once more and looked outside.

There was a smoky dent in the steel corridor, the walls bulging outward slightly. However there was no sign of the droid, only a scattering of partially melted machine parts littering the floor.

"Wh-what a piece of drek," J.B. panted, swinging the Uzi behind his back to reclaim the scattergun. "A sec droid would have been much tougher to chill." Taking spare cartridges from the shoulder strap, he worked the pump and fed them into the weapon.

"True enough," Ryan countered, squinting his good eye to try to see into the shadows beyond the nimbus of the road flare. "But we better stay on triple red. If this thing had caught us in the open, we'd have bought the farm for sure."

Just then, the road flare sputtered and died.

Cursing under his breath, Ryan pulled out his last flare and scraped it across the rough wall until the tip sparked. The flare gushed into smoky flame.

"I just hope this is some sort of a redoubt and not a predark warship," Krysty stated, thumbing fresh rounds into her blaster. "Those were actually designed to be a maze of corridors, ladders and passageways to confuse any potential invaders."

"Quite so, dear lady," Doc muttered. "There is little chance of us successfully finding the egress in an unfamiliar locale through pitch darkness."

"Finding what?" Jak asked, arching an eyebrow.

Doc smiled tolerantly as if addressing a student. "The exit."

The teen nodded. "Gotcha."

"Well, we wouldn't be in absolute darkness," Mildred retorted, releasing her butane lighter and tucking it into a pocket. "Not quite, anyway."

Rummaging in her med kit, the woman unearthed a battered flashlight and pumped the handle of the survivalist tool until the batteries were recharged, then she pressed the switch. A weak beam issued from the ancient device, and she played it around the war-torn corridor, making sure there were no still functioning pieces of the war machine.

With his blaster at the ready, Ryan eased into the corridor, listening closely for any creaks or groans from the floor. The dented metal seemed stable, but he had been fooled before. And even a short fall onto steel could ace him just as sure as lead in the head from a blaster.

Past the blast zone, the metal corridor was covered with pale filaments that he soon recognized as roots. They covered the ceiling, and hung thick on the walls, extending out of sight in either direction. Scowling, the man glanced at the wall opposite the ready room. In every redoubt, that was always the location of a wall map showing new personnel where everything was to be found. The lack of a map, or any sign that a map had once been there, was proof positive to him that this was not a redoubt.

"Okay, anybody got an idea which way we should try?" Ryan asked, looking in one direction, then the other. Both went on for a hundred paces to end at an intersection with a ladder.

"Left," Jak stated confidently, jerking his Colt in that direction.

"Now, how do you know that?" Mildred asked curiously, warily hefting her ZKR.

Stoically, the albino teen shrugged. "Roots thinner to the right, thicker to the left. So that way out."

"Elementary, my dear Watson," Doc said appreciatively.

Having heard the quote many times before, Jak merely smiled in reply.

"You do know that Holmes never actually said that, don't you?" Mildred asked. "Not in the books, anyway. Only the movies."

"I am literate, madam," Doc replied with a sniff.

Ignoring the banter, the companions sidled carefully around the blaster crater, and Ryan took the lead. Heading to the left, the companions found a lot of closed hatches along the walls. If there had been time, they would have eagerly done a fast recon for anything useful. But right now, getting outside was the goal.

Spying some lumps on the floor up ahead, Ryan slowed his advance, but soon he saw they were only a couple of crumbling skeletons covered with roots, the tendrils entwined among the loose bones and moldy strips of clothing. A gold ring glistened on the finger bones of a hand no longer attached to anything, and silver dots shone from the loose teeth inside a lopsided skull.

"This might tell us something," Mildred said, kneeling to inspect the plastic ID badge still pinned to a piece of uniform lying on a skeleton. Reverently, she lifted the rectangle from the morass of plant roots and human remains. "It seems that we are inside a U.S. Navy ship after all, the—" she bent and angled the badge to try to catch the light better "—the…USS *Grover Harrington.*"

"Indeed, and who was that, madam?" Doc asked, craning his neck for a better look. "Some politician, perhaps?"

Placing the badge down, the physician stood. "Never heard of the guy. He must have been an admiral."

"Don't care who, what is?" Jak asked pragmatically.

"Sorry, again I have no idea," the woman replied honestly, wiping off her hands. "This could be anything from an aircraft carrier to a missile frigate."

"Well, at least we know it's a boat," Ryan said, easing his stance slightly. "Which means up is the way out."

Reaching the intersection, Ryan paused at the sight of a wide breach on the metal floor. The hole didn't appear to have been caused by an explosion as the edges were feathered with corrosion, not bent and twisted from the force of a detonation. That was when he heard the slow drip of water from above. A split second later, a drop plummeted past the man, directly through the hole and into the darkness below.

Kneeling slightly, Ryan lowered the flare into the darkness and froze at the sight of another robotic droid, apparently the same model as the one they had just aced. However, this one was in even worse shape, the dome already cracked, several of the rusty arms lying on the deck nearby, and a broken tread was hanging limply off the gears.

"Not much of a danger there," J.B. said with a touch of satisfaction in his voice.

"Not unless we trip over it," Krysty agreed.

"What are those boxes behind it?" Mildred asked curiously, angling the beam of her flashlight.

The weak beam did little to alleviate the murky interior, but slowly their sight grew accustomed to the darkness. Lining the rust-streaked walls in orderly rows were stacks of plastic storage boxes, faded numbers stenciled along the sides to identify the contents.

"Those are full of MRE food packs!" Ryan exclaimed. "And those others contain ballistic vests!"

"I see some Hummers and an LAV in the back!" J.B. called, grinning widely. "And the boxes over here are full of boots, field surgery kits, radios…there's even one marked for freaking LAW rocket launchers."

"Excelsior!" Doc whooped in triumph. "We have hit the motherload of supplies."

"This much ordnance must have been en route to a military outpost when the world ended," Mildred guessed, chewing a lip. "Perhaps even a redoubt."

"Quite true, madam."

"Maybe," Ryan muttered, in taciturn agreement. This was turning into one of the richest jumps they had ever made. But the man automatically distrusted anything this easy. If something looked too good to be true, it almost invariably was.

"Looks good, but how reach?" Jak said with a frown,

estimating the distance to the floor below. "That fifty-foot drop. How reach?"

"We can't," Krysty stated flatly, shifting her attention to the flare. It was already half consumed. "But once we get outside, we can come back with torches and rope. Even if there are no villes in the area, we can easily make those ourselves."

Starting to agree, Ryan paused as there came a soft thumping. Fireblast, that sounded like a hydraulic pump. It seemed that some small part of the warship was still in working condition.

Something moved in the shadows. Ryan scowled as another droid rolled into the light.

This new machine was perfect, not a speck of rust or a scratch on the chassis. Even worse, instead of buzz-saws and hammers, this model sported a tribarrel Gatling gun in lieu of a left arm, the enclosed Niagara-style ammunition belt going into a wide hopper attached to the back of the droid.

Grunting at the sight, Ryan froze as the domed head instantly swiveled upward at the small noise to look directly at him, the Gatling swiveling, giving off a hydraulic sigh as it copied the gesture.

Lurching into action, Ryan threw his arms wide to push the other companions out of the way. They cleared the hole and a split second later, a chattering maelstrom erupted out of the opening. The noisy column of hot lead hammered along the riveted ceiling, blowing off the layers of corrosion, a barrage of ricochets musically zinging away in every direction. Mildred cried out and Jak grunted loudly as they both were hit by the misshapen slugs.

Yanking a pipe bomb from his bag, J.B. started to light the fuse, but then paused. They were sitting over a cargo hold packed with military ordnance. One bomb could easily start a chain reaction of detonations that would remove this ship, and the companions, from the face of the Earth. They couldn't even shoot back without risking a damn explosion!

Suddenly the blasterfire ceased, and there was a series of hard clicks, then silence, almost as if the machine had run out of ammo.

Scowling in disbelief, Ryan took a spent brass from his pocket and flipped it toward the hole. As it hit the rusty edge, there immediately came a fiery response. He nodded in grim satisfaction. Yeah, thought so. Pretending to be out of brass was an old trick to try to lure an enemy into sneaking a peek so that you could blow off his or her head. The droid was well-programmed in military tactics. He would remember that when they returned.

Silently motioning the others to follow, Ryan crawled away from the jagged opening until they were at the base of the ladder.

"That damn machine was playing possum!" Krysty said angrily. At the soft words there came a short burst from the hole, but it soon stopped.

"Which probably means it can't come after us," J.B. stated, removing his fedora to smooth down his hair before jamming it back into position. "This droid didn't activate until there was an explosion. This is the reserve force. It's not going to leave that cargo bay under any circumstances."

"Then we should be safe until trying to enter," Doc rumbled, using a thumb to ease down the hammer on the LeMat.

"Unless there are others," Ryan countered, grabbing the lowest rung of the old ladder. He shook it hard, and when nothing fell off, the man stood and holstered the SIG-Sauer. "But that's tomorrow's problem. We'll find some way to take out that droid later."

"If ship still here," Jak added dourly, pressing a handkerchief to the bloody score along his neck. The teen couldn't see the damage, but knew that it was only a flesh wound.

"And if those boxes aren't empty," Mildred rejoined, tying off a field dressing on her forearm. An inch higher and the ricochet would have taken off her elbow.

"Paranoid," Doc sniffed in disdain.

"Cynic," the physician corrected, finishing the bandage.

Seeing the others were ready, Ryan started to climb up the ladder, holding the flare so that it stuck out to the side. It was pretty low by now, and he had no intention of stopping for anything until they reached daylight.

After twenty feet or so, they reached the next deck. Rising from the access hole, they checked for any more droids, then proceeded directly to the next ladder. Having done some exploring in other predark warships, the companions found this familiar territory.

As they ascended, the roots became thicker. Soon, more of the predark crew was discovered, the tendrils deeply embedded into the moldy remains. Mildred fought off the urge to rip out the plants, while Krysty found the sight comforting. People ate plants to live, and when they died, the plants consumed them in return. It was the circle of life.

Five decks later the first of the leaves appeared, diamond-shaped and dark green with a thin blue stripe. Obviously a mutie, but the smell was that of ordinary kudzu. Both Ryan and J.B. checked the rad counters clipped to their lapels, but there was no discernible background radiation.

Reaching a remarkably clean level, the companions quickly passed by the security office, the pile of spent brass and skeletons on the deck proclaiming a major firefight. There was even some wreckage from a couple of the droids. However, there was no way of telling if the fight had been the crew repelling hostile invaders, or staging a mutiny. Or even worse, a rebellion by the machines. J.B. fought back a sigh as they climbed higher. There was probably a wealth of weaponry inside the office, but time was short and—

With a wild sputter, the last flare died.

Pumping the handle of her flashlight, Mildred passed the device up to Ryan, and he tucked it into his shirt pocket. The beam was very weak, but a lot better than trying to climb while holding a candle. Now, their speed increased, and as the reek of the flare dissipated, they began to detect the smell of freshwater, along with the dulcet aroma of flowers.

At the next level, Ryan saw there were no more ladders, and allowed himself a smile as a cool breeze came from the darkness to the right. However as he advanced, the flashlight revealed that the passageway was blocked solid with plant life, the walls festooned with orchids of every color imaginable. The place resembled a rainforest more than the inside of a battleship.

Drawing the panga, he hacked and slashed a crude path through the foliage until finding an open hatchway. Sheathing the blade, Ryan drew the SIG-Sauer and stepped over the jamb to emerge into bright sunlight. Blinking against the harsh glare, he braced for an attack.

Nothing happened. The deck was covered with a thick carpet of moss, and flowery vines hung from above.

Ryan could only vaguely detect a railing, marking this as an observation balcony. Then he changed that to a battle station at the sight of a large lump of rusty machine parts that could have been a machine-gun nest, or perhaps even a Vulcan minicannon, but there was no way of telling anymore. There was a bird nest perched on top of the debris, and a small pine tree grew out sideways, the trunk molded into a twisted spiral by the gentle ocean wind.

Stretching in front of the man was a large body of blue water, low waves cresting onto a wide pebble beach. Hills rose to a rocky plateau, and then abruptly jutted upward into snowcapped mountains. A thick fog moved stealthily along the lowlands, masking any signs of civilization.

Stepping into view, Krysty blinked at the sunlight, keeping a tight grip on her blaster. "That looks like the ocean," she said hesitantly. "But there's no smell of salt. Could this be some sort of an inland sea?"

"Makes sense," Ryan replied tersely. "Or at least a bastard big lake."

"Some of them are as big as an ocean," Krysty commented, walking over to the railing and looking down. It was an easy hundred feet from the balcony to the choppy surface of the water. She scanned the shoreline for the remains of a dockyard, but there was nothing in sight. Now she understood why the vessel had never been looted. From stem to stern, keel to radar mast, the dense foliage completely covered the ship. She could not tell the size, or shape, of the vessel, much less where it stopped and the land began. To anybody passing, the ship would simply seem another irregular foothill, just one lost among a dozen others.

With the scattergun leading the way, J.B. came next, followed closely by Mildred, then Jak and Doc. The companions moved with practiced ease, each keeping a safe distance from the others to not offer an enemy a group target. There were a lot of ways to get aced, and stupidity was the most common.

"Looks like Oregon," Mildred said, closing her jacket. The damp air was cold, almost enough to make her breath fog. That was when she noticed the play of colors from above and looked skyward. "Good Lord, that's an aurora borealis!" she cried in delight. "John, are we near the North Pole?"

"Could be Canada," Jak stated coolly. "Been before."

"Or Iceland, or even Siberia," J.B. said with a frown, remembering the time they had jumped to Russia.

"Nonsense, dear lady, it is much too warm for either

of those icy locales," Doc replied, turning up his collar. But then he paused. "However, since we have found deserts in Japan, and swamps in Nevada, we could be anywhere."

"Well, I can't take a reading through these clouds," J.B. said. "But we'll find out where this is, sooner or later."

"This is a magnificent view, though," Doc commented, looking over the oceanic vista. There seemed to be some small islands far ahead, but he could not be sure at this range.

"Hell of fall, too," Jak retorted, glancing over the railing into the waves so very far below. It had to be an easy fifty feet, maybe more.

"We're not going to jump, that's for damn sure," J.B. stated. "Any sign of stairs or another ladder?"

But before any of the companions could start a search, a strident roar of blasterfire annihilated the curtain of vegetation hanging over the exit. Lightning-fast, the companions took cover behind the pile of corroded machinery and leveled their blasters at the smoking hatchway.

"By the Three Kennedys, the dastardly machine did come after us!" Doc bellowed, thumbing back the hammer of the LeMat.

"No room to maneuver here," Ryan snarled. "Gotta shut that door. Cover me!"

As the companions sent a hail of lead into the hatchway, Ryan charged around the debris and crossed the balcony in under a heartbeat, to throw himself flat against the vine-covered wall. From inside the corridor, he clearly heard the rumble of armored treads over the constant ricochets of the incoming barrage. Holstering his blaster, Ryan grabbed the old portal and shoved hard. Nothing happened. He tried again with the same result, then saw that the hinges were hopelessly choked with rust and tiny vines.

Shoving two fingers into his mouth, Ryan sharply whistled and made a motion at the open hatchway. Nodding in understanding, J.B. pulled a pipe bomb out of his munitions bag and tossed it over. Making the catch, Ryan pulled out a butane lighter, bit the bomb fuse in two, and started the nubbin burning.

Knowing what to do next, the rest of the companions pulled out their spare blasters and sent a double fusillade of hot lead into the open doorway. Raising a splayed hand, Ryan silently counted down from five, and as he dropped the last finger, the others instantly stopped firing. He tossed the pipe bomb into the corridor, getting only a very brief glance inside as the explosive charge clattered along the floor to stop in the middle of the four hulking guardians jammed into the narrow corridor. Nuking hell, he thought, the cargo droid had to have called in reinforcements!

Jerking out of the hatchway, Ryan barely got behind steel when the pipe bomb violently detonated, the concussion shaking the vessel for yards.

"There's four of them!" Ryan bellowed at the top of his lungs.

Startled at the news, J.B. grimaced as he pulled out a gren, flipped off the arming lever, pulled the pin and whipped the bomb forward in a sideways pitch. The military sphere hit the door and bounced inside to erupt into a searing light, and writhing tongues of chemical fire bellowed out from the hatchway, the volcanic heat wave withering the vines for yards as hundreds of leaves turned brown and fell away to expose the bare hull underneath.

"Okay, the thermite will hold them for a few minutes," J.B. stated. "But that was my only gren."

"Move with a purpose, people," Ryan commanded, heading for the bow. The foothills were only a short distance from the ship, and once on land, the companions could easily disappear among the boulders and trees. Even if the machines followed, their treads would become hopelessly mired in the soft ground, making them easy pickings.

However, there was no clear way off the balcony, the stairs or access ladder, which were hidden under multiple layers of moss, flowering vines and bird droppings. Risking a step off the balcony, Ryan saw his boot punch straight through a leafy canopy to reveal only open space. He tried again with the same results.

Holstering their spare blasters, the companions pulled out blades and wildly slashed at the plants. But there only seemed to be more vines underneath, layer after layer, in an endless procession. Going to the railing, Ryan looked down at the choppy water of the lake and tried to guess the distance. Roughly fifty feet.

Unexpectedly, a sizzling beam of light stabbed through the wall alongside the roaring conflagration. Steadily the power beam drew a line in the ancient metal, rising up from the deck about twelve feet, and then slowly starting to move sideways.

Caught reloading the ZKR, Mildred almost dropped a handful of brass at the horrible sight. Sweet Jesus, the robotic sons of bitches were cutting themselves a new exit around the thermite! A hundred possibilities flashed through her mind like riffling playing cards, and she chose the most logical. The prime rule with every machine in existence was that electrical circuits did not like water. Therefore, her decision was made.

"Follow me," Mildred shouted, jumping over the railing to hurtle toward the choppy water of the lake. Without pause, the other companions were right behind the bold physician.

Plummeting through the chilly air, the fall seemed to take the companions forever, as if the universe had slowed to aid the escape. But they knew better and hugged their belongings tightly, trying to brace for the coming impact, which was going to be bad.

A cataclysm of pain engulfed the companions as they plunged into the turgid lake, the biting cold almost stealing the breath from their lungs. The agony was unbelievable. It was as if every inch of their bodies was being stabbed with tiny knives.

As expected, their clothing resisted for only a few seconds, then quickly soaked through, a fresh wave of cold reaching their vulnerable skin as their weight increased tenfold.

Half expecting to hit the bottom and shatter their legs, the companions rode the wave of torment, preparing for even worse.

An unknown length of time passed and incredibly their descent began to slow, and the companions started to sluggishly rise. Fueled by a fierce determination to live, the companions forced their limbs to move, desperately swimming for the surface, the ancient scuba mantra of "always follow the bubbles" keeping them going in the right direction.

Erupting through the waves, the gasping companions greedily drank in the bitterly cold air, then shivered in renewed torment as a chill invaded their aching lungs, sapping away even more of their failing strength. But that was of no real concern. They had survived. Now it was only a dozen yards or so until they were safe on shore.

Swimming in steady strokes, Ryan quickly glanced around to see if everybody was present and accounted for when a large metallic object violently smacked into the choppy water, the armed guardian promptly disappearing below the lolling waves.

Chapter Three

Standing on the lee of the rocky shore, a blonde woman lifted a wooden flute to her lips and began to softly play.

Made of whalebone, the delicately carved musical instrument had been a parting gift from her father, just before Mad Pete threw her off a cliff.

The music slowed as she almost smiled at the memory. Oh, it was true that the old man had been triple crazy. Yet he was also oddly wise, and always gentle. It took years before the child could understand that her loving father had acted more insane than he really was to keep the baron from taking her to his bed. Not a marriage bed, just the one he kept hidden from his wife in a stone shed behind the Citadel, where nobody else could witness what happened to other young girls in the dark of a foggy night. Named Victoria by the baron, but called Summer Liana by her father, her first lesson in life had been that deception could be more useful as a knife. Mad Pete had taught the young girl many secret things in the privacy of their hut, patiently waiting until she became an adult of eighteen winters before casting her into the world to live free or die. It was cruel, but necessary.

May the moon goddess bless you for that brutal act

of kindness, dear father, Liana prayed silently in her mind. As a well of raw emotion made her throat tighten, she accidentally blew a sour note on the flute. Instantly the subtle motions in the lake stopped.

Frowning, the teenager redoubled her concentration, blocking out the bittersweet memories of her lost childhood and the fierce stabs of hunger in her belly. Thrown into the sea wearing only the rawhide dress and soft slippers of a slave, Liana now wore a warm robe made of moose hide and waterproof beaver-skin boots. A grass rope was tied at her waist, and a large wooden knife was sheathed at her hip, with another tucked into her left boot. A spear rested in the dirt nearby. There was even a flat stone with a razor-sharp edge hidden under her rawhide dress in case of emergency. Such as, if somebody got a look at her eyes. A woven bag of river reeds hung across her back, bulging with everything she possessed, which sadly wasn't very much.

There had been no berries to be found on the mountain bushes, potatoes in the fields, frogs in the swamp, snails, or even eggs in the bird nests hidden along the north cliffs. Liana was accustomed to feeling hungry, as food was always in short supply for a runaway slave, but this winter was particularly lean and the teenager knew that she had to learn how to forage for herself or else join her beloved father on the last train west.

As her stomach grumbled loudly once more, Liana forced her mind to relax, and the music flowed clear and sweet across the misty bay. The wind ruffled the long blond hair hanging across her face, almost pushing it aside, but the lard carefully rubbed into the strands kept them in place. Since her birth, nobody had ever gotten a good look at her face, which was why she was still alive. Her eyes revealed the awful truth, and throw-backs were slain on sight.

Soon there was an answering tug in the back of her mind and she almost smiled at the sight of a black snake rising to the surface and coming straight toward her. Excellent!

Stepping back slightly, Liana continued to play the flute. The snake blindly charged her, going over the edge of the small pit and tumbling to the bottom. Startled, the snake lashed about, trying to get out, but the sides of the hole were much too steep. Hissing in unbridled fury, the snake eventually calmed, moving to the rhythm of the music, and then bizarrely fell asleep.

Overjoyed, Liana could not believe the sight. The song was working! Her father had been right once again. While he could see the future, she was able to command the lower animals. Never again would she be hungry. What a glorious day!

As a young girl, Liana dimly remembered her grandy scoffing at the notion that she could summon snakes with a musical instrument. "Snakes ain't got no ears!" she raged, waving her walking stick. "I've eaten enough of them to know that! How can you summon a thing with music if it can't hear?" And it was true, the snakes had no discernible ears. Yet her father had insisted that someday they would come to her call. Nothing else, just snakes. But that was enough to fill her belly, even in the bad times after the acid rains came to burn the land clean.

Wishing to test the range of her new ability, Liana played on, using her mind to probe into the murky depths of the cold sea. She found more snakes, and several eels, a rare delicacy reserved purely for those of royal blood. What a feast she would have back in her little cave!

Deciding that she could not wait that long, Liana tucked away the flute and yanked the spear from the ground. Stabbing a particularly fat snake in the pit, she hauled it out impaled. The dying creature thrashed for only a few seconds, then slumped and went still.

Using her belt knife, the young woman carefully peeled off the valuable skin and placed it aside, then scooped out the guts and tossed them into the weeds for the creatures of the field. Nothing bloody was ever allowed to fall into the lake, as that could summon a kraken, the most horrible creature in the world.

Using a piece of flint and some dry grass, Liana soon started a fire and fed the tiny blaze sticks, then branches, until it was a roaring campfire. Savoring the warmth, she stuck the snake on a greenstick and put it over the flames, the delicious aroma of roasting meat a tantalizing torment. Her empty stomach rumbled in anticipation, and she stole a tiny piece of the raw flesh to hold it in abeyance for just a few more minutes.

Humming happily to herself, Liana only vaguely heard a whooshing noise from behind when there was a terrible pain at the back of her head, and blackness filled the universe.

She never quite fully lost consciousness, but she fell helpless to the ground, the snake falling into the flames to disappear in an explosion of embers and smoke.

Dimly through the hammering in her ears, Liana could hear the sound of boots crunching on loose pebbles, and rough hands flipped her over. Dark shapes stood nearby, and she tried to speak, but could only manage a sort of wet burble. Her tongue felt thick and the world kept spinning around.

"Hot damn, look, boys, it's a slut!" A man chortled. "Guess we got a meal, and a ride!"

Cold horror exploded in her guts at the casual pronouncement of rape, and Liana blinked to try to clear her vision. The savage pounding at the back of her head made it difficult, but she ordered the pain away and suddenly could see once more.

There were ten of them, large men with beards, wearing dirty robes of mismatched furs. Their hair was matted with sticks and mud, with grisly necklaces of dried human ears hanging around their throats. Each was heavily armed with stone weapons, knives and axes, plus each carried a crossbow slung over a shoulder. Goddess protect me, she prayed. These were Hillies.

Kneeling alongside her, a redheaded man was binding her wrists with lengths of rawhide, while another cleaned the blood and hair off a boomerang on his sleeve. Dimly, she recognized it as her own blond hair, and cursed herself for a fool. Struck from behind! Hunger had distracted her for a few minutes, and now she would have to pay the ultimate price.

Feebly, she tried to resist and the cold edge of a stone knife was pressed against her throat.

"Stop wiggling or I'll gut you like a fish," a Hilly

snarled, displaying rotten teeth, his breath fetid with shine and wolfweed. "That won't ace ya, but you'll sure wish it had. Savvy?"

Liana nodded her understanding, her mind racing to find some way to get loose, get free, escape. But if she struggled too hard, it might show them the truth, and death would swiftly follow.

Finished binding her wrists, the Hilly began running his hands over her clothing, taking away everything in her pockets, and then cutting away the rope belt to spread open her coat. Shivering from the rush of cold air, Liana felt sick at the leering faces of the mountain savages looking down at her.

"Hey, lookit there. Bitch has got a whole pit full of snakes," a blond man muttered, kicking some loose dirt into the hole. The snakes awoke and hissed angrily. "How the frag did she do that without a net?"

"Don't know, don't care," a bald man said. "Ask her after we're done, but I wanna start pumping right now."

"Wait your turn, gleeb," the redhead barked, sheathing his blade. "Now strip the bitch, and make sure she ain't hiding a blade."

"We already know what she's hiding!" the fat Hilly said, rubbing a hand across his mouth.

Trying not to burst into tears, Liana winced at their raucous laughter, and the stone knives slashed away her clothing, soon leaving her exposed on the cold, hard ground. Filthy hands fondled her as the last of her clothing was removed, then the Hillies jerked away as if she had suddenly become red-hot.

"Well, nuke me," a tall man whispered, tossing away

a shredded piece of her rawhide dress. "Looks like we got us a runaway slave!"

"That's the mark for Anchor ville," another said in wonder, rubbing a finger along the chained eagle burned into her shoulder. "The baron there will pay a fortune in steel for this little bitch."

"I…am a singer," Liana croaked, knowing there was nothing to try but the truth. "I can summon snakes. All you want, at any time. I'll…I'll be a good slave. Y-your ville will never go hungry again!" She swallowed hard. "But don't send me back. Please!"

The faces of the Hillies underwent a variety of expressions as they considered the matter from every angle.

"We got enough food," the leader said, loosening the belt around his waist. His pants fell away, revealing that he was more than ready. "Grab her legs, boys, I'm going in!"

With those dire words, fear filled her mind and Liana knew that her only escape would be on the last train west. So be it. She could at least rob the bastards of their fun. Shaking her head as hard as she could, the woman felt her long bangs shift and the Hillies recoil in horror.

SLOSHING OUT OF THE OCEAN, the cresting waves knocking them forward, the bedraggled companions staggered onto the shore, panting for breath and drawing their blasters.

Weakly shuffling behind some boulders for cover, the friends caught their breath as yet another droid rolled off the balcony of the warship and plummeted into the water, only to vanish beneath the surface and then violently explode. A few moments later, a boiling geyser erupted upward, only to come back down to spread outward as a warm and gentle rain.

"Triple stupe feebs." J.B. sneered in disdain, lowering the Uzi. "If that keeps up, there'll soon be no more droids on the bastard ship." The man was drenched, his hair and clothing steadily dripping water.

"Lake bigger than ship," Jak agreed, his white hair plastered to his head, giving him a vaguely corpselike appearance.

"The bastard comps must have gone haywire over the decades," Ryan said, fighting a shiver.

"Personally, I was thankful for the wash," Doc stated, visibly trembling. "I was starting to name my flies."

It was an exaggeration, but everybody understood the feeling. The past couple of redoubts had not possessed working showers, only hot water in the kitchen, and the companions had washed using the kitchen sink. But in spite of that, they had started to become noticeably ripe. A dunk into frigid water was no shower, but it would do for the moment.

"We need a fire quick, or we're going to get sick," Krysty stated, her soggy hair flexing as if trying to dislodge the water droplets. "There's enough driftwood about, but this wind is going to ace us eventually."

Just then, another droid rolled off the ship, the machines still in hot pursuit of the invaders. There was the usual underwater detonation and rain.

"Okay, these things aren't going to be troubling us any," Ryan decided, shouldering his Steyr longblaster. "Let's get into the forest and find some bastard shelter before we freeze solid." Flexing his hands, the man gently rubbed a finger under his eyepatch. The cold was making the old wound ache something fierce.

"Shelter and coffee," Doc countered, holstering the useless LeMat. The Civil War handcannon had many positive attributes, but it was not waterproof like a modern-day blaster. After their immersion, the black powder in the cylinder was dribbling out of the barrel like dark blood. The weapon would be useless until thoroughly dried, cleaned and reloaded. The Ruger was still in his frock coat pocket, but he was saving that until needed. There had been no chance to thoroughly clean the blaster yet, and it was possible that pulling the trigger would be the very last thing his right hand ever did in this world.

Taking hold of his walking stick, Doc twisted the lion's-head newel to unlock the mechanism and draw his sword.

Starting to offer a suggestion of digging a pit, Jak caught a movement in the air and smiled. A bat! Spinning, he strode toward the nearby cliff and there it was, a large opening in the side of the rock formation.

Whistling sharply for the others, the teenager drew his blaster and butane lighter, then carefully proceeded inside. Caves were natural shelters, and also one of the most dangerous places in existence. Aside from the possibility of a cave-in sealing a person inside, or tumbling into a cavern, or getting lost, bears liked to hibernate in caves, as well as rats, bats, lions, wolverines and a host of muties who delighted in eating human flesh.

However, Jak soon saw that the precautions had not been necessary. The cave ended after a hundred feet or so, narrowing into a crevice too small for anything larger than a mouse to traverse. Obviously the bat had not come from this particular cave. Fair enough. With all of those boulders outside, the cliffs were probably honeycombed with caves and tunnels.

Off to the side of the cave was a small pool, only a few inches deep, the crystal-clear water full of albino crayfish. Since the companions had plenty of food, Jak ignored the tiny creatures, leaving them in peace. A real hunter never aced for pleasure, but only to put food on the table.

Suddenly there came a whistle from behind, and the teenager answered without even turning. Soon, there came the sound of boots on stone.

"Dear God, it feels good to get out of the wind," Mildred said, playing about her flashlight. "Any occupants in here, Jak?"

"We alone," the albino teen replied, then gestured with his blaster. "Right now, anyway." There was the remnants of a campfire and a few gnawed bones tossed into a corner. Clearly, somebody had used the cave as a campsite once.

"Looks fine," Ryan said, studying the smooth ceiling. "Good job, Jak."

The teenager shrugged. "Easy find cave, know how."

Softly in the distance, there came another watery explosion.

"Well, I'll cook dinner if somebody else gets the firewood," J.B. offered, easing his sodden munitions bag to the rocky floor. The spare blasters clattered as they came to a rest.

"We better find something to block the mouth first," Mildred corrected. "Let's try to roll one of the smaller boulders in first to help block the wind."

"And keep in the heat." Krysty laughed weakly, then she frowned unexpectedly.

"Something wrong, lover?" Ryan asked, pausing in the act of removing his fur-lined coat. Soaked with water, the garment felt like it weighed a hundred pounds.

Her hair flexing in a wild corona, Krysty said nothing as she looked around the cave, then suddenly lurched back outside with a drawn blaster in her hand.

"Krysty?" Ryan repeated in growing concern, joining her outside the cave.

The woman gave no reply, lost in a private world. Just for a second, there had been a flutter in her mind. Screwing her eyelids shut, the woman blocked out the distractions of the world—the sound of the ocean, the cold wind, even the voices of her friends, concentrating solely on the ghostly sensation.

However, strain as she might, nothing more could be felt. Then she heard a faint cry from the direction of a low dune. Surging into action, the woman pelted in that direction. Whatever was happening, that had not been a cry of surprise or gladness.

A steep embankment formed a dune that sloped upward to a grassy plateau. Krysty took it at a run, her breath visibly puffing as she reached the top. The rocks were slippery under her muddy cowboy boots and she nearly fell several times before reaching the top of the steppe. A split second later Ryan and the others arrived, staying quiet and letting her take the lead.

Hesitantly, Krysty moved forward, a blaster in each hand.

The area was thick with scraggy grass, along with tall reeds. To the left was the forest of pine trees, the air sweet with their scent. That seemed a logical place for somebody to make camp, but the cry had come from the right, so she raced back toward the lake.

Bushes and reeds blocked her view, but the woman cried out in pain once more, and then there came the curse of a man.

Redoubling their speed, the companions crested a low rise to come upon a small clearing filled with hairy men surrounding a blond woman waving around a fishing spear. She was completely naked, her body covered with bruises, but the men were slashed in a dozen places, blood trickling from shallow cuts in their fur coats. Her wrists were lashed together, but the men seemed to be getting the worst of the fight. One big man had missing teeth, his jaw still dripping blood, another had a broken nose, and a third was missing a large patch of hair, his scalp oozing a clear fluid. Every time they tried to get close she would jab for their hands, and the men retreated, sucking the wounds. However, they did not go very far.

Forcibly holding Krysty back, Ryan went low in the reeds to stay out of sight for a moment to gauge the situation. Rushing into the unknown was a good way to get aced. This looked like a gangbang, but things were not always as they seemed. The blonde could have been a gaudy slut bought for the night and the men had caught her stealing. Acing her would only be justice. On the other hand, this could be a trap to lure in passing travelers.

Grunting savagely, one of the men rushed forward, and the blonde thrust the spear toward him, then slashed it sideways. Caught by surprise, the man cursed as the blade opened his cheek. Blood gushed out, and he quickly retreated.

Spotting the companions, the blonde smiled in obvious relief, then her expression darkened. "Run," she screamed, raw terror in her husky voice. "Run for your lives!"

As those exact words repeated inside her mind, all doubt was gone, and Krysty knew for a fact this was the source of the previous cry for help. We're coming, sister, Krysty mentally shouted back, but if the blonde heard, she gave no indication.

Hesitantly glancing backward, unsure if this was a trick of some kind, the hairy men recoiled at the sight of the companions, then cursed vehemently and dived for their dropped weapons.

"Sec men," a tall coldheart shouted, grabbing a boomerang and whipping it forward. "Ace 'em, boys!"

Spinning across the campsite, the edge of the wooden boomerang glinted with sharp pieces of glass, and it parted the reeds at throat level, leaving a clear path behind.

But the companions were already gone, ducking among the weeds and bushes. Instinctively they expected to hear the crackle of blasters, but there only came another boomerang, closely followed by a spear, and then a flurry of crossbow arrows. However, the barrage did nothing, not even coming close to the crouching companions.

Encouraged by that, Mildred stood and fired both the Beretta and the ZKR.

Hit in the arm, a coldheart cursed and dropped his crossbow. But the next man spun fast, and something small flashed across the clearing, getting wider every second.

Before she could dodge, Mildred was hit by a bolo, the stones and rawhide strips wrapping tightly around her throat. Unable to breathe, the physician clawed at strands on her neck. Snarling in rage, Jak lunged for the woman with a knife in his hands.

Hauling up his longblaster, Ryan shot two of the men dead before he had to take cover again as another boomerang cut through the reeds. Rolling to the side, the one-eyed man took cover behind a fallen log, and felt it shake from the arrival of several arrows, the stone tip of one going all the way through and missing him by inches.

Appearing from behind a tree, J.B. fired the shotgun. Catching the blast full in the chest, a coldheart went sailing off the cliff to disappear below.

"Did ya see? Did ya?" a man shouted excitedly.

"By the sky gods…" a coldheart whispered. "They have blasters! Working blasters!"

"Get that steel!" their leader bellowed, surging forward.

Yanking a gren from her pocket, Krysty primed the bomb and tossed it at the charging group of men. Incredibly, one of them reached up to catch the explosive charge.

"Hey, this ain't no sleepy bomb," he said in growing astonishment. "It's…it's made out of metal. They be throwing metal at us!"

"Don't be a feeb," the leader snarled, reloading his crossbow.

But the coldheart started walking. "No, looky here." Then the grenade detonated, and the man was violently reduced into a gory cloud, steaming gobbets of flesh wetly smacking into the rocks and trees.

"Boomers!" a coldheart gasped. "They got boomers!"

"Frag 'em!" the leader shouted, firing blindly into the reeds. "Just get that steel."

Standing, Doc leveled the Ruger and triggered a fast six shots, the .357 Magnum blaster bellowing smoke and flame. Three of the coldhearts fell with gaping wounds in their chests, but the other two were only nicked by the Magnum's rounds, the sixth shot going wild. Cursing the inaccuracy of the unfamiliar weapon, Doc crouched and started thumbing in more rounds. Then from out of nowhere, a boomerang sliced through the reeds at knee level, smacking the wheelgun from his grip and sending him tumbling into the grass, his hands torn and bloody.

The cry caught the blonde woman's attention, and

she saw the handsome face of the silver-haired man for only a moment before he vanished into the reeds. Her heart leaped at the sight, then Liana jerked her attention back to the fight. Biting a lip, she shoved her hands toward the rocks forming a circle around the campfire, and began to saw her bonds back and forth along the rough edge of a jagged stone. The heat from the fire was almost intolerable, but she kept doggedly at the action until the rawhide strips parted and fell away. She was free!

"Hey," Liana shouted.

Cursing, a coldheart turned fast, furious that he had forgotten about the slut for this long. But as he looked her way, she threw the fishing spear and it thudded directly into his groin.

Shrieking insanely, the coldheart dropped his weapons to grab the wooden shaft obscenely jutting from the ruin of his manhood.

"You fragging bitch!" another coldheart roared, throwing a boomerang. Oddly, it came apart in mid-flight to reveal that it was actually two pieces.

Desperately trying to get out of the way, Liana managed to avoid one of the sections, but the other caught her in the forehead with a hard crack. Sighing, she slumped to the dirt, feebly twitching.

As if infuriated over the act, the snakes in the pit started hissing louder than ever, sounding as if they were being boiled alive.

Rising from the reeds along the edge of the cliff, a grinning coldheart stood with Mildred's dropped blaster in his grip. Fumbling with the Beretta, he sent several booming rounds at the companions, then J.B. cut him in two with the shotgun.

Spinning a sling to nearly invisible speed, another coldheart let fly a stone. It missed Doc, but hit a nearby rock and shattered into a thousand pieces, the shrapnel peppering the time traveler. Spitting a curse, Doc fired back and missed. As the coldheart began to spin another rock to chilling speed, Ryan took him out with a hollowpoint round to the knee. Letting go of the sling, the wounded man cried out as he stumbled into the campfire. As his clothing caught fire, Doc aimed, using both hands, and blew away most of his throat, cutting off the wild shrieks of pain. Still aflame, the body tumbled off the cliff.

With the blonde out of the way, J.B. leveled the Uzi and opened fire, burning through a full clip of 9 mm Parabellum rounds. The shocked coldhearts were torn to pieces.

Moving forward, fast and low, the companions swept across the bloody campsite, chilling every coldheart they found with ruthless efficiency. Tucking away the Ruger, Doc used his sword to slash the throat of every man, just in case one of them was only pretending.

While Ryan and J.B. stood guard over the campsite, Jak and Krysty gathered firewood and Mildred knelt alongside the unconscious woman to check for any serious damage. Privately, Mildred fumed over losing her weapon, but concentrated on the task at hand. Thankfully, the blonde seemed fine, just undernourished, and with a knot on her head that was going to be very tender for quite a long time. The pretty blonde was going to have a monumental headache when she awoke, but that was infinitely better than the alternative. However, now that the rush of battle was over, Mildred's wet clothes were starting to feel clammy once more; every gust of wind from the ocean sent a shiver through the woman.

"How is she doing?" Krysty inquired, dumping an armload of loose sticks onto the dying campfire. The dully glowing embers pulsed into life under the deluge of dry fuel, rapidly building into a roaring blaze.

"She'll be fine," the physician declared, realizing slightly under the waves of heat. "Just battered and bruised."

"They not ride?" Jak asked, adding more fuel to the fire.

Brushing back the long hair of the woman to expose her face, Mildred wearily smiled. "No, we got here in time."

"Glad about that," J.B. said, handing the physician the dropped Beretta. She accepted it gratefully.

"The filthy blackguards," Doc growled, the sound of hate thick in his voice. "They perished too quickly for justice. A nice long hanging would have been their reward back in Vermont."

Cleaning off his sword on a headless corpse, Doc sheathed the blade and started to remove his damp frock coat, but then he paused and instead kicked over the body of the largest coldheart to strip the corpse of its dry furs. He draped them over the woman, covering her naked body.

"Looks like they ambushed her while cooking dinner," J.B. said, studying the footprints in the dirt. "Guess she forget to rig a trip line."

"Stupe place for a campsite, anyway," Ryan agreed, resting the plastic stock of the Steyr on a hip.

"Wonder if this was her first time outside a ville," J.B. added, rubbing his jaw. The lee side of the cliff sloped down to the water, the other end rising high above the rocky shore, which meant that when the coldhearts had attacked, she had nowhere to go aside from jumping onto the rocky shoreline. Glancing over the edge of the cliff, the man saw the crumpled bodies of several coldhearts sprawled on the beach, their red guts splayed across the shiny pebbles, only inches from the cresting waves.

"Even then, she held off ten coldhearts all by herself," Krysty said, feeling a strange touch of pride at the act. "Naked and alone, she fought ten men. She may not be very experienced, but she's got guts."

"A mighty tough lady," Ryan agreed, giving his highest compliment. Then he scowled and kicked away a snake wiggling across the ground.

That was when the hissing pit caught his attention, and Ryan strode over for a closer examination. The hole was only a few feet deep, but absolutely jammed full of live snakes. He looked around for a net, but there were none in sight. Now how the frag did she catch this many snakes without using a net? Ryan knew how to tickle a fish out of water, but you couldn't do that with a damn snake. It would just twist around and bite you. Then he saw something in the grass and lifted a small bone flute into view.

"She singer!" Jak exclaimed.

"Maybe," Krysty agreed hesitantly. "I heard her in my mind back in the cave. That's how I knew to come here."

"She asked for help?" Ryan said suspiciously.

"Not in actual words, no." Krysty smiled ruefully. "It was more like a feeling of desperate need."

Grunting in reply, Ryan tossed her the flute, and Krysty tucked it into a pocket for safekeeping.

"All right, let's get my patient off this exposed butte and back into our cave," Mildred directed, rising stiffly. "I want to get some hot broth in her as soon as… What the hell?" With a jerk, the woman kicked away a snake that had been circling around her boots—a water moccasin.

The deadly snake went sailing to land a few yards away, but immediately went straight back.

"Don't let bite!" Jak cried, and threw a knife. Rising for a strike, the snake was beheaded and dropped limply to the ground.

But even as it died, several additional snakes came out of the reeds, hissing angrily. Most were harmless black snakes, but mixed among them were several larger varieties that shook rattles or brandished long fangs that glistened with venom. The astonished albino simply could not believe it. Snakes never attacked in groups! How was this possible?

Swinging up their blasters, the companions shot down the first wave of poisonous snakes, ignoring their nonlethal cousins. But more of the creatures kept coming up the dune, completely cutting off any possible route to the mainland. Maintaining a steady barrage, the companions aced the deadly reptiles, while the harmless black snakes circled their boots, to converge on the unconscious woman. Hissing constantly, the black snakes crawled over the woman, trying to get between her and the companions.

"Dark night, they're here for her!" J.B. said, swinging around the scattergun. "She wasn't calling you, but summoning an army!" Every boom of the shotgun announced the demise of a score of snakes, but more were coming out of the lake in an endless swarm.

"But she asleep!" Jak snarled, blowing the guts out of another water moccasin.

"Tell them that!" Krysty retorted, shooting in a two-hand grip.

As the snakes crawled over the aced coldhearts, they paused to savage the warm bodies, biting the aced men repeatedly in the face, hands and throat, often carrying away tiny morsels of raw flesh.

"Fireblast!" Ryan cursed, firing his blaster nonstop. Cut off from the mainland, the companions were trapped, neatly boxed on the crest of the sloping dune. The grass was alive with tiny eyes full of hate. Then another wave of snakes washed onto the shore, heading for the dune.

"Mildred, wake her up, or blow her brains out!" Ryan commanded, dropping a spent magazine to hastily reload.

Dropping to her knees, Mildred slapped the woman twice. "Wake up!" she shouted, then grabbed her by the shoulders and shook hard. "We're friends! The coldhearts are aced! Call off your snakes!" There was no response.

"It's no use," Mildred declared. "She's too far out of it for me to ever rouse in time."

"Sister, help me." Krysty spoke calmly, putting every ounce of her strength into the heartfelt plea.

There was a pause, and then the woman fluttered her lids, but nothing more.

However, the physician took heart at the reaction, small as it was, and shifted her aim to fire the Check ZKR right alongside the ear of the blonde, the roar of the concussion actually riffling her hair.

Abruptly jerking awake, Liana looked around in confusion at the companions shooting snakes, then she saw Doc hacking at the swarm of reptiles, the gory blade rising and falling. It was the tall man who had aced the leader of the Hillies!

Instantly understanding what was happening, Liana weakly tried to summon the strength needed for a song, but the pain in her head swelled in response, and she fell once more into a pool of deep black that seemed to have no bottom.

ROLLING TO THE EDGE of the battle station, the last guardian droid paused, then decided to go no farther. It would stay with the ship.

The military programming inside the core CPU re-acted strongly to that, but buried under the millions of lines of code coursing through the memory banks, the ancient, original command of self-preservation surged to overwhelm the hastily written dictates of the U.S. Navy High Command.

Trundling back into the battered corridor, the

guardian proceeded toward the elevator. Pursuit had failed to apprehend the invaders. Now it would assume a passive role and wait....

Chapter Four

Soft voices murmured to each other in conversation. There was the scent of pine in the air, and the crackle of a campfire. The smell of cooking snake meat was mixed with the aroma of something else…something new, and deliciously powerful…then there came a guttural laugh.…

With a violent lurch, Liana awoke to find herself inside a small cave. Five strangers, two of them women, were sitting around a low campfire, laughing and talking, their hands full of plates piled with food or steaming plastic cups. A wide assortment of weapons that she could not identify hung off their belts, along with some odd knives, the glass blades having a strange blue tint, almost as if lake water had been solidified hard as rock. Bizarre. Even more strange, the women also carried weapons and were not chained in any manner that Liana could see, and were talking directly to the men as if they were equals and not slaves. Perhaps these were sec men from Northpoint. That was the only ville on the world with a female baron. In most other places women were merely sluts, only good for cooking and cleaning, birthing and bedding.

That gave her some hope, then a dull pain throbbed

in her head and the memories of the fight came rushing back. These were the outlanders who had saved her from the Hillies. Then she scowled. Saved her for what, was the question. She had heard tales of people who actually ate other people as if they were animals. And there were terrible legends about the mainlanders who did even worse things, ghastly, ungodly things, especially to pretty young girls. Even a mutie like me, she thought.

With her heart pounding, Liana looked around for the tall man with silver hair, but he was nowhere to be seen, and her fledgling hopes and dreams collapsed like a felled tree. Obviously, he had sold her to these others.

Trying not to make any noise, Liana eased a hand down her body and was startled to discover that she was fully dressed. The unseen garments were as soft as the clothing of a baron, and there was something on her feet even more comfortable than a pair of deerskin moccasins. She wanted to see, but did not dare to attract any attention.

Surreptitiously, the woman examined between her legs, but there was no pain or soreness, not even dried blood. Clearly, she had not been taken while unconscious. That sent a wave of cold through her guts. It could only mean they were going to bring her back undamaged to Baron Griffin for the reward. Dear goddess no, anything, she prayed, but that.

Desperately, Liana looked about for some way out of the cave, but the only opening was past the five coldhearts, and partially blocked by a large boulder and an odd arrangement of torn bushes lashed together into a

crude curtain. Was that done to keep out the night fly-
ers who lived in caves? How very clever!

"Ah, I see you are finally awake," Mildred said, stirring the contents of a simmering pot with a green stick.
"I was hoping that the smell of food would bring you
around. Hunger is one of the most powerful of the pri-
mordial triggers."

Hunkering lower into the fur blankets, Liana said
nothing, having no idea what the majority of those
words meant.

"How is your head? Feeling any better?"

Ever so slowly, Liana nodded.

"Hope you don't mind, but we took all the snakes,"
Ryan said, stuffing a forkful of blackened meat into his
mouth. "Didn't want food going to waste."

"Fresh snake." Jak grinned happily. "Been long time.
One of my favs."

"Want some food, or coffee?" J.B. asked, proffering
a cup. "It's not coffee-sub, either, but the real stuff from
a predark tin." That wasn't exactly correct, but the Armorer was guessing that the woman would probably
think an MRE food pack was magic. Or worse, evil.
Lots of folks these days still held tech, any tech aside
from blasters, in extremely low esteem.

Unsure of what to do, Liana waited, and then finally
shook her head. She had no idea what "coughy" was,
but the smell was so good she assumed it had to be some
sort of a drug, like jolt or wolfweed.

Turning away from the cheery fire, a tall woman
with long red hair smiled in a friendly manner, and
Liana found herself instinctively responding in turn.

"I've never met a singer before," Krysty said. "That is a mighty valuable talent."

"No, please, don't ace me!" Liana cried in terror. "I'm not a mutie. I'm not! I found those snakes. Honest!" From sheer force of habit, she reached up to touch her face and found that her hair had been combed to the sides. These newcomers could see her eyes. They knew the truth.

The terror on her face was plain for everybody to see, and the companions could easily guess the reasons why. There had to be a rad crater in the area, and for decades children had been born horribly malformed. Over time, any deviation from the norm would be unclean, maybe even blasphemous, and more than sufficient justification for being aced on the spot, even newborn babes.

"Oh calm down, we know that you are not a mutie," Mildred said soothingly in her best doctor-to-patient manner. Lifting the stick from the pot of stew, she took a lick, then added some pepper.

The casual nature of the statement took the blonde by surprise. "You…do?" she whispered.

"Shitfire, think me mutie just 'cause my skin?" Jak asked with a laugh, taking a sip from his cup.

"No, of course not, master," Liana replied hastily, bowing her head in respect.

"Cut that drek out right now," Ryan snapped irritably, furrowing his brow. "Nobody here is a baron or a sec man. We're just folk, same as you."

Liana started to speak, but nothing would come out. Did…did they really consider her a norm?

"Dear God, girl, do people think you are a mutie because you are Oriental?" Mildred admonished curtly, laying aside the plate to fill another.

Utterly confused, Liana said nothing.

"Your eyes," the physician explained patiently. "Do folks believe you are a mutie because of how your eyes are shaped, and the color of your skin?"

A long moment paused in tense silence.

"Yes," Liana said in a very small voice, almost bursting into tears.

"Horse shit," Jak drawled, draining the cup. "Double horse shit! Just part Japanese, or Chinese, or something. Seen hundreds like you. Nothing special."

"Really?" she asked, hope thick in her voice.

"Sure." Which was only a partial lie. He had seen a lot of folks with Asian blood in their veins, but only a handful of them also with blond hair.

Astonishing herself, Liana managed to screwed up the courage to ask, "Where did you see them, sir?"

Ignoring the honorific, Jak refilled his cup. "All over the Deathlands," he said honestly. "Front Royal, Two-Son ville, Hammertown, Norleans, IronHat, near the Washington Hole…" He grinned. "Would tell how many, but can't count high."

She seemed relieved at the news, then excited. "I don't know any of those villes," Liana said, trying to control her emotions. "Where on the world are they?"

The odd turn of phrase caught Ryan's attention. On the world, not in the world. He was starting to get a crazy idea about this place, but it couldn't be confirmed until the dawn when J.B. could check their location on his sextant.

Wiping her mouth clean on a handkerchief, Krysty accepted a second plate of snake stew from Mildred, then added some salt and dug in with gusto.

Astonished, Liana could only gasp at the wanton display of wealth. Metal, now salt. And there was so much, they mixed it into food! Not even the barons were that rich. Just who were these people?

"So, what ville are you from?" Ryan asked, watching her reactions carefully. So, salt was valuable stuff, eh?

"I was born in the wildwoods," Liana said, the words spoken far too quickly. "Never even seen the inside of a ville."

"Yeah, me, too," Ryan lied in return. "By the way, don't you want your stuff?"

"Stuff?"

"There on your right."

Looking down, Liana gasped. Lying on a clean piece of white cloth was her beloved flute, as well as a sheathed knife, a crossbow and a quiver of arrows.

"Your share of stuff from acing the coldhearts," Ryan said gruffly, returning to his interrupted dinner. "You're not a slave, or our new slut, or any damn thing else. If you want to leave, there's the door."

"We won't stop you," Krysty added. "You have my word on that, little sister."

Completely flummoxed by the incredible offer, Liana couldn't think of what to do next. Ryan and Krysty exchanged a fast smile. Yeah, they both had thought so. The woman probably had never owned a thing in her life aside from that flute, plus the clothes on her back, and maybe not even them. The companions would need a local guide to show them what baron could be trusted, where the rad pits and stickie nests were hidden, and so on, and this was the easiest way to get the woman on their side. It was a bargaining tactic Ryan had learned from his days with the Trader long ago. Give the other person everything they wanted, but ask for nothing in return, and they would bend themselves over double trying to repay you with info. It would be a matter of honor.

Hesitantly, Liana reached out to touch the items, then looked at the companions as if asking permission. They artfully paid her no attention whatsoever, and the woman hurriedly dragged everything out of sight under the furs.

"By the way, the name is J. B. Dix," the Armorer said, putting aside his plate.

Liana started to reply with the name she had used all of her life in Anchor ville, the hated Victoria, the family name supposedly a dark secret. But something deep inside made her feel that would be wrong, and she yielded to the urge. "I'm Liana," she replied.

"No last name?" Jak asked.

"Me? I'm no baron," Liana scoffed.

Warming his hands to the fire, Ryan stored that info away. Never use a last name here. Already, the woman was paying for all the brass they had used chilling the coldhearts.

In short order, introductions were exchanged as the woman strapped on her new weapons. The crossbow was as familiar as air to the woman, but the knife…gods of the atom, she had never seen bone this hard and sharp. It shone bright like winter ice.

"Well, it's time for me to go stand guard duty," J.B. said, slinging the scattergun and taking one last sip of coffee. "See you in a couple of hours."

Going to the entrance, he pushed aside the curtain of thorny bushes and eased into the night.

"There is still plenty of food," Mildred offered once more, taking a seat on a rock, her coat folded on top as a cushion. "Mostly, it is just snake, but we also have some rice mixed with canned veggies."

Eagerly scooting closer to the fire, Liana accepted a plate, marveling over the strange material it was made from until the smell of the stew hit her, then she dug in with gusto using her fingers. Tactfully, the others said nothing about the nearby fork and spoon.

"Goof!" Liana mumbled happily, barely able to speak from the sheer volume of food stuffed into her mouth.

Allowing the starving woman to eat in peace for a while, Krysty then started the conversation going in the direction she wanted. As her mother always said, give a little, get a lot.

"Well, Liana, I'm very impressed with your ability," Krysty said, resting an elbow on her knee to lean forward. "Have you always been able to summon snakes?"

Blinking, the woman swallowed. "Sure. I've always been a singer."

"Can you summon anything else?" Mildred inquired, adding some powdered milk to the predark coffee.

"Only ever needed snakes," Liana answered simply.

Fair enough, Krysty supposed. Those were a handy source of meat and leather. "What about the fog? When does it clear?"

Licking her hand clean, Liana seemed confused by that question. "Fog?" she asked hesitantly.

The lack of a reply caught Krysty off guard. "The…you know, the stuff out there that looks like smoke."

"You mean, the air?" Liana said with a frown.

Annoyed, Ryan scowled. Fireblast! If the locals didn't even have a word for the fog, then it probably never went away. There had to be a rad crater, or a volcano, in the vicinity boiling a section of the ocean into steam, creating a permanent shroud over the land. That was bad news. Without a clear view of the sun, J.B. would never be able to find out exactly where they were this time.

Just then, there was a rustle from the entrance and Doc entered, sliding the massive LeMat into a holster.

"Do I smell coffee?" he said as a greeting. He saw Liana and smiled widely, displaying his oddly perfect teeth. "Ah, I see that our guest has finally left the land of Nod! Welcome back, dear lady, I trust you are comfortable?"

"Fine, yes, no damage," Liana said in a rush, feeling oddly naked, even though she was fully dressed. The tall outlander affected her in the most disturbing way. He was very handsome, almost striking, and while the silver hair made him appear to be a wrinklie, this close she could see that was wrong. The tall man carried himself with the assurance of a seasoned sec man. But there was something in his face that she could not readily define.

"Doc, say hello to Liana," Mildred said with a mischievous grin. "Miss Liana, may I present Dr. Theophilus Algernon Tanner."

"Charmed, dear lady," Doc said, giving a courtly bow.

Looking into his smiling eyes, Liana saw something that she had only known from her father, something she scarcely even had a word for—kindness. Somehow, the woman felt sure that this was a man who would never harm her, no matter what.

"I saw what you did to those coldhearts," Liana blurted, blushing slightly. "For some of the fight, anyway."

"Indeed? Well, I am always glad to assist a damsel in distress," Doc demurred gallantly, suddenly feeling very awkward.

"Thank you," Liana whispered, throwing her arms around his neck and hugging tight. Then she unexpectedly burst into tears.

Standing as if hit with a poleax, Doc did nothing for an inordinate length of time. Then ever so slowly, the scholar placed his arms around the young woman and gently returned the gesture, moving as if he were afraid that something might break, and not necessarily the beautiful young woman in his arms.

Outside the cave, there came a flash of lightning, closely followed by a crackling peal of thunder, and then it began to rain, the shower rapidly escalating until the wild maelstrom that sounded like the end of the world.

Chapter Five

Once, it had been the skull of a kraken, but now it was the terrible throne room of Anchor ville. The mouth and eyes had been closed with stout wooden shutters, and the interior walls delicately carved with scenes of victorious battle, along with the legendary downfall of the predark world. At this time of night, the throne room was normally full of people, sec men, servants and stewards. But by the command of the baron, it had been completely emptied for a very special visitor.

Standing uncomfortable in the palatial grandeur, the bearded Hilly was completely dressed in badly cured furs, their pungent reek almost overpowering. As a sign of goodwill, none of his stone weapons had been taken. However, both of the other people in the throne room were armed with working blasters.

"Exactly how much metal are we talking here?" Baron Wainwright asked, leaning back in her throne. The carved symbol of a holy maple leaf framed her head perfectly. "A pound? Two pounds?"

"My lady, more than the weight of a man," the Hilly replied, uneasily hitching up the rope belt around his waist.

"How much?" sec chief LeFontaine retorted. "I should ace you on the spot for lying to my baron!"

"No, it's true!" the Hilly cried, raising his hands in protest. "I watched the jacking from the bushes in the forest. Planned on taking whatever was left behind. But I saw that the outlanders were covered with metal, all different kinds! There was metal in their backpacks, on their faces, around their necks, mixed into their clothing…"

Listening to the rambling of the outcast, Wainwright and LeFontaine said nothing, but their expressions clearly stated that their interest was quickly fading. Metal worn as mere decorations? What utter and complete drek.

"An' they had blasters like I never seen!" the Hilly went on, feeling the sale slip away between his fingers. "I know it sounds crazy, but the things shot faster than a dozen imperial crossbows, and spit out tiny gold pieces of metal that sparkled in the firelight!"

That caught the baron short, and she studied the man with renewed intent. That sounded like the outlanders had working rapidfires. Could that possibly be true? What few blasters existed on the world came from mainlanders who accidentally landed here after storms. However, nobody had arrived on these shores for a long time. Years, decades!

"These blasters," LeFontaine said carefully. "The golden pieces came out the bottom, right?"

Puzzled, the Hilly frowned. "No, they popped out the side. Kinda made an arch as they flew away."

"How did they load them?"

"Shoved in little boxes." Then he added, "But first they had to move some kind of stick on the top. Dunno what it did."

An arming bolt! That was enough for the baron. There was no way this unwashed feeb could possibly know how a rapidfire worked, unless he had actually seen one in action.

"All right, little man, I'll pay your price," Baron Wainwright said eagerly. "Fifty horses, fifty slaves, ten crossbows and a hundred arrows."

"Two hundred."

"One-fifty."

"Done!" She smiled, then spit on a palm and they shook to seal the deal. "Now, tell me more about these outlanders. Tell me everything."

IT WAS LONG after midnight before the thunder and lightning finally began to recede, the pounding rain easing into a gentle patter before stopping entirely as the autumnal storm slowly moved out to sea.

Ryan was on guard duty inside the cave, sitting on a rock with the Steyr leaning against the nearby cave wall. The SIG-Sauer was tucked into the holster of his gunbelt, and he was testing the action on his new acquisition from the Navy ship, a Desert Eagle. The big-bore weapon was a real handcannon, the wide magazine holding only seven fat .50-caliber rounds. The recoil would be awful, but anything hit by the weapon would be aced, probably damn near blown in two. Unfortunately there was only the one magazine of seven rounds, so Ryan planned to save the handcannon in case they returned to the ship.

Setting aside the Desert Eagle, Ryan rose and grabbed the Steyr to check outside. The clouds were gone from overhead, and in the east the sun was just starting to rise. Excellent!

Grunting in satisfaction, Ryan went back inside the cave to quickly walk around the blazing campfire.

"Hey," Ryan said, nudging the bare foot of the Armorer with his combat boot.

Instantly the man was awake, and the U.S. Army blanket shifted to reveal the Uzi machine blaster in his grip.

"Trouble?" J.B. asked, squinting. His glasses were on a natural shelf set into the rocky wall, safe from any possibility of getting rolled on and crushed during sleep. Lying right next to the glasses was the recently cleaned and oiled 9 mm FN Hershel blaster. The logo on the checkered Zytel grip marked it as the property of NATO, but what that was doing inside an American warship was anybody's guess.

"Better." Ryan grinned. "We've got sky."

J.B. threw off the blankets. Hastily pulling on and lacing his boots, J.B. donned his glasses and grabbed the dry munitions bag to hurry outside.

The morning air felt crisp and clean as a yawning J.B. sloshed across the sodden ground to reach the shore. Black storm clouds rumbled on the western horizon, but a glorious sun was rising in the east, the reddish sky brightening into dawn. Unfortunately the ever-present cloud of toxic chems and rads was already starting to roll in from the south, and J.B. knew that he only had a few minutes to get this right. There would be no second chances.

With Ryan standing nearby as protection, the Armorer set the Uzi on top of a damp boulder, and swung the minisextant to his eye. Expertly focusing it on the rising sun, he then carefully placed the mirrors and started working the numbers.

Watching the area for any possible danger, Ryan said nothing, letting the man work in peace. A few moments later the rest of the companions stumbled from the cave, their hands full of blasters and rolls of bog paper.

Muttering equations under his breath, J.B. pulled a plastic-coated map from the munitions bag.

"Okay," he said, biting a lip. "We are…yep, we're on Royal Island in Lake Superior, smack between Canada and Michigan."

"That lake?" Jak asked with a scowl.

In the morning light, the albino teen could clearly see for miles in every direction, and there was nothing in sight but flat open water to the misty horizon.

"Well, technically it is a lake," Mildred replied, closing her jacket. "But really it is an inland sea, hundreds of miles wide and over a thousand feet deep in some spots."

"Good God, madam, that would make it roughly the same size as England!" Doc espoused, his tousled hair sticking out in every direction. His clothes were rumpled, but the LeMat was spotlessly clean, primed and ready.

"Pretty damn close," Mildred agreed, stomping her boots to encourage circulation.

"Fireblast! There's no way we are ever going to paddle across that on a raft," Ryan stated, resting the Steyr across his broad shoulders.

"Not and survive," J.B. agreed, folding the map before tucking it into the plastic bag. "Now, Canada is to the north, and only a few miles away. However—"

"Travel in that direction is forbidden because of Red Mountain," Liana interrupted, shifting uncomfortably in her new clothing. The spare denim pants and sneakers had come from Mildred, the socks and shirt from Krysty. The clothing was a little tight in some spots and a tad baggy in others, but it was still the finest clothing she had ever worn.

Adjusting his eyepatch, Ryan scowled darkly. Red Mountain, that was the local name for what had to be a major volcano. The woman had told them about that after dinner. The volcano was huge, probably a series of volcanoes, the lava flow boiling the lake for several miles and generating the eternal fog that was already starting to creep across the landscape once more.

Oddly, Liana had also said that was the direction that most of the muties on the island came from, and that anybody traveling toward the mountains soon died coughing blood with their hair falling out. That strongly indicated the chain of volcanoes was not natural formation, but had been caused by skydark. The whole bastard world had been changed forever by the bombs of the last war. Mildred called it nuclear landscaping, or nukescaping for short.

Red Mountain. A rad mountain was more likely, Ryan thought. "Not much of a choice here," he stated. "Canada is closer, but fragging unreachable. Which makes the only safe way to travel being south to Michigan."

"Across two hundred miles of open sea," Doc rumbled, smoothing down his unruly hair.

Suddenly there came a faint cry from the trees on the rill of a nearby cliff, and a stingwing lanced down to splash into the lake, and then reappear almost instantly with a wriggling fish impaled on its needle-sharp beak. Flying back to the trees, the stingwing tore the fish apart, blood and entrails raining out in a hellish contrail.

"Looks like we use Jak's plan," J.B. stated, shifting the munitions bag on his shoulder to a more comfortable position.

"Looks like," Ryan agreed. "We either buy or steal a boat from some ville."

"Only Anchor and Northpoint have boats large enough to carry seven people," Liana started, then paused nervously. When nobody objected, or corrected her math, she continued with an excited feeling in her stomach. Except for her father, the young woman had lived alone her whole life. Now to have companions made her feel different somehow, bolder, more alive.

"Think they'd be interested in doing some biz?" Ryan asked, turning her way.

Addressed directly, like an equal, Liana almost lied, wishing to please the big man, then paused and told the brutal truth. "Not Northpoint, they don't want anybody else to own boats," she said. "But…Anchor might. The baron is a fool."

"That is where you formerly served as a slave?" Doc asked gently, leaning on the ebony stick. The previous night, Liana had been given a blanket near the fire, but sometime during the night she had moved it closer to him, right alongside, almost touching. That both pleased and troubled the scholar, his mind awhirl with conflicting emotions.

"No, I was a slave at Northpoint," Liana stated. "But by now the birds have spread the word of my escape, and I'm worth a full pound of metal to any ville that takes me live so that Baron Wainwright can strap me to the learning tree." Involuntarily she shuddered at the possibility, and the rest of the companions clearly got the idea of what would happen—death by slow, public torture.

"Then you'll just wait in the hills with everybody else until we return," Ryan stated, sensing the fright in the woman. "If they think you're a mutie because of those eyes, they'll think the same thing about Krysty and Jak."

"There is nobody like them in any of the villes," Liana agreed.

"Nobody good as, ya mean." Jak grinned confidently.

"And is there anybody like me?" Mildred asked pointedly.

Liana blinked. "There's plenty of women in the ville," she answered, unsure of the question. "Do you mean the beaded hair?"

"Never mind." Mildred smiled. If the girl didn't even understand the question, then her skin color would not be a problem.

"And I can't go because of these," J.B. added, touching his wire-rimmed glasses. "I'm not blind yet, but near enough to matter in a fight."

"Besides, we'll need to keep watch in case Ryan

and Mildred get into trouble," Krysty stated. "Always have to prepare for the worst, as Doc likes to say."

"Hope for the best, but prepare for the worst," Doc corrected her. "Ben Franklin was a very wise man."

"You…you want me to help guard him?" Liana asked in frank disbelief, staring up at the one-eyed man. Ryan was easily twice her size, with hands that looked capable of squeezing a kraken to death.

"Anybody can get captured," Krysty commented sagely. "Besides, we never divide the group unless absolutely necessary. Those coldhearts could have friends. Left here alone you'd be easy pickings for them. Best to keep everybody together."

That would also remove the possibility of her running ahead to tell the baron about the companions to earn her freedom, J.B. noted privately. He didn't think that was likely, but he had been fooled before. A pretty face sometimes hid an ugly mind.

"At the very least, you will need to show us where the ville is located," Doc said with a gentle smile.

Eagerly, Liana nodded. "I can do that easy."

As if unaware that there was anybody else on the lakeshore, Doc beamed in unabashed pleasure at the younger woman and she responded in kind.

"Any good with crossbow?" Jak asked teasingly.

In a blur, the woman turned and fired, the arrow flashing past the teenager so close that it shook the feathers along his jacket. A split second later, there was a small cry of pain and a squirrel dropped out of the branches of a pine tree to land twitching on the ground, shot directly through the head. Almost instantly, a swarm of black beetles converged on the body and began tearing it into pieces.

"She-et," Jak drawled, giving the word two syllables. "Do fine!"

Already reloading the weapon, Liana preened under the unaccustomed praise.

"Breakfast before anything else." Mildred yawned. "Empty bellies make empty minds."

"Well, it's my turn to cook," Ryan said, rubbing a hand across his unshaved jaw. He would have liked to shave, but it would be better if he looked rough when negotiating with folks who didn't have any metal. "Is there any of the stew left?"

"Nope," Jak said with an apologetic shrug.

Knowing the appetite of the teenager, Ryan accepted that. "Fair enough. I'll use some of the MRE packs."

"Be glad to help," Liana offered. "I'm a very good cook."

"Me, too," Ryan replied tolerantly. "This time you watch, learn how we do things, then you can make lunch. Fair enough?" The man understood her eagerness to be seen as a valuable member of the group. But he wasn't quite ready to trust the newcomer enough to consume anything she made out of sight.

"Done and done," Liana said, and offered a hand, as if sealing a deal.

The smiling man and serious woman shook, then got busy gathering more driftwood, while the others took their turns in the bushes and washing in the cold lake.

Seeing his refection in a tide pool, Doc decided to

shave. Using a scrap of soap recovered from a distant redoubt, he worked up some lather, then used his belt knife, running the flame of a butane lighter along the edge first to make sure it was clean. Over the years, the blade had been thrust into far too many bodies, both norm and mutie, to risk using without sterilization.

Soon, the time traveler was freshly scraped, his face shiny pink, with only a small cut on his chin. A single red drop of blood fell into the water and faded away from sight into the murky depths.

Chapter Six

Leaving the cave behind, the companions trundled inland, going high into the foothills then across a woodsy glen.

Breakfast had been MRE envelopes of pancakes and syrup, French toast and scrambled eggs, plus packets of hot chocolate. Liana marveled over the foodstuff, but passed on the hot chocolate for some of the coffee, savoring the dark roast Colombian as if it was made from precious salt. From her sounds of pleasure, it clearly tasted even better than she had imagined.

As the day progressed, the thick fog returned, masking the landscape until it was impossible to see more than a few yards in any direction.

Irritably, Ryan realized this condition made the scope of his Steyr useless. Any chilling on Royal Island would be up close and personal, knives and blasters only.

Preparing to bargain with the local baron, Ryan and Mildred had already removed anything they carried that was made of metal: belt buckles, rad counter, belt knives and such, including their combat boots. The footwear wasn't made of metal, but was in far too good shape. The spare Army blankets had been converted into crude ponchos, held in place by pieces of hemp rope, with additional pieces lashed into place around their bare feet as crude rag boots. Doc said the idea came from the Middle Ages.

Trying to look the role of sec men from one of the outer islands, both Ryan and Mildred were armed with a crossbow and quiver, stone knives, wooden boomerang and bolo. However, secreted inside their shirts, under their ponchos, were their blasters and a few grens, just in case of emergencies.

The two companions also carried a couple of gifts for the baron, hopefully more than enough to buy a boat and fishing nets. The companions had no conceivable use for the nets, but since it was forbidden to leave the island, they would make for a good cover story, as Mildred liked to say. A reasonable lie used to hide the uncomfortable truth.

Slowly the hours passed as the companions crossed a wide field of daisies growing in wild profusion around the corpse of what might have been a mutie spider, but it was impossible to tell anymore. Just to be safe, J.B. primed a Molotov and watched the trees for any unusually large webs.

Reaching the forest once more, the companions climbed a ragged hill covered with pine trees only to quickly go around a small bay, the rad counters of Ryan and J.B. both clicking steadily upward.

"That's Dead Man Bay," Liana said with a shiver, making a protective gesture in the air. "It looks safe, but drink that water, or even eat a fish from there, and all you hair falls out, then you start bleeding from the gums."

"And then?" Krysty prompted. The bay seemed perfectly normal, but the counters were almost off the scale.

"And then the sec men shovel dirt over you," the blonde replied. "They used to feed the bodies to the crabs, but then the women started having bad babies for some reason, so the baron made them stop."

"Crabs eat corpse, then you eat crabs?" Jak asked, shifting his backpack.

"Sure. Why?"

"That reason," he replied succinctly.

"Heavy metal poisoning," Mildred explained with a sigh. Strontium, thulium, cobalt, the list of lethal isotopes was nearly endless. Most likely, the bay had been hit by a Russian MIRV, a warhead containing not a single, massive, thermonuclear bomb, but a dozen tactical nukes. However, she knew better than to raise the possibility to the others. They simply did not care. A nuke was a nuke, end of discussion.

"Are you a whitecoat?" Liana asked sharply, her eyes narrowing in suspicion.

"Healer, just a healer," Mildred replied, sensing possible danger.

After a while Liana nodded in acceptance and continued walking, her legs moving fast as she tried to keep abreast of Doc with his long stride.

The masked sun was in the afternoon sky by the time the companions started to run across traces of the ville—repairs done to the dirt road from the summer rains, farmland already harvested for the coming winter, acres of tree stumps with the splintery stumps giving mute testimony to the backbreaking task of using a stone ax, and a crude bridge spanning a dry ravine that was probably a raging torrent in the spring.

Finding a relatively secluded area, masked from the surrounding hills by a copse of maple trees, Ryan and Mildred divested themselves of their larger metal items, the spare blasters and brass going to Jak, the Steyr to Krysty, and the med kit to Doc. Double-checking each other for anything metallic, Ryan and Mildred then rubbed some loose dirt into their hair and clothing to enhance the idea that they had walked to Anchor from the far end of the known world.

"Okay, we part company here," Ryan said, hefting a loaded crossbow. The weight was awkward, so he shifted the grip until it properly balanced. A small detail like that could easily get them aced if the local sec men were any good at their jobs. "Whether we get a boat, or not, we'll meet you at the grotto that Liana told us about."

"We'll be there," J.B. replied earnestly, stashing away the possessions. "And if you're not back by midnight, we'll come looking for you."

"Damn well better."

"Watch out for the *Wendigo!*" the blonde warned again, knowing that she was repeating herself, but feeling it was necessary. She had once seen the terrible thing in action, and her new friends had not. It was not a sight the woman would ever forget.

"The *Wendigo?*" Krysty asked with a scowl.

"Unless I am mistaken, that comes from a Canadian myth about an unstoppable monster," Doc replied. "A trapper went mad from hunger, ate a friend and the Indian gods cursed him forever."

"Unstoppable monster." Jak nodded. "Good name war wag."

"Hopefully it is just advertising, and not an accurate description," Mildred said, double-checking her clothing one last time. The rag boots were surprisingly comfortable, but the physician knew that would cease at the first touch of moisture. Rain puddles were now to be avoided like landmines.

As the companions slipped into the bushes, Jak waited until they were past before following along behind, a leafy branch in his pale hands erasing any trace of their passage.

"The Trader used to do something similar with sage bushes," Ryan commented. "Said he learned it from the Sioux when he was a kid." The one-eyed man almost smiled. "Seems kind of funny thinking of the Trader that way, learning things, instead of teaching others."

"Even the great Socrates had a teacher as a child," Mildred replied. One of her professors had said that civilization was merely the accumulated wisdom of everybody who had ever lived. Smart words. With all of her heart, the physician hoped that in the future people would be smart enough to never allow another sky-dark. The universe rarely gave anybody a second chance.

When the others were completely out of sight, Ryan and Mildred stolidly returned to the main road, then walked back toward the lake for a mile, before turning and starting for the ville again. Along the way, the man and woman sharply watched the trees and hillsides for any signs of perimeter guards, sentries or outriders, but saw only songbirds, stingwings and an abundance of squirrels. Whatever else was wrong with the island, at least food was plentiful, which was a nice change from the vast sterile deserts of the western Deathlands.

A few miles later the ville rose into view. Situated on the side of a cliff, the walls were composed of irregularly shaped stones, joined with a blue material that was probably river clay. Sec men and women armed with crossbows walked along the top of the structure, and a guard tower rose high above the ville, the pillbox on top bristled with wooden spears like a frightened porcupine.

"Protection from the kraken?" Mildred asked out of the corner of her mouth.

Adjusting his eyepatch, Ryan merely nodded in agreement. Perhaps the bastard lake muties really were as large as Liana had informed them. If so, that could put a real crimp in their plans to reach the mainland in a fishing boat. The journey would be tough enough without dodging a hungry mutie larger than a predark warehouse.

The front gate of the ville was made of interlocking logs, the bark stripped off and the smooth bare wood studded with wooden spikes and shiny pieces of volcanic glass. Only the hinges were metal. Then Ryan looked again. Correction, two of the six hinges were metal, the rest were carved from stone.

Unlike every other ville Ryan and Mildred had ever encountered, the front gate was wide open, with no guards in sight. However, there was another log wall just past the gate, neatly blocking any view of the ville. That was standard in most villes. The second wall was a shatter zone, designed to break the charge of any invaders and to give the ville sec men an excellent place to shoot at the enemy from relative safety.

Strolling closer, Ryan could hear the sounds of ville life, raised voices, a dog barking, laughter and cursing, a drunk was singing, a newborn crying, and there was the steady, never-ending chopping of wood.

When they were only a few yards away, a muttered curse came from off to one side and a sec man scrambled out of a brick kiosk, holding a large crossbow. Each brick in the kiosk was a different color, showing they had been salvaged from several ruins, and there was a firing slit in the side, subtle movements on the other side showing the gatekeeper was not alone.

"Hold it there, outlanders!" the sec man commanded, swinging up his weapon until it wasn't exactly pointing in their direction, but close enough to be used if desired.

The guard looked dangerous, but Mildred internally sighed at the sight of the large black man, his skin even darker than her own. Once more, Liana was right. She was just regular folks here.

The huge sec man was dressed in thick furs, with a stone-throwing ax hanging from a thong at his side. The leather-wrapped handle was old and worn, the stone blade nicked in several places, but polished to a mirror sheen. It was clearly a deadly weapon that saw a lot of constant use.

"Sure thing," Ryan said in an even tone, his own

crossbow pointing at the ground, but with an arrow notched and ready.

"What's your biz in Anchor?" the sec man demanded, a finger resting on the trigger of his weapon.

"Just here to buy a boat," Ryan replied, trying to appear anxious.

"Buy a boat?" That seemed to confuse the man. "What for? They're easy enough to make out of bark."

"Don't want a fragging canoe, we need a fishing boat," Ryan answered curtly. "A big one. Got a whole ville to feed, and mine got swept out to sea in a storm last week."

"Along with our master carpenter," Mildred added on impulse. "You ever try to make one of those things without any tools?"

"Hell, no, and don't ever wanna try, either." The guard chuckled, changing the aim of his weapon. "Well, come on in. Guess you're telling the truth. We do have the best carpenters on the world. A man can notch that into his crossbow!"

"Everybody knows that flies straight," Ryan agreed, resting his crossbow on a shoulder. "Is there a toll?" This was a weak point in their masquerade as locals, and he just had to bull through. As a slave, Liana had never entered the ville by the gate, and thus had no idea if there was payment due.

"Toll?" the sec man asked, puzzled over the word.

"We heard from a Northpoint sec man that folks had to give the payment of a good arrow to get into Anchor." Mildred ad-libbed, trying to cover the gaff by playing on the natural rivalry of the two largest villes. "We thought it was a lie, of course, but still…" She shrugged, but didn't finish the sentence.

"Those, dirty, inbreed, mutie-kissing, sons of bitches," the gatekeeper growled in clear hatred, his hands twisting on the wooden stock of the crossbow. "No, there ain't no nuking toll. Never even heard of such a triple crazy thing before."

"Hey, you know Northpoint," Ryan said with a shrug.

"You got that right, friend." The guard barked a laugh and stepped aside. "Welcome to Anchor. No riding a slave unless you ask permission first. Knife fights ain't allowed in the gaudy house, only bare fists. Piss in the lake, not the street, or else you get ten lashes. Twenty for lying to a sec man, fifty lashes for refusing to obey a direct order. Savvy?"

"No prob," Ryan replied amiably, thumbing the safety on his weapon. "Where would we find the baron, anyway?"

"Don't worry about that, he'll find you!" the guard replied gruffly, going back into the kiosk.

Ambling through the gate and around the shatter zone, the two companions were instantly immersed into a living mandella of noise, smoke and motion. The air was redolent with the smells of baking bread, frying fish, horse dung and boiling laundry. The perfume of civilization.

Laughing and cursing, pushing and shoving, civies and sec men were everywhere, each going in a different direction. Squealing children ran underfoot chasing rats, then a falcon swooped down from overhead and stole their prize. Sitting around in clusters, elders nimbly stitched repairs to ripped fishing nets, their conversations lost in the overlapping din. A burly woman walked by with a yoke across her wide shoulders to support a pair of large buckets full of freshly made charcoal, the blackened lumps still smoking. Inside a circle of rope, two men had stripped down to the waist and were having a bloody fistfight, while other norms watched and placed wagers. A smiling stone worker slapped his apprentice on the back in congratulations as the teenager successfully split a piece of granite into a set of perfect knife blades.

In the open doorway of a log cabin, a beautiful young woman with an infant suckling at her breast was stirring a cauldron of bubbling maple syrup, the aroma so sweet to the companions that it was almost sickening. Crystallized sticks of maple candy hung from the eaves. At another cabin, a man was diligently smearing fresh mud along a wide split in a seam.

The busy ville was alive with commerce, and nobody paid attention to the companions as they strolled along. Which was just fine by them—the less they were noticed, the better. However, Mildred secretly reveled in the commotion. Any kind of civilization was better than none. Then the physician saw the dreaded learning tree, the wooden stocks and wide leather straps darkly seasoned with overlapping blood stains, and she quickly revised her opinion. Clearly some societies were better than others.

"Found it!" Ryan said in grim satisfaction, moving quickly in a new direction.

Lurching forward, Mildred rushed to stay close as the one-eyed man slipped into the bustling crowd and disappeared from sight.

Chapter Seven

Down in the bowels of the *Harrington,* the ceiling lights sluggishly flickered several times, then they came back on, filling the engine room with a blinding corona of power.

Surveying the assorted wreckage to the main engine and primary tokomac power reactor, the sec droid made a command decision. Several small hatches opened in the armored chassis of the machine and out rushed a score of small repair robots. Resembling mechanical spiders, the robots looked at the massive damage and started to rush forward when the sec droid issued an electronic command to override their programming.

Pausing for only a nanosecond to digest the new information, the robots changed direction to converge on the auxiliary power plant. Crawling over the hulking machine, they conducted a preliminary assessment, noting every nick and ding, then patiently waited until the sec droid gave them permission to start the repairs.

Instantly their dozens of small lasers pulsed into life, cutting away the dented access panels. As one of the heavy pieces of shielding came loose, the robots scuttled inside and crawled everywhere, measuring, testing and probing, to finely analyze the internal damage.

Patiently, the sec droid waited for their detailed report. Soon enough, power would be restored to the entire vessel. Then it would immediately turn the power back off, making the *Harrington* appear to be dead once more, a helpless prey for the invaders. When they eventually returned, the power would come crashing back on and every hatch would slam shut, trapping them inside. That was when the sec droid would attack. The invaders would be confused, and frightened, easy prey for the military juggernaut.

However, if for some unknown reason it seemed that the invaders might destroy the droid and seize control of the vessel, it would have no choice but to detonate the scuttling charges hidden inside the keel of the carrier. They were only atomic charges, no more than a few kilotons yield. But that would be more than enough to destroy the *Harrington*. Either way, win, lose or draw, the mat-trans would never fall into the hands of the enemy.

With the patience of steel, the machine began to run a systems check on its various weapons systems. Everything was under control. Now it was only a matter of time.

REJOINING RYAN, Mildred matched his long stride, one hand artfully brushing the pocket of her dirty furs to check on her ZKR blaster. With any luck, they wouldn't need weapons today. But luck had been evading the companions lately, and it was always wise to be prepared for trouble. The heavy gren in her pocket was a comforting weight.

Moving among the mob of civies, the armed sec men were easy to spot in their matching uniforms—all of them were shaved bald and sported a small goatee. Ryan could only assume they did it to help recognize one another even in the thickest fog. Actually, it was a bastard smart idea.

The homes in the ville were the expected conglomeration of rebuilt predark structures, log cabins and ramshackle huts. But they were all laid out in neat lines, the streets wide and paved with loose white stones. Harnessed elks pulled crude carts loaded with wood, and a sec woman rode by on a horse, a long line of slaves hobbling along behind. Lengths of rawhide were tied between their ankles and a thick rope was attached to wooden collars. In spite of the chill, they were dressed in rags, and hauling a wheeled cart full of giant arrows over ten feet long.

"So they have an arbalest," Mildred muttered, glancing at the rooftops. "That's good to know." If she remembered correctly, the weapon had a tremendous range.

Grunting in reply, Ryan studied the ville, trying to get the feel of the place. A smart man could learn a lot with his eyes open and his mouth shut. Even if Liana had not told about the shortage of metal on the island, the companions would have figured it out for themselves in short order. Everything was either made of wood, stone or leather.

On a corner, drunken laughter came from a tavern, and gaudy sluts lounged in the second-floor windows, smoking home-rolled cigs, their breasts exposed for potential customers. In a large corral, a herd of bleating goats was being milked by somber teenagers intent upon their task, and nearby lay huge wheels of cheese drying in the weak sunlight, the rind thickly coated with beeswax. Past that, a butcher was chopping apart the carcass of a moose, a line of civies waiting impatiently for the big woman to finish, their arms full of empty wicker baskets.

In the far corner of the ville was a row of gallows, the killing bar extended over the wall, a rotting corpse dangling from a noose and swaying gently in the breeze.

"Smart," Mildred said, impressed. "Just leave the body there as a warning to newcomers, and when the flesh rots, it'll simply drop off."

"Plus, that high up, the wind would help reduce the smell," Ryan agreed, trying to see through the bustling throng for the *Wendigo*. But so far, there was no sign of it.

Situated behind a split-rail fence, a sec man was sitting in a rocking chair, a loaded crossbow in his hands and a massive black wolf-dog panting on the ground near his boots. A spiked leather collar announced that the beast was a pet, and not a wild animal.

Protected by a stout wooden fence, the companions could just barely see a large iron kettle with a roaring fire underneath. A coiled copper tube attached to the top to slowly drip a clear fluid into ceramic jugs. The tangy smell of raw alcohol was thick around the still, almost overpowering.

"If the shine is here, the *Wendigo* must be close,"

Ryan noted, looking around the ville, through the hustling mob.

"Over there," Mildred said, tilting her head.

Sure enough, the dreaded machine stood less than a hundred feet away, sitting in the middle of the ville square, for everybody to see and marvel over.

"Smart. Newcomers have probably never seen that much metal in their whole bastard lives," Ryan sagely guessed.

"The *Wendigo*," Mildred said, the name suddenly having resonance now that she could see the war wag. "This would really put the fear of the baron into their bones."

Ryan grunted in agreement. According to Liana, Northpoint ville ruled the sea with their infamous steamship, *Warhammer,* but Anchor was the undisputed master of the dry land from the eastern shore to the western mountains with the deadly *Wendigo.*

Supposedly named after a mythical beast, the war wag was huge, as large as any predark tank, boasting overlapping armor plating and eight huge tires. There was no cannon, but it was armed with a brace of heavy machine guns, and what could only be a crude flamethrower. Blasterports dotted the sides, and two fluted exhaust pipes rose from the rear of the machine. Each was protected by a hood and surrounded by a small iron cage to prevent anything from being thrown into them and into the vulnerable engine.

Sitting motionless on the green grass, the *Wendigo* radiated a feeling of lethal power, and no fence or guards were necessary to keep the civies from getting too close. In a land almost completely devoid of metal, the armed might of the *Wendigo* was disturbing, almost obscene.

"Now where is… Yeah. There he is," Ryan said in quiet satisfaction. "I knew he'd be close."

"The master likes to keep his dogs close at hand," Mildred noted dryly.

Only a few paces away from the hulking war wag was a wooden dais topped with a pair of thrones. The chairs were ornately carved with an endless motif of eagles and stars, the backs draped with beautiful white wolf fur. Sitting in the thrones and holding court over some bound prisoners were the absolute rulers of the ville, Baron Griffin and his lady.

Stroking the feathers of a falcon resting on the arm of his throne, Baron Nolan Griffin was heavily muscled and covered with tattoos, more closely resembling a sailor than a ruling baron. His clothing was spotlessly clean, and he wore several pieces of metal to show his wealth, a thick silver necklace, a high school signet ring and a large predark wristwatch in remarkably good condition. A crude half-circle of hammered iron served the baron as a makeshift crown and two holstered blasters rode low in a fancy gunbelt.

Clearly much older than her husband, Lady Barbara Griffin was as plump as a gaudy house madam, yet her breasts were so small that they disappeared behind an embroidered leather bodice. Her auburn hair was long, and hung loose around a stern face that held no trace of mercy. The woman wore a flowing gown trimmed in white fur, with a silk scarf wrapped about her pudgy throat. A sawed-off shotgun rode in a large holster that had to have been specifically designed for the ungainly blaster. Metal rings were on every finger, and silver loops hung from both of her ears.

Standing alongside an iron brazier full of glowing hot charcoal was a large man with a blond crewcut, his bearing, scars and holstered blaster proclaiming that he was either the only son of the baron or the sec chief.

Kneeling on the cold ground in front of the baron and his wife was a pair of men, their hands and legs lashed together. Their clothes were in tatters, and bloody welts crisscrossed their backs.

"But, my lord, I reported this man for stealing the salt from the barracks of the sec men!" one of the prisoners called in a hoarse voice. He had a full head of hair and wore the loose clothing of a civie. "Why am I also being punished?"

His head bowed, the other man said nothing, his fate already sealed. He could only hope for the clemency of a swift execution on the gallows.

"Why? You dare to ask that? Because you are also a thief!" Lady Griffin growled in barely contained rage. "You were seen licking the block when you thought nobody was watching!"

"B-but I had to make sure it really was salt…" the man said lamely.

"Don't you have a nose?" Sec chief Donovan snarled in open hatred. "My lord, let me ace this fool here and now!"

Surreptitiously, Ryan and Mildred exchanged glances. Salt was in short supply, eh? That only made sense on an island in the middle of a freshwater lake. They had seen what a lack of salt did to a person out in the broiling desert of the Deathlands. First came a terrible thirst, then mounting weakness, closely followed by mental confusion, and finally death. It was an ugly way to get chilled.

Placing the falcon on a nearby wooden perch, Baron Griffin thought about the request. "Granted," he said without any trace of emotion. "Slit his throat and boil him down to recover the salt."

Grinning, the sec chief leaped off the dais, pulling out a blade. The prisoner had only a moment to gasp in shock before the blade flashed through the air and he fell gurgling to the ground, his hot blood steaming as it pumped onto the cold grass.

Wiping the blade clean on the clothes of the dying man, Donovan sheathed the weapon, then hawked and spit on the fool.

"As for you…" the baron said, turning to address the thief. "Twenty-five lashes for the theft, and ten more for trying to escape."

Prepared for much worse, the prisoner could not believe his good luck. Was that all? He was going to live!

"Then take his eyes so that he won't be able to ever steal again," Lady Griffin added, a hint of a smile playing on her full lips.

The surrounding crowd roared their approval and the terrified prisoner began wildly twisting and turning, trying to get free.

Snapping his fingers, sec chief Donovan pointed at the bound man and a gang of sec men descended upon him with raised clubs and proceeded to pound every trace of defiance out of the condemned thief. Battered and bruised, the prisoner fell gasping to the ground, openly weeping. Then the hooded figure of the ville executioner walked out of the crowd, a curved blade held in a gloved hand.

Some of the civies watched in fascination, others turned away in disgust, but soon the odious task was done, and the unconscious prisoner was dragged off to the learning tree to wait until he woke to receive the rest of his sentence.

"Well, you were right," Mildred said, shifting the boomerang in her belt to a more comfortable position. "The baron does like to hold court in sight of his war wag."

"That's just common sense," Ryan replied, involuntarily touching the patch on his face in sympathy. "You always have to make the people remember you're the greatest victory, or their own mortality. Sec men chill with blasters, but a baron rules through fear."

Judging this was as good a time as any, Ryan raised an arm high and began walking toward the dais. "Metal!" he shouted. "I've got metal for the baron!"

As the startled crowd got hastily out of the way, the baron and his wife glowered at the stranger walking boldly forward. The black-haired man was not familiar to them, and carried himself with the calm assurance of a seasoned warrior.

Carefully studying the man, sec chief Donovan rested a hand on his blaster. He had no idea who the fellow was, but his guts said this was a nuke-storm of trouble coming.

"And who are you?" Baron Griffin demanded.

"Finnigan, sir," Ryan replied, using the name of an old friend who no longer walked the Deathlands. "And this be my wife, Holly."

Trying to appear humble, Mildred gave an awkward curtsy.

"Odd accent. Where are you from?" Donovan asked in a hard tone, his fingers tripping the handle of the big bore blaster.

"Saddle Brook," Ryan replied. "A little fishing ville on the outer islands, near the Broke Place." He had no idea what that meant, and neither did Liana, but she claimed that was all anybody called it, the Broke Place.

Incredibly, Lady Griffin perked up at that. "Saddle Brook? Why, I was born there!"

Keeping his face neutral, Ryan internally cursed the bad luck, then saw the baron fight to hide a smile. Clever bitch, it was just a trick to try to expose a liar. Whatever else they might be, these people were not fools.

"Sorry, my lady, but I don't seem to recall ever seeing you there," Ryan said in mock apology. "Could have sworn that I knew everybody from the Saddle." He shrugged. "Guess I was wrong."

Nodding in satisfaction as if the stranger had just passed some kind of a test, Baron Griffin dismissed the matter with a gesture. "You two can talk about old times later," he said, leaning forward. "Now, what was this about metal, eh? Found a tin can, did you? Or perhaps a nail?"

"We can always use more of those," Donovan sniffed in marked disinterest.

"Show the baron, woman!" Ryan barked, jerking a thumb at the baron. "That be why we here!"

Meekly, Mildred stepped forward, offering a small wad of folded cloth.

Scowling uncertainly, the baron hesitantly took the bundle and unwrapped the oil cloth to gasp out loud. Lying in the palm of his hand was a blaster. Not the rusted remains of one, but an intact blaster, the steel as smooth as polished bone.

Lifting the blaster, the baron felt a visceral thrill surge through his gut at the weight of the steel in his hand. His own weapons were nowhere near as heavy. This blaster was a monster! Easily twice the caliber of the one he inherited from his father, and he from his father before, possession of the weapon going all the way back to skydark.

"Careful, my lord, it be loaded," Ryan warned.

The baron raised an eyebrow at that, and warily cracked the cylinder to extract a live brass, the metal shiny bright, the lead cut into the deadly cross pattern of a dum-dum. It was incredible. Live brass! He checked and found two more in the weapon, plus two empties. Five brass, three of them live!

"This is truly quite a find," Lady Griffin said, seemingly unable to catch her breath. "You did well, outlander, to bring it directly to us. Failure to do so is a slow death on the learning tree. Or worse, the slave pits."

In dark harmony, there came the distant crack of a bullwhip, followed by the anguished scream of a slave.

"That is as it should be, my lady," Mildred answered

quickly, spreading her arms. "Only barons and their sec men should touch metal." She smiled, and hoped it didn't look like a grimace. The fragging boomerang was digging into her hip again, and bothering a sore rib she had acquired when the companions abruptly departed from the warship in the bay.

If the baroness noticed anything wrong, she made no comment. But she looked steadily at the physician in a most unnerving manner.

Sensing that something might be wrong, Mildred decided to not speak again unless spoken to directly.

"Well, Finnigan, this is the prize of a lifetime," Baron Griffin stated in heartfelt honesty, removing the cartridges to spin the cylinder, then load it again. "So tell me, what do you want as a reward? A year of easy living in the gaudy house? Two horses? Ten crossbows? A hundred slaves?"

Pretending to scratch under his eyepatch, Ryan struggled to not show his disgust at the callous hierarchy of life. "Just a boat, my lord, one large enough for fishing, and six nets," Ryan said, putting a touch of eagerness into the words. "Plus, all the food it can carry. My boat sank in a storm last week and now…" He shrugged.

"The ville is starving without the boat." The baron nodded in understanding, passing the blaster to his sec chief. "Yes, I see, of course."

Accepting the weapon, Donovan tucked it away for later cleaning and a thorough examination. Nobody was going to fire the new weapon until it had been completely disassembled and checked for traps. The fat slut Wainwright was triple clever, and not above sending one of her sec men to pose as an outlander with a trick blaster as a gift to ace her cousin. The baron of Northpoint never attacked straight-on, but always hit from the side, like a damn lake snake. The joke among his troops was, if you hear nothing in the fog, it had to be Wainwright on the move.

"A boat and two nets, you said?" Baron Griffin asked, deliberately getting the numbers wrong.

Instantly, Ryan felt his long years of training under the tutelage of the Trader flare into action as the negotiations began in earnest. "Beg pardon, my lord, it was six nets and a ton of food," he said incorrectly.

"Oh, yes. Six nets and ten barrels of dried fish."

"Twenty barrels and five more of grain."

"Ridiculous! Ten and five."

"Six, ten and ten."

"Done!" The baron grinned in pleasure. "We have a deal, outlander." He paused and then added, "You could have asked for more."

Knowing that was true, Ryan shrugged. "I only asked for what was needed, my lord. Not going to ask for a horse if I can't ride."

"Wise words," the baron acknowledged, then spit into his palm and offered his hand. "My sec men will escort you to the dockyard, and you can choose a boat from my fleet. Anything under twenty feet is yours. Slaves will deliver the food and nets before nightfall."

"Thank you, my lord!" Ryan said, accepting the hand and shaking to seal the deal.

"Please also allow me to give you a small gift," Lady

Griffin purred, sliding a worn plastic bracelet off her wrist.

"Thank you, my lady," Mildred replied with a forced grin, trying to appease the woman. In her time, the garish trinket was the kind of thing you could buy from a vending machine for a quarter.

However, as the physician reached out to accept the bracelet, Lady Griffin roughly grabbed her hand and pulled Mildred closer, staring intently at her face, and then nodding in grim satisfaction.

"Yes, I thought so!" Lady Griffin shouted in triumph. "Look there, metal! The outlander bitch has steel in her mouth!"

Jerking free from the grip, Mildred stared at the woman as if she were insane, then the truth of the matter hit her like an express train. Her fillings! She had completely forgotten about the fillings in her back molars.

"Steel in her teeth?" the baron asked with a frown, then his face hardened. "Mainlanders! Only mainlanders do that twisted perversion!"

Snapping his head around at the wild accusation, sec chief Donovan started to frown, then saw the grim expression on the face of the outlander. So it was true, these were mainlanders! "Close the gate!" the man bellowed, drawing his blaster. "Protect the baron!"

But as fast as the sec chief was, Ryan matched his speed, whipping out the SIG-Sauer in a blur of motion, and the two men fired simultaneously at each other in point-blank range.

Chapter Eight

The fog was heavy along the shore, and with their crossbows leading the way, the Northpoint sec men warily pushed aside the curtain of thorny bushes to enter the dark cave.

The last to enter was the Hilly, the mountain man brandishing a weapon in each hand, his every sense alert for the presence of the one-eyed giant who led the pack of outlanders. He had seen the nuking bastard in action, and had no wish to ever face the big man in battle. A knife in the back would do just fine.

As the sec men moved deeper into the cave, their torches revealed nobody hidden inside the rocky passageway, only the remains of an abandoned campsite, a few broken arrows, some food scraps and a wad of strange paper that smelled like food but was as shiny as metal.

"What the frag is it?" a sec man asked in obvious confusion.

"Dunno," sec chief LeFontaine muttered, fondling a piece. The material was as soft as leather, and made a sound like dry autumn leaves being crumpled when he closed his fist. Yet when the man opened his hand, the stuff sprang back into the original shape. Bizarre.

"We better bring that back to the baron," a beefy sec woman stated. "Just in case it's…ya know…"

"Yeah, guess so," LeFontaine agreed. It gave him a thrill to think there might be a wad of metal in his pocket.

"Well, whatever that drek is, there's no big honking pile of blasters waiting for us, that's for damn sure," a sec woman declared irritably, playing the light of her torch around the cave. "I always did think that inbred throwback was shitting in our ears."

"No, I swear the outlanders were here!" the Hilly cried.

Frowning, a sec man chuffed him to the ground. "Shut the frag up," he growled menacingly. "Or ya get more!"

"No need for that yet," LeFontaine growled, then paused to retrieve something shiny from the cold ashes of the campfire.

At first, he couldn't quite identify what it was, never having seen anything like it before. Then his mind co-alesced around the object and he gasped in astonishment. It was a spoon! A bent spoon made of solid metal, left behind with the trash as if it was of no importance whatsoever, completely worthless.

"Release the Hilly," LeFontaine ordered, marveling over the incredible utensil. "He was telling it straight, boys. The outlanders were here, and packing more steel than even the lord high bastard Griffin his own damn self!"

The hand that had hit the Hilly now reached out to offer him assistance to get back on his feet. Ignoring it, the mountain man stood and dusted off his ragged furs. There were a million things he wanted to say, but now was not the time or the place.

"So what are we waiting for?" the Hilly demanded. "Let's go track down the mutie lovers, and get those blasters!"

The sec men cheered, and LeFontaine led the way outside to the waiting horses.

Climbing onto his mount, LeFontaine shook the reins and started forward at a slow walk. "All right, I want a full recce of the beach!" he said gruffly. "They probably swept the dirt to disguise which direction they went in, but nobody can do it forever. Spread out! Find their damn tracks, and it's a week of beef, bed and beer for the man who does!"

The sec men burst into eager smiles at the generous offer, but then their expressions melted into frowns as a mountain of mottled hide rose from the nearby lake, the colossal figure of the kraken blotting out the foggy sun.

Snarling virulent curses, the sec men swung up their crossbows to cut loose with a flurry of arrows. They hit the mutie hard, the wooden shafts going into the fletching. Ignoring the attack, the monstrous thing howled as dozens of ropy tentacles snaked out of the waves to grab a horse by the legs. Screaming in terror, the animal was hauled into the lake and disappeared beneath the choppy surface.

"Retreat!" LeFontaine bellowed, kicking his horse in the flanks and charging for the nearby forest. The sec chief had a full five rounds of live brass in his wheelgun, but against a kraken he might as well be throwing pinecones.

Galloping off the beach, the Northpoint sec men raced for their lives. If they could just get deep enough into the trees, the sheer size of the mutie would prevent it from following. They knew it was a desperate gamble, but there was no other choice. Only a feeb fought a hopeless battle.

Oddly, the Hilly did nothing, standing motionless near the mouth of the cave, a hand covering his mouth.

Astonished, LeFontaine and the sec men had no idea what the feeb was doing, and didn't nuking care. If the Hilly wanted to see a kraken from the inside, that was his choice. But they were going to live!

Bent over their animals, trying to urge them to greater speed, the sec chief and his troops were near the tree line, when suddenly they were engulfed in writhing tentacles.

Indiscriminately, random men and horses were grabbed and bodily dragged back to the lake. Briefly, they shrieked in raw terror, then were hauled below the waves and out of sight.

Reaching the forest, the rest of the sec men sighed in relief, and slowed their advance to keep from getting knocked from their horses by the endless array of low-hanging branches.

"Think we're safe now?" a sec woman panted, not daring to look backward.

Before anybody could reply, a mottled tentacle lifted her out of the saddle and into the sky. The other sec men heard her scream, but not for very long.

Realizing escape was impossible, LeFontaine reined

his horse to a halt under a large oak tree and slipped out of the saddle. Stepping away from the animal, he covered his mouth with a hand and tried not to breathe too loudly. With his heart pounding in his chest, the sec chief burned to tell the others what to do, but knew that would only mean his own demise. They had to figure it out on their own, or buy the farm.

"What the frag are you doing, sir?" a sec man demanded, and then was gone. A few seconds later a bloody boot descended from the sky, the foot still laced tightly inside.

As comprehension dawned, the few remaining sec men brought their horses to a standstill and clambered off, to creep away from the animals as quietly as possible. Set free, the horses bolted deeper into the forest and, one by one, their death screams could be heard from the sky above, heading back toward the lake.

Only a few seconds later, the sec men were alone in the dim forest, a chilly breeze murmuring through the pine needles and stirring the carpet of oak leaves around their boots.

Nobody dared to move, or speak, for an inordinate length of time. Then a new sound began to permeate the woods. Looking curiously around, the sec men blanched as they saw the deadly tentacles of the kraken wiggling along the mossy ground, the questing tip probing every tree, rock and bush in an orderly search for the hidden food.

AS THE TWO MEN FIRED, the soft chug of the SIG-Sauer was lost in the thunderous discharge of the Colt revolver, and they both jerked backward, Ryan grazed across the throat, Donovan spraying blood from a shoulder wound.

"Blasters! The outlanders have more blasters!" Baron Griffin shouted, fumbling for his twin weapons.

Knowing the jig was up, Mildred ruthlessly shot the man smack in the chest. Dropping one of the weapons, the baron staggered backward, splinters showing from the ragged hole in his shirt.

The crafty son of a bitch was wearing wooden body armor, she realized. Now aiming at the baron's face, Mildred quickly switched targets as Lady Griffin unlimbered her sawed-off shotgun and thumbed back the hammer. Neatly, the physician blew the weapon out of her hands with a well-placed shot from the ZKR. Mildred knew it was foolish, but she still hesitated to ace another woman without provocation, a terrible moral holdover from the twentieth century.

Torn from her grip, the shotgun discharged into the back of a throne and slammed the startled baron off the dais. Screaming in pain, Lady Griffin dropped to her knees, clutching a broken hand to her ripped bodice.

Shooting the sec chief in the chest with a similar lack of results, Ryan triggered his blaster at the falcon, and the bird exploded over Donovan, covering the man with blood and feathers. Blinded, the sec chief clawed at the gore on his face while waving his Colt around and shooting randomly. Feeling the breeze of a passing round on his cheek, Ryan put hot lead into the big man. Crimson erupted from the sec chief's knee, and from the sleeve of the muscular arm frantically rubbing at his face.

Falling to the floor of the dais, a badly wounded

Donovan shot back once more and knocked over the brazier, pieces of flaming charcoal spraying out like a meteor shower as a swirling cloud of black soot filled the chilly air.

By now the ville was in total chaos, screaming civies running around madly, horses whinnying in terror, elks bawing, dogs barking. But the cry of "outlanders" and "blasters" steadily grew louder as it spread across the ville.

Putting a fast five rounds into the roiling smoke covering the fallen sec chief, Ryan heard an answering grunt of pain, then hastily reloaded and turned his attention to the onrushing squad of sec men. He took out the people loading crossbows, then something came at him from his blind side, and Ryan ducked as a boomerang spun by, missing him by inches.

In the distance, Baron Griffin was limping into a squad of sec men and shouting orders. Brandishing weapons, the troops charged toward the dais, firing arrows and twirling deadly bolos overhead. Gunning them down, Ryan felt a brief urge to be furious at the physician for nuking the scam. But that brass wouldn't load. They had made a mistake, and now had to pay the price. That was life. And death, he added solemnly.

Stepping out of the thick smoke masking the dais, Mildred appeared with the Czech ZKR at the ready, her other hand holding the collar of the panting Lady Griffin. In ragged stages, the barrage of arrows and the spears coming their way slowed and then stopped completely, the ville sec men unwilling to harm the baron's wife, augmented by their clear terror of the working blasters.

"Let us leave, and she lives!" Mildred bellowed, then fired into the tumultuous crowd edging the ville green. With most of his face removed, a sec man fell back, the bolo spinning in his hands going high into the trees.

Doing the same thing in the other direction, Ryan started to ask a question when he saw Lady Griffin pull a hidden knife from within her bodice and press the sharp stone tip against her own throat.

"You're never gonna take me to that bitch Wainwright alive!" she growled defiantly, her fist tightening in preparation.

Seeing the raw determination in her face, Ryan knew there was no use trying to convince the woman they had nothing to do with the other baron. In a world of paranoids, nobody believed the truth. "Okay, then we surrender," the one-eyed man said, dropping his blaster.

Gasping at the action, Lady Griffin eased her muscles, and Mildred swung her blaster hard and fast, the barrel cracking across the temple of the other woman with surgical precision. Giving a little shudder, Lady Griffin released the knife and slumped unconscious to the cold grass.

Around the green, the sec men paused, not sure if their ruler was aced or not, then rushed forward in a wave, pulling out knives and axes. As Ryan and Mildred mowed them down, there unexpectedly came a long trumpet from the guard tower high above the ville, and the gate in the wall began to slowly rumble closed.

Then the sec man blowing the horn seemed to jump out of the tower to plummet to a grisly death. A moment later, there came the crack of the Steyr longblaster rolling down from the nearby foothills. However, the gate continued moving until it boomed shut.

"Fireblast, only one way out of here now," Ryan muttered, snapping off shots. Swinging an arbalest around, the sec men fell, clutching red bellies.

"Yeah, I know," Mildred growled, dumping out spent rounds to hastily reload. She closed the revolver with a snap of her wrist. "Lead the way, my friend."

While Mildred laid down suppressive fire, Ryan pulled his only gren from a pocket, yanked loose the arming pin, flipped off the safety lever and threw the deadly explosive charge at the *Wendigo*.

The military sphere hit the grass and rolled directly underneath the war wag just as a swarm of sec men piled into the machine. With a sputtering roar, the diesel engine came to life…and the gren detonated. The strident blast blew the *Wendigo* apart, flaming chunks of men and machine flying outward in every direction.

Even as everybody ran away from the explosion, Ryan and Mildred raced toward the wreckage, using the expanding cloud of dark smoke as makeshift cover. Now that they were away from the baron's wife, there would be nothing to stop the sec men from attacking with everything they had. Unless, of course, the companions were long gone.

As Ryan and Mildred pelted cross the field, the Steyr spoke again from the foothills, abruptly ending the life of a sec man struggling to aim a black-powder longblaster. Stopping a few yards away from the burning wreckage, Ryan snapped off rounds from the SIG-Sauer, as Mildred prepared her gren and lofted it high to sail over the fence surrounding the bubbling still.

As it landed inside the barricade, the guards raced away in terror, but it was already too late. The military charge cut loose and the huge still erupted, hundreds of gallons of shine igniting into a staggering fireball. Shrapnel tore the fence to pieces, and the limp bodies of the sec men went airborne, the deafening concussion of the double explosion echoing among the rows of cabins and tents throughout the entire ville sounding louder than doomsday.

Waiting for the concussion to dissipate, Ryan and Mildred once again ran toward the explosion, the SIG-Sauer and ZKR removing any potential opposition. Halfway there, they changed direction and headed toward the gallows. There were few sec men in this area of the ville, but that was only to be expected. Nobody considered the execution yard a weakness in their defense. What prisoner would ever rush pell-mell toward his or her own demise? But that mistake would serve the companions well this day.

Holding a throwing ax, a young sec woman valiantly tried to block their way with a wooden shield. Shooting her in the boot, Ryan and Mildred ran past the yelling teenager and proceeded up the long flight of stairs.

Behind them, thick smoke was extending across the ville, the descending umbrella of burning shine setting the roofs of a dozen buildings on fire. Horses, elk and herds of terrified goats were running rampant in the streets, trampling civies and sec men alike, and seriously hindering the clumsy efforts to battle the spreading conflagration with buckets of water drawn from the artesian well.

Halfway up the stairs, the two companions saw a group of sec men climb on top of the only brick building in the ville, obviously the baron's home. Three of the men attacked with their crossbows, but the half-arrows were unable to reach the staircase, and arched down into the chaos of the streets. However, the third sec man lit the fuse on a thick bamboo tube, then began to swing the homemade gren overhead at the end of a rope.

Both Ryan and Mildred cursed and quickly took aim. Before they could shoot, the man crumpled and the sizzling bamboo tube sailed away to land near the empty dais, violently exploding and throwing out chunks of wood and other debris.

Resuming their hectic sprint up the stairs, the two companions could only assume that had been the work of the Steyr, but the report of the longblaster could not be heard over the growing riot in the streets of the beleaguered ville. The destruction of the still had inadvertently set the slaves loose, and they were extracting a swift and terrible revenge upon the brutal overseers before running toward the gate, their hands dripping blood. Some of the sec men were trying to stop the mass escape, but without orders from their baron or sec chief, their efforts were proving futile, and often disastrous.

Reaching the top level of the gallows, the companions paused to catch their breath. "Good luck, guys,"

Mildred panted, watching the slaves battle it out with the sec men near the shatter zone.

"They should have stolen some weapons first," Ryan countered, untying a rope from a cleat. Handing it to the physician, he took another for himself. Checking the distance, the companions jumped off the gallows to swing out over the stone wall and simply let go.

Their journey forward seemed impossibly brief compared to the fall from the *Harrington,* and knowing what to expect, Ryan and Mildred braced themselves just before splashing into the freezing water of the Great Lake.

The icy shock banished the exhaustion from their bodies and galvanized their efforts to start swimming toward the surface even before slowing to a stop. However, it was a good thing that the companions had left most of their heavier items behind as the cloth boots soon became soaked, the cold numbing their feet and slowing their efforts considerably.

Fighting to the surface, Ryan and Mildred gasped for air and instantly started for the shore. Irregularly shaped boulders dotted the expanse of the wide bay, waves crashing against them and throwing out an icy mist that nearly formed snow. There was also the gentle tug of a tide below the surface, both Ryan and Mildred surprised that such a thing could exist in a lake, no matter how large.

Suddenly there was a flurry of motion above and a hail of arrows stabbed into the surface around the companions, the wooden shafts oddly hissing as they disappeared into the water. Firebrands! Then from under water, there came a muffled whomp, and a small geyser bubbled upward.

More firebrands arrived as the companions struggled onto the pebble beach and finally out of range. Shaking the water off their bodies, Ryan and Mildred saw that the beach was covered with hundreds of blue-shell crabs, most of them sitting directly under the dangling corpse, patiently waiting for the ripe meat to fall. Remembering the advice from Liana, they moved carefully through the colony, trying not to step on any of the creatures. Just then a large rock plummeted from above, smashing onto the beach and chilling a dozen crabs. That seemed to wake the rest of them, and the army of crabs scuttled forward to examine the new arrivals.

Brushing back her wet plaits, Mildred cursed at the realization that the sec men were now dropping rocks on them from the wall. Clever bastards.

Trying to kick a crab aside with his wet boot, Ryan saw the thing attach itself to the cloth and start crawling up his leg. Quickly drawing the SIG-Sauer, he shook the blaster to make sure there was no water in the barrel, then blew the crab off his boot with a well-placed shot.

Every crab on the beach went motionless at the sound of the weapon, then the smell of fresh blood reached them, and they wildly converged upon Ryan, their pinchers clattering and snipping. After all, everything that fell from the sky was dead, and easy pickings.

Low on ammo, Ryan had to place his shots, the hollowpoint rounds making the body of each crab explode.

Pulling out the Czech ZKR, Mildred shot the largest crab in the face, hoping to intimidate the rest. The soft-lead punched a neat hole in the mouth, then came out the back end in a grisly spray of pale flesh and slimy organs. Still horribly alive, the squealing creature began to crawl in a circle, going nowhere fast. In a rush, some of the other crabs attacked it, savagely removing legs and eyestalks, consuming it alive.

Now shooting only to wound, the companions soon cleared a path to the base of the cliff, the scuttling horde turning upon itself in a cannibal frenzy. Soon the battle became pandemic, quickly spreading across the beach like some horrible new disease.

Ryan and Mildred quickly reloaded, then stomped their sodden blanket boots, trying to squeeze out the excess moisture.

Incredibly, there was a splash from the lake as a sec man dived into the water.

Quickly aiming their blasters, the companions relaxed as they saw a crimson red pool rise to the surface, the wellspring of life spreading outward in every direction.

Almost instantly, the army of crabs abandoned their internecine combat and rushed into the bloody lake, disappearing below the choppy waves.

Taking advantage of the distraction, Ryan and Mildred raced along the base of the cliff until reaching a low rill. Clambering over the lava ridge, they dropped down the other side only a moment before a hail of half-arrows peppered the barrier. Suddenly a massive arrow from an arbalest slammed into the rill, smashing through and plowing deep into the pebble beach on the other side.

Keeping to the lee side of the larger boulders on the beach, Ryan and Mildred dodged from one to the other, staying constantly on the move, until the natural curve of the island finally took them out of the range of the ville crossbows.

Chapter Nine

A thick carpeting of lush green grass covered the wide hill, a copse of tall oak trees standing on the crest like an arboreal crown. A feathery rainbow of songbirds twittered in the leafy branches, and a cottontail coney darted among the laurel bushes in search of food. Off to the side, a hulking stone gargoyle sat amid a plethora of clover. The decorative statue was cracked across its weathered visage, giving the fantastic creature a lopsided grin.

Oddly, there were no other remnants of a predark city in sight, and so it was impossible to tell if the gargoyle was all that remained of a once-mighty metropolis, or if the statue was merely windblown trash, just a chunk of debris that tumbled down from the sky into the sylvan field from a thermonuclear explosion a thousand miles away.

Suddenly, a long black tube extended from behind the gargoyle to sweep along the rocky coast.

"Okay, they made it to dry land," Krysty announced, her relief painfully obvious. Lowering the yard-long Navy telescope, she compacted it back to the size of a soup can.

Crouched on the other side of the protective statue,

J.B. lowered the longblaster. "That's good to know," the wiry man said, working the arming bolt on the Steyr to open the breech and insert a fresh magazine. "Because the damn smoke is so thick in the ville, I can't find anybody else to ace."

"Nobody worth live brass," Jak corrected, squinting into the distance. There were still a lot of sec men running around on the wall, but shoot too many of them, and the fall of the bodies would reveal the direction of the attack. The prime rule for sniping an opponent was to never let them know where you were hidden.

Opening a canteen, the albino teen smiled. Liana had been right. The hilltop was perfect to recce the ville. The wild bushes gave good cover, and the statue of the predark mutie would confuse anybody looking for snipers.

"Unfortunately, I fear that a choice of targets will not be a problem, John Barrymore," Doc rumbled, wiping the loose dirt from his hands. "Because here come the Visigoths!"

Promptly, J.B. and Krysty swung up their optical devices, but it wasn't necessary. The companions could clearly see that the huge front gate of the ville was already in motion, swinging outward. A dozen sec men on horseback galloped out of the ville hard and fast, the riders hellbent for leather, the big mounts huffing in the chilly air.

"I only hope the diversion works," Kristy said, pulling off her gloves and flexing tired fingers.

Cradling the loaded crossbow, Liana started to speak when a large pack of cougars charged out of the gates to disappear in the thick bushes.

"Blind Norad, the baron released the cats!" she cried out in fear. "They'll find Ryan and Mildred long before the riders do, and maul them bad."

"Only maul?" Krysty asked, surprised. "The cats don't chill their prey?"

The blonde woman shook her head. "No, ma'am, they just cripple them for the sec men to take alive."

Tucking away the telescope, Krysty frowned. That sounded like real trouble.

"Not if I can help it," J.B. said, swinging up the Steyr and searching for the cats. But they were gone, vanished into the bushes edging the dirt road.

"All right, let's move," Krysty said, drawing her two revolvers and heading into the trees.

"Are we going to rondee with the others at the natural bridge?" Liana asked, staying close to the tall redhead. "That's a good place to stage a fight. The sec men can only attack us from one direction."

The staggering disadvantages of fighting on an open bridge were so many that the companions decided simply not to comment. She would soon see the truth of the matter for herself.

"No, my dear, we shall rendezvous with them near the cliff," Doc rumbled, rotating the cylinder of the Ruger to check the load, and then doing the same to the LeMat. "It is never wise to surrender the high ground."

"Then why didn't we just stay here, and roll those boulders down on the sec men as they rode past?" Liana demanded, shifting her grip on the crossbow.

"Maybe we would have aced them, and then again, maybe not," J.B. replied, aiming the Steyr down the hill, his finger resting alongside the trigger. "But with the valley below us blocked, now they have to go through the forest."

Squinting in that direction, Liana looked at the wide expanse of trees. "Hoping they'll get lost?" she asked vaguely.

"Hardly." Krysty snorted. "See that area with no bird nests, no squirrels?"

"Yes," Liana answered hesitantly.

"Then watch and learn, my dear," Doc said, scowling darkly at the wide expanse of forest, the branches of the trees stirred only by a gentle breeze coming in from the Great Lake.

STAYING IN A TIGHT FORMATION, the Anchor sec men rode fast along the old dirt road, their blasters out and primed. The baron had armed them with the unheard-of bounty of ten live brass, and an order to chill on sight. Naturally, they would have preferred to take them both alive for a little payback, but orders were orders.

Oddly, a recent avalanche blocked the way to the stone bridge, but the road through the apple orchard was wide and clear. Wary of more snipers, the sec men slowed their mounts and closely watched the shadows for any hostile intentions.

"Funny there ain't no birds or nothing in the trees," a sec woman noted tersely, her body rocking to the motion of her horse.

"Don't like that," an elderly sec man muttered.

Spotting motion in the thick canopy of branches, a corporal fired his crossbow upward. "They're in the trees!" he yelled. As the arrow disappeared, there came an answering smack, and something large fell to the ground, pulsating and undulating.

"Flapjack!" a sec woman screamed, her horse rearing in terror.

The flapjack touched the belly of the nearest horse, and the animal immediately went motionless in incredible pain. Then the creature's boneless limb began to pump red, siphoning blood from the animal.

Snarling in rage, a sec man fired his crossbow directly at the mutie, but the feathered shaft went straight through the gelatinous creature, only to bury itself deep underground.

"Blasters!" the corporal bellowed, hauling out a revolver.

Just then, the leaves rustled and another flapjack fell directly onto the startled man, completely covering his head. The corporal gave a muffled scream and raised both hands to paw off the amorphous creature. But his arms become instantly mired in the sticky ooze covering the flapjack. The mutie tinted crimson with the corporal's blood as his hair and eyes disappeared, followed by his ears and lips.

Shrieking insanely, the corporal went silent as the amorphous mutie flowed into his mouth, ramming a path down his throat. Still in the saddle, the corporal violently shuddered as the thing started to dissolve him from the inside, the flapjack nearly purring as it feasted on the raw flesh and brains.

Leveling her blaster at the nightmarish mutie, a sec woman aimed and fired, the rounds blasting a deep furrow through the flapjack and blowing apart the partially consumed head of the corporal. Cursing vehemently, another sec man took aim with his shotgun and stroked the trigger. In a thunderous bellow, the flapjack was blown apart, along with the remains of the aced corporal, gobbets of the weird translucent flesh flying about the forest to smack into the trees and ground.

Almost losing control of his stallion, a large sec man burbled in terror as a piece of the mutie hit his cheek, the thick beard turning white under the furious assault of the organic acids.

"Don't touch it!" a sec woman commanded. Pulling out a throwing ax, she expertly swung it, cutting off the bushy beard, the wad of pulsating hair falling to the leafy ground.

"Th-thanks," the sec man panted, clutching the reins in both hands.

That single word seemed to be the clarion call to war for the flapjacks as they dropped from the shadowy boughs by the dozens, the gelatinous killers landing on the sec force and its horses.

Shooting blasters and slashing with their stone knives, the dying sec men and women fought for their lives, but it was hopeless, and soon the forest trail was strewed with dissolving bodies, humans and horses alike buried under the pulsating mounds of the gorging flapjacks.

"Retreat!" one of the few survivors commanded, reining in her dappled mare to neatly avoid a plummeting flapjack.

As it lay there on the ground, she started to shoot,

but since the thing had no visible targets such as a brain, or heart, the sec woman held back and kicked her horse into a gallop. The urge was to simply ride over the thing, killing it beneath the sharp hooves of the animal, but she had seen what these monsters could do, and decided not to take the risk. There were old sec men, and there were bold sec men, but nobody ever heard of any old, bold sec men.

As the four remaining sec men wheeled their mounts around to head back to the ville, small flapjacks pelted from the trees, the infant muties smacking all over the horses. As the acid started to burn, the animals reared, kicking wildly, and the riders were thrown to the hard ground.

Hastily scrambling to their feet, the sec men fired their blasters at anything nearby, a growing panic stealing their years of training. A horse was mortally wounded and instinctively kicked back. A sec man's knee cracked audibly and he dropped to land face-first onto a flapjack.

As he began to thrash around, the nearest man swung his ax down to sever the spine of the doomed man, then swung the ax sideways to slam into the ribs of a sec woman. Caught in the act of aiming the blaster at the man, she doubled over from the impact of the stone blade, the blaster firing into her own boot.

Burbling blood, she collapsed to the leaves and several flapjacks immediately started undulating toward the smell of fresh meat.

Glancing in every direction, the last sec man saw that he was momentarily in the clear, and tossed away the

ax to increase his speed as he desperately sprinted for
the edge of the forest. The horrible sounds of the feasting grew dimmer as he sprinted along, then there came
a subtle movement from above. Instantly, he dived to
the side, and a flapjack missed smacking into him by
the thickness of a prayer.

Rolling under a thornbush, the sec man came out
scratched, but alive, and began to zigzag through the
trees, never moving in a straight line for more than
three paces. More muties dropped from above, but each
one missed. Suddenly the sec man exploded out of the
shadows and slowed to a stumble, unable to believe his
fantastic luck. He was out of the forest and in the clear.
Made it. He had made it, and was going to live!

CENTERING THE CROSSHAIRS on the face of the panting
sec man, J.B. stroked the trigger of the Steyr and a
7.62 mm hollowpoint round sent the coward tumbling
into the eternal.

"By the lost gods," Liana breathed, not sure if she
was impressed or not. "You aced them all with a single
shot!" The former slave had trouble speaking the next
words. "How…how did you know this was going to
happen?" Plaintively, Liana looked in their eyes hoping to see a glimmer of her father's abilities, but the
companions merely smiled, completely unaware of the
silent question.

"Readiness is all," Doc said in a singsong tone.

"Didn't know trick would work," Jak said, turning
away from the ghastly feeding in the trees. "Just hoped.
Good plans do."

"And whenever possible, try to use any natural features of the land against your opponent," J.B. added, clicking the safety back on the Steyr and slinging it over a shoulder. "Slow them down in mud, try to get them to take cover in a bush you know has a beehive in it, that sort of thing."

"The earth is always a powerful ally," Krysty added, lengthening her stride down the sloping foothill.

As the group proceeded down the hill and into a wild bramble of laurel bushes and tall weeds, Liana tested the wisdom of the new words, and found them strong, so stored the information away for later. If she was going to stay with these coldhearts—companions—then she had better start getting razor triple fast.

Shyly sneaking a look at Doc, Liana made a decision and surreptitiously reached out to grab several handfuls of the pretty flowers to stuff into a pocket. Better safe than sorry.

Crossing a wide field, the companions encountered hundreds of irregular chunks of concrete, the material weathered almost to the point where it resembled natural stone. There were even a few more pieces of the gargoyles scattered around, along with the shattered remains of a granite cross. This was the debris from a destroyed church. Doc sighed at the desecration, while the others simply kept walking, the dead past of no more interest to them than the unreachable stars.

The sound of the crashing waves on the beach was discernible long before the companions saw the Great Lake. Studying the area carefully, they decided it was safe enough to proceed, but Jak stood guard while the others began to slide down the sloping hill on the seat of their pants, boots and hands alone keeping them from tumbling head-over-heels.

When the companions reached the beach, Doc and Krysty stood guard while J.B. swung around the Uzi to keep watch over Jak as he slid to join them.

Slapping the dust from her clothes, Liana was very happy the others had given her pants to wear instead of her usual dress. They really came in handy holding off scratches from brambles and such, and pockets were a marvel all by themselves. Slaves were not allowed such things, but she had them now.

Because I am a slave no more, Liana thought in a rush of comprehension. Live or die, I am free! Timidly, she touched the crushed flowers in her pocket, and amused herself with some private thoughts about their eventual use.

Reaching the edge of the slope, Jak jumped the last few feet and landed in a crouch, the impact driving the loose dirt off his clothes. "Now where?" he drawled.

"This way to the Dragon," Liana said, pointing her crossbow.

But before the companions could move, Ryan and Mildred stepped into view from behind a gigantic rock roughly the shape of an alligator. For a long moment nobody moved or spoke.

"Hey, Adam," J.B. called in a friendly voice, his fist tight around the pistol-grip safety of the machine pistol.

"Sorry, the name's Charlie," Ryan replied, not moving an inch, a finger resting on the trigger of the SIG-Sauer.

Easing his stance, the Armorer grinned in relief that the coded greeting proved all was well. "Hey, mine, too!"

With that, everybody eased their stance and the companions rushed back together, then moved closer to the sloping hill where the chilly spray from the lake was the weakest. Along the shoreline, several blue crabs scuttled about, looking for anything edible, but only finding lake foam and some loose strands of dead kelp.

Accepting the Steyr, Ryan worked the bolt to check the magazine in the breech before slinging it over a broad shoulder. "Any trouble?"

"Nothing that a flock of feasting flapjacks did not fix," Doc answered, holding his frock coat protectively over the LeMat. The .44 Ruger revolver was in his other hand, the gunmetal sparkling with tiny dew drops of moisture.

"Then nobody is coming after us?" Mildred asked, fighting off a shiver and stomping her sodden boots on the polished stones.

"Not this life," Jak stated proudly. "Aced."

"Good," Ryan grunted, sitting on the damp rocks and pulling out a knife to slash away the leather straps holding the soaked boot blankets in place. The man desperately wanted a fire, but that wouldn't happen until they were very far away from the seacoast ville.

Taking a position alongside the man, Mildred did the same to her boots, then they both gratefully dried their feet with handkerchiefs before slipping on dry socks and donning their combat boots.

Staying a little bit away from the others, Liana wondered why the men had called each other by the wrong names before? Perhaps it was some sort of a password like the sec men used during the changing of the guards. That was the only logical answer. They trusted nobody, not even each other. For some reason, that made her feel better.

Stiffly standing, Mildred stomped the boots into a comfortable position. "At last, my feet are complete!" She chuckled, then shrugged when nobody else laughed. Too many of her jokes were obsolete these days, the book and movie references gone with the wind, somewhere in time, lost in space....

Gathering the loose pile of rags and leather, Liana ran to the shore and lashed them all together with a large stone in the middle of the bundle, then heaved it far into the lake. It hit with a splash, and promptly sank out of sight. Instantly the crabs dived into the waves, intent upon investigating the submerged object.

"Smart," Jak said, brushing back his damp hair. "Cats no follow smell now."

"What cats?" Ryan asked, and the teenager explained.

"We better make tracks," the man growled, standing. "Okay, Liana, which is the fastest way to Northpoint?"

"That way," the blonde replied, pointing a finger.

"Okay, but this time no disguises, or cutting deals," J.B. declared firmly. "We simply nightcreep the place, jack a boat and leave."

Nodding in agreement, Liana started to reply when she caught sight of a lone bird circling high in the sky. A hunting falcon! Quickly swinging up the crossbow,

Liana aimed and fired in one smooth motion. There was a squawk, and a moment later the impaled bird tumbled down to wetly impact on the Dragon.

"That was one of the baron's falcons," she said, panting for breath. "It would have kept circling above us until the sec men arrived."

"Does he have any more of them?" Mildred asked.

"Oh, yes, many."

"Damn, would the cats also check what the falcon was circling?" Ryan demanded brusquely, studying the cloudy sky.

"I…have no idea," Liana replied honestly, fumbling to reload the crossbow. It was made for a sec man with much larger hands, and she had trouble just carrying the bulky weapon. Still, it was much better than a wooden knife.

"Fireblast," Ryan growled. This trip was fast becoming an absolute mutie-shag, and neither he nor Mildred were in any shape for a prolonged battle. "All right, we can't take the chance they might have, so let's get moving. Double time, people. We have to get away from here as fast as possible. J.B., take the point. Doc, muddy our trail."

"Yes, of course," the scholar said in resignation, and pulled out his pouch of black powder to start sprinkling it behind the companions. With the smell of fresh blood on the rocks near the shoreline, and the reek of black powder in the opposite direction, unless the animals were exceptionally intelligent, the companions should not be bothered by the big cats.

"Okay, which way should we go?" Ryan asked,

studying the face of the former slave for any sign of betrayal.

"Toward the mountains," Liana said, gesturing with the crossbow.

After a moment Ryan nodded in agreement, and the companions immediately took off in that direction, J.B. taking the point position.

Quickly leaving the beach, the companions headed inland across a field of wildflowers. Reaching a small creek, they sloshed along for a while to mask their tracks, then retreated a distance, before going onto dry land once more.

All the while, Ryan kept a close watch on the newcomer. The one-eyed man knew that sec men might change their allegiance purely for jack, or revenge, but slaves would mistrust everybody until they chose a new master. Then he saw Liana look longingly at Doc, and knew that decision had already been made. Fair enough.

"Krysty, give her a piece," Ryan decided, stepping over a fallen log, the deadwood alive with insects.

Expecting that decision, the redhead pulled out a spare blaster recovered from the battleship. "Here, this is for you," she said, offering the revolver. "You're good with that crossbow, but this has a lot more chilling power." Personally, Krysty was glad to be rid of the weight. She was carrying too many blasters.

"Besides, you have earned it," Doc added proudly.

Slinging the big crossbow over a shoulder, Liana accepted the weapon as if it were made of dried leaves and a single breath would blow it away. It was an actual blaster. A real, live, metal blaster!

Get FREE BOOKS and a FREE GIFT when you play the...

LAS VEGAS

GAME

7

7

*Just scratch off
the gold box with a coin.
Then check below to see
the gifts you get!*

YES! I have scratched off the gold box. Please send me my 2 **FREE BOOKS** and **FREE GIFT** for which I qualify. I understand that I am under no obligation to purchase any books as explained on the back of this card.

▼ DETACH AND MAIL CARD TODAY! ▼

366 ADL EVMJ

166 ADL EVMU
(GE-LV-09)

FIRST NAME	LAST NAME

ADDRESS

APT.#	CITY

STATE/PROV.	ZIP/POSTAL CODE

7	7	7	Worth TWO FREE BOOKS plus a FREE Gift!
🍒	🍒	🍒	Worth TWO FREE BOOKS!
🔔	🔔	♣	TRY AGAIN!

Offer limited to one per household and not valid to current subscribers of Gold Eagle® books. All orders subject to approval. Please allow 4 to 6 weeks for delivery.

The Gold Eagle Reader Service — Here's how it works:

Accepting your 2 free books and free gift (gift valued at approximately $5.00) places you under no obligation to buy anything. You may keep the books and gift and return the shipping statement marked "cancel." If you do not cancel, about a month later we'll send you 6 additional books and bill you just $31.94* — that's a savings of 15% off the cover price of all 6 books! And there's no extra charge for shipping! You may cancel at any time, but if you choose to continue, every other month we'll send you 6 more books, which you may either purchase at the discount price or return to us and cancel your subscription.

*Terms and prices subject to change without notice. Prices do not include applicable taxes. Sales tax applicable in N.Y. Canadian residents will be charged applicable provincial taxes and GST. Offer not valid in Quebec. Credit or debit balances in a customer's account(s) may be offset by any other outstanding balance owed by or to the customer. Offer available while quantities last.

BUSINESS REPLY MAIL

FIRST-CLASS MAIL   PERMIT NO. 717   BUFFALO, NY

POSTAGE WILL BE PAID BY ADDRESSEE

GOLD EAGLE READER SERVICE
3010 WALDEN AVE
PO BOX 1867
BUFFALO NY 14240-9952

NO POSTAGE
NECESSARY
IF MAILED
IN THE
UNITED STATES

"Always keep the first chamber empty," Krysty said, touching the cylinder. "That's for safety. I'll guess that you are not overly familiar with the operations of a revolver."

"A what?" Liana asked, totally confused.

"That's another name for a blaster," Doc explained.

"There's no brass in the cylinder right now," Krysty stated. "So it's okay to dry fire it a few times. Pull the trigger a little bit, the hammer cocks. See? Now pull it all the way back, and the hammer drops, firing the brass."

Carefully, Liana did as she was instructed, trying to get the feel of the clicking metal thing. The blaster was heavier than a boomerang, and carried a strange feeling of deadly power. She could guess why. A hammer had a dozen uses, rope was good for a hundred purposes, and a knife even more, but this tool was made only for chilling and nothing else. It was a solid piece of death.

"Save for close range," Jak advised sagely. "Then shoot into belly."

"Not the head?" Liana asked with a frown. "I've heard the sec men say that was the best place to ace somebody, even a mutie."

"It's also the hardest to hit," Krysty said. "The barrel of the blaster will jump a little when you fire. That means a beginner will miss a head shot every time."

"I see," Liana said slowly, testing the weapon in her hand. The checkered grip slipped into her palm as if it had been designed just for her and nobody else. Simply amazing. "So if I shoot for the belly, and miss, I'll still hit the chest?"

"You learn fast, little sister," Krysty said with a smile, passing the woman a leather gunbelt, the loops full of live brass. Then the redhead showed the blonde how to load the blaster.

It took Liana a few times to learn how to open the cylinder and then insert the brass cartridges while walking, but she finally got the task accomplished and closed it with a satisfying click. Suddenly the blaster felt alive and potent.

Keeping the barrel of the Colt pointed away from the others, Liana tried to thumb back the hammer the way she had seen the companions do just before a fight. However, it was much heavier than expected and slipped away from her to hit the cylinder. Instantly, the blaster jumped as the brass fired, the round loudly ricocheting off a rock to zing into the distance. Horribly embarrassed, the woman cringed and started to offer the weapon back.

"Don't worry about it, no corpse, no crime," Mildred said in a soothing tone, patting the blonde on the shoulder. "Besides, everybody does that their first time. Damn near blew off my own foot as a beginner."

"Will somebody teach me more later on?" Liana asked eagerly, hefting the weapon.

"Well, Doc is the best shot," Ryan lied, not looking backward as he stepped over a fallen log.

Quite surprised by the untruth, the scholar raised a questioning eyebrow and grinned in understanding. Clearly, Ryan wanted to keep the newcomer at a distance in case they were forced to leave her behind. However, the answer to that problem was simple.

"Dear lady, would you be so kind as to shake my hand?" Doc asked politely.

Timidly, Liana did so, and was rudely surprised when the tall scholar began to squeeze hard. As the pain grew, she almost cried out for him to stop, but then saw something in his gentle eyes, and gamely fought back, trying her utmost to give as good as she got.

After several minutes, Doc finally let go, and beamed a wide, contented grin. "By Gadfrey, miss, you'll do fine!" He chuckled. "You are clearly more than strong enough to handle the recoil of that weapon."

So that had been a test? "If strength is important, why don't I use a two-hand grip?" she asked eagerly.

"Ah, but you should!" Doc exclaimed, and demonstrated how, one hand holding the grip of the blaster, the other holding his own wrist for additional support.

Clumsily, Liana copied the hold, then shifted her position slightly and suddenly the blaster felt an integral part of her arm. It was amazing! Nearly bursting with questions, Liana tried to get them out one at a time, and the lessons continued over the long miles as the seven companions marched into the misty hills, leaving the seacoast ville far behind, the hazy smoke of the burning buildings fading into the distance.

Chapter Ten

Slowly the old healer rose from the tattered form lying on the churned earth, and reverently laid a white fur coat over what had once been a living, breathing woman.

"She's gone, lord," the healer said, bowing his head.

"No...impossible...." Baron Griffin whispered, dropping to his knees. His clothing was torn and dirty, a great chunk of fur missing from his cape. His left arm was nestled in a crude rope sling, and a crimson streak was smeared across a cheek from the barrage of shrapnel that exploded from the destruction of the *Wendigo*.

"My love?" the baron whispered, reaching out a trembling hand to stroke the bloody arm of his wife. But there was no reply, and he knew there never would be again.

Opening his mouth to speak, the healer decided it was better to say nothing and moved away, looking for anybody his seaweed potions and cloth bandages might be able to help. Nearly half the people in the ville had wounds of some sort or another, but most of them had been caused by the sec men shooting blindly at the escaping outlanders. However, that was the sort of comment that got a man hung and fed to the crabs. With every wound he stitched shut, the healer wisely cursed the cowardly outlanders and praised the brave sec men.

Seeing one of his wife's favorite plastic rings where it lay near her body, Baron Griffin reverently slipped it back on the stiffening finger, the wild maelstrom of raw emotions inside the tormented man too complex and powerful to ever put into simple words. Gone, Barbara was gone forever.

A long time passed, but none of the sec men surrounding the tableau dared to speak and disturb their mourning baron. There was only the background cries of the wounded, the wail of civies over their deceased husbands and wives, and the steady crackle of the burning log cabins. Arrows stuck out of the ground like winter weeds, the spent brass of the outlanders' blasters clearly showing their escape route through the ville. The smoldering wreckage of the *Wendigo* lay scattered across the ground for a hundred yards. A thick column of black smoke rose from the roiling inferno of the annihilated still, the cooking bodies of the shine crew sizzling horribly inside the raging fire, the meaty smell both oddly appetizing and utterly repulsive at the same time.

"What should we do now, lord?" sec chief Donovan demanded, thumbing live brass into his blaster.

The chest of the big man was covered with tight leather wrapping to ease the pain of his broken ribs. A fat bandage sat on his wounded shoulder like the pet bird of a sailor, a rivulet of red seeping out from underneath to trickle down his arm. His once handsome face was covered with blisters from the spray of red-hot coals, but there was a fierce determination in his dark eyes.

"Do?" Baron Griffin repeated, as if he had never heard the word before. Then withdrawing his hand from the cooling skin of the ragged corpse, he slowly stood, the mounting fury giving him new strength. "What we do is track down the mutie-loving outlanders and skin them alive!"

"I already have a full team of horsemen out searching for them, as well as the cats and falcons," Donovan replied curtly, closing the blaster with a snap and tucking it into a holster.

"Send more," the baron commanded, looking at his hands, tightening them into fists and releasing them again. "Send out everybody who's still alive."

"No, my lord, that would endanger the safety of the ville," Donovan countered. "We're already down to the newbies and green recruits on the wall."

Turning, the baron wanted to scream at the sec chief to do as he was told, but then cold reason countered the hot rush of anger. Yes, the ville had to be protected at all costs. If only so that he could cut out the beating hearts of the outlanders over the grave of his wife, and soak the ground with their blood. The baron knew the old legends. Only the blood of the living enemy could sooth the soul into the next world.

"Yes, a prudent move," Baron Griffin growled, his face jerking with a nervous tick. "Have the children recover the arrows, send the oldsters to put out those damn fires, reload the arbalests in case of an attack, and then…" He smiled, the tick coming back to turn his visage into a feral mask. "And then send out every messenger pigeon we have! Inform every ville on the entire world about the coldhearts. Offer a reward of fifty pounds of steel if they are captured and brought back to me alive."

"F-fifty!" a sec man gasped. "But, my liege, that's the entire royal treasury!"

"Not anymore," the baron commented dryly, waving a hand at the steaming debris of the shattered *Wendigo*. "Gather every scrap, every piece, and start rebuilding the boiler. We may need to take it as trade in case—"

Whatever the baron was about to say was truncated by a low, inhuman growl from the direction of the cliffs. Instantly everybody scrambled for weapons as the noise came again, louder this time, and much closer.

THE LONG DAY FADED into a cool afternoon, but the companions kept moving deeper into the rugged terrain, steadily climbing ever higher into the foggy mountains. The air was crisp and clean, and wildlife abounded in the thick foliage.

Thick forests of pine trees dominated the rolling landscape, but there was also a steady scattering of maple trees, copses of apple and nectarine trees, and an endless variety of fruit-bearing bushes—blueberries, loganberries and several species that not even Krysty could identify.

"No starvation here," J.B. said, wiping his glasses with a cloth as they marched along. "I'm surprised that the island isn't choked with people."

"Have there been a lot of wars?" Ryan asked.

"There's always fighting," Liana replied, lengthening her stride to keep abreast of Doc. If the scholar noticed her efforts, he gave no sign. "But even in the good times, breeding ain't allowed unless the Book says so."

"Bible?" Jak asked as a wild guess. He knew of several villes that lived by the old rules.

Glancing at the teenager, Liana frowned as if she had never heard the word before. "The Book of Blood," she explained. "It's the only thing that all of the barons agree on. Every family is listed, and nobody can breed unless they're three births away from each other."

"Interesting," Mildred mused, rubbing her chin. "The island must have survived the war with a very small gene pool, and somebody was smart enough to keep track. You can safely have children with a relative if you're third cousins. Any closer and you would start to get terrible inbreeding."

"The innies, yeah, they're bad," Liana agreed with a hard expression. "Most of the babes…well, the midwife aces 'em right there on the birthing bed." After a moment she added, "Sometimes the villes swap folks around, send five men here, or ten women there. Not sure why, but the babes born afterward are always bigger and stronger than usual. Sec chief Donovan is one of those, and he's bastard strong."

"I noticed," Ryan muttered, touching the bandage on his throat.

"Sadly, there must also be the occasional mutation," Doc added, clearly thinking out loud.

Trying not to blush at the dirty word, Liana agreed.

"I...I always thought that I was a...a mutie," she said in a rush. "Don't look like either of my parents."

"Just a recessive gene," Mildred explained. "There must have been some Asian blood in your family once, and it resurfaced in you."

"Why?" Liana asked in a sudden surge of interest.

Briefly, the physician considered trying to explain Mendell, the laws of heredity and DNA, then decided not to even try. "Just nature's way of keeping us all different," she said affably. "Like when two ugly people have a beautiful child, or two really smart people have an incredibly dumb kid."

"I see," Liana said slowly.

Leaving the field, the companions trudged higher into the mountains, the air becoming steadily colder. Along the way, Liana kept drawing her blaster and pointing it at targets: rock, tree, bush. She got faster, then slower as her muscles got tired, then a little bit faster once again through sheer determination.

Slowly, night descended and once more the dancing lights of the aurora borealis filled the sky. As if they were entering the clouds, a heavy fog spread across the land, more dense than any Deathlands sandstorm. Soon the cicadas began their eternal song, and in the far distance, a wolf howled at the silvery moon for reasons unknown since the dawn of time.

Suddenly, Krysty raised a clenched fist and everybody instantly stopped moving. Walking a few yards ahead of the others, the woman squinted into the distance. "There's a ville over there," she announced hesitantly.

"Better stay away from there," Liana stated firmly. "That's Hill ville."

"Friendlies?" Jak asked, thumbing back the hammer on his Colt Python.

"Aced, they're all aced," Liana replied. "They were triple crazy and defied the Book of Blood, marrying and breeding with anybody they wanted." She scowled darkly. "Or could catch. The barons of both Anchor and Northpoint sent troops to attack the ville one night, and they chilled everybody, man, woman and child."

"Even the civvies?" J.B. asked, pushing back his fedora.

"Everybody," Liana repeated. "Only a handful escaped alive. Dunno how." She turned to the tall mountain in the east. "Some folks say they took refuge in the Forbidden Caves, but anybody going there to see don't come back."

"And thus were created the Hillies," Mildred said in a rush of understanding. She had assumed that the name was merely a bastardization of the term hillbilly, but actually it came from the name of their former ville.

"Anybody there now?" Ryan asked, pulling out the Navy longeye.

"Sky gods no!" Liana replied, shocked at the mere suggestion. "The ville is cursed. Baron Griffin sent some pilgrims once, and they went mad, screaming, running around naked and clawing out their eyes. Couple of years later Northpoint tried, and the same thing happened. Since then, Hill ville has been avoided like a mutie in a rad pit."

"Sounds like some kind of poison to me," J.B. stated. "I'm guessing the locals soaked a cord of wood with something, and when the invaders started a campfire for dinner, the fumes took them out neat and quick."

"Makes sense," Ryan agreed, sweeping the ville with the longeye. "Unless they had a stock of nerve gas." The outer wall of fieldstones was still standing and seemed in good repair, but the front gate was gone. Dimly, he could see some log cabins inside, but there wasn't even the dimmest glow of candles, torches or cook fires. There was only a deep, unbroken blackness.

"Nerve gas? That is most unlikely, my dear Ryan," Doc rumbled in his deep stentorian bass. "Military-grade nerve gas must be stored in glass-lined metal containers to protect it from moisture."

"And in this blighted island the containers would be more valuable than the gas," Mildred finished. "However, there are all types of poison you can make from plants and such." She waited, but J.B. gave no indication that he heard. "More likely they used poisoned firewood, or maybe the wooden seats in the ville lav."

"The place sounds damn near perfect," J.B. said. "Good strong walls to keep out the night hunters, and lots of empty houses for us to choose from. The baron's is probably in the best condition…no, frag that. The invaders would have burned his home when they first attacked the ville."

"Sec chief," Jak stated, easing down the hammer.

"Yeah, the home of the sec chief would be the next best," Ryan agreed, collapsing the longeye and tucking it away. "At the very least, it'll get us out of this bastard cold."

"How can you know these things?" Liana asked curiously as the group started forward.

"We've done this sort of thing once, or twice, before," Mildred stated.

Just then, an owl softly hooted in the gloom, sounding eerily like a stickie. The companions drew their blasters and braced for a rush of the humanoid muties, but then the owl called once more and noisily flapped out of the bushes, taking to the misty sky.

Easing their stance slightly, the companions kept their weapons out and primed as they proceeded toward the distant ville.

It was night when the companions reached Hill ville, and the moon bathed the landscape in an ethereal glow. With their blasters at the ready, the companions did a fast recce around the outer wall for any signs of recent breaks or, worse, repairs. But the weathered fieldstone wall seemed untouched, the base hidden by thick grass.

Taking the point position, Ryan proceeded to the gap in the wall where the front gate should have been. Even through a thick growth of weedy grass, the one-eyed man easily spotted the gate on the ground. It had been thoroughly smashed into kindling from some sort of explosion, or possibly a salvo of those giant arbalest arrows. However, the hinges were missing entirely, which clearly meant that they had to have been made of metal, and thus taken by the invading sec men.

"We're not gonna find a nail in this place," J.B. muttered, the Uzi held steady in a two-hand grip.

Easing inside the ville, Ryan nodded his agreement. "Looted to the wall" was the phrase the Trader had taught them, and it would never be more accurate than on this triple-crazy island.

Passing by the ruins of a sandbag nest, Ryan saw several skeletons inside, their skulls smashed in, a spider spinning a web among the jumbled collection of ribs.

Next came a split-rail fence surrounding a large corral, the number of cow pies covering the ground showing that the locals had owned quite a large herd at one time. But not anymore. Every animal, whether alive or chilled, would have been jacked by the victorious invaders.

Every cabin, water trough, outhouse, shutter and shingle was elaborately covered with detailed carvings: animals, misspelled words, trains, planes, winged horses, lightning bolts, giant spiders and mushroom clouds, a phantasmagoric mixture of fanciful myths, old legends and hard reality of the postwar world. If nothing else, the Hillies were ace woodcarvers.

Past the empty corral were neat rows of small log cabins radiating from a large pool of water encircled by a low stone wall. A bamboo pipe rose from the middle of the pool, and the water bubbled out steadily, the splashing sounding oddly like rain.

Approaching the pool, Ryan and J.B. checked their rad counters, but the devices remained silent. Holstering her blaster, Mildred swung around the med kit to unearth a small water testing kit she had salvaged from a department store in the Bikini Islands. The kit was designed for checking the PH balance of water, but it was the only chemical test the physician owned. As she dipped in two strips of litmus paper into a little test tube, the blue did nothing, but the red strip turned a brilliant shade of electric blue.

"Alkaloid poison," she declared, tossing away the water and strip. "Can't know for sure, but from the prevalence of fungi on the cow pies in the corral, I'd guess they used some sort of magic mushroom. Psilocybin is a powerful hallucinogenic, and would easily drive anybody not familiar with the effects over the edge." Tucking away the kit, Mildred frowned. "And if it's a mutie form of the mushroom, then anything is possible. Even death."

"All right, don't eat anything in the ville, and only drink from your canteens for tonight," Ryan added.

Most of the cabins were just piles of blackened timbers and loose stones, only a few were still standing. None of them had an intact door or window. Every cabin had been thoroughly ransacked, anything of value taken, and everything else smashed in an orgy of destruction.

Incredibly, the easily identifiable pattern of bullet holes were everywhere in the wooden carvings, the holes enlarged with blunt instruments, probably stone knives, to retrieve the crumpled wads of precious metal. Blast craters dotted the ground, telling of the use of high explosives. Bones were everywhere, scattered randomly, many of them clearly gnawed upon by wild animals or, worse, by even more wild people.

As the cold night wind blew over the ville, nobody spoke, and no words were necessary. The ruthless slaughter of Hill ville had been complete. It was a terrible price to pay for straying from established rules.

Moving carefully among the dead, the companions tried not to step on any of the bones, not out of respect, but to not announce their presence with a loud crunch.

The ville was dead, long deserted, but the natural shelter would be very attractive to many creatures: wolves, bears, muties and even the former residents. What better place to hide than the very ville you had been chased out of so many years ago?

Doing a fast recce of the small ville, the companions found the place totally deserted, aside from some field mice and a colony of fat coonies.

That was when the companions spotted the hanging house. A score of ropes had been tethered to the ground, the ends thrown over the roof of a large log cabin. A dozen skeletons hung from the knotted ropes, the bodies supported by the slanted roof. It was a chilling sight. Death would have come from slow strangulation, or from starvation, not the fast, clean break of a proper noose.

"Bad way to get aced," Krysty said, her hair flexing wildly.

"There is no good way to die, my dear lady," Doc retorted grimly, making the sign of the cross and muttering something in Latin.

"Amen," Mildred added, bowing her head for a moment.

Curiously, Liana watched the strange proceedings, but said nothing. They paid homage to the dead as if they were a baron on his throne. She had never heard of such a thing. Then the woman relented as she recalled her own prayers to her aced father. Maybe she had more in common with these people then she had ever considered before.

Returning to the pool, the companions located what

might have once been the home of the local baron, but now there was only a large burned area on the ground, milkweeds growing in profusion amid the charred timbers, smashed window shutters and splintered roof shingles.

However, off to the side was a smaller log cabin in relatively good condition, aside from the lack of a door or any windows. The inside was carpeted with wind-blown trash and piles of jumbled skeletons, many of the bones gnawed upon by rats or something equally small.

"These are sec men," Doc said, gesturing the LeMat at the bare feet. "The invaders didn't take the boots of the civies. This must have been their last stand."

"Then it'll do fine for tonight," Krysty said, sliding off her backpack. "I'll get some food ready, if somebody else clears away the bones."

"I can do that," Liana offered, also dropping her pack.

"Okay. Doc, stay with them and keep a watch out for anything," Ryan commanded, hefting the Steyr. "Jak and Mildred, check the firewood for any additional poisons... No, forget that. Use the busted window shutters and furniture. Those should be safe. J.B. and I will close the front gate."

"Make barricade?" Jak asked.

"This is more my style," J.B. answered with a grin, pulling a pipe bomb into view from his munitions bag.

Everybody got busy, and soon the cabin was cleaned of human debris and a brisk fire was blazing just outside the front door, the smoke trailing up to vanish into the foggy sky. In short order, the interior was warm and dry, and Krysty started cooking. Wisely, Jak and Mildred decided to take no chance on any split firewood, and gathered only the already burned timbers from the other cabins. Any dangerous chemicals in that wood should have been completely burned off long ago.

With Ryan standing guard, J.B. rigged a trip wire across the opening in the wall, each end attached to a lead pipe bomb filled with bent nails as shrapnel. Anything or anyone trying to come through the wall was going to be removed from this plane of existence. Then they laid a spare blaster on top of the sandbag nest, and wired it to another pipe bomb. Anybody trying to night-creep the ville would grab the invaluable blaster, and his or her violent demise would give the companions plenty of notice that trouble had arrived.

Dinner was simple, just some MRE food packs, a few self-heat cans of tomato soup and plenty of coffee.

Since Ryan and J.B. rigged the trap at the front gate, Doc took the first shift of standing guard, snatching a cup of black coffee to hold him.

Unearthing a wooden spoon from within her borrowed clothing, Liana did what she could to help in the preparation of the meal, quietly marveling over the casual display of metal utensils. It was the wealth of a baron, and yet the companions treated the steel as if it was as common as wood. In spite of common sense, she was starting to get the feeling that everything they had said was true. Maybe the world really was just an island in a lake, like a stone sitting in a small puddle. The thought made her mind reel, and she concentrated on making dinner, trying not to fantasize about a world of mountains, lakes and valleys.

When the food was ready, Liana gamely helped Krysty dish out the spaghetti and meat balls, but she was utterly repulsed by the sight of the wormlike food, in spite of the wonderful smell. However, Liana found the tomato soup delicious, and sopped it up with canned bread with gusto.

During the meal, the companions asked Liana a thousand questions about Northpoint ville, and the best way to acquire a boat. In the end, they decided that the wisest choice was to simply jack one from the docks, and then head due south. Thunder Bay in Canada was just a dozen or so miles to the north, a lot closer than the United States. But that direction was also where the kraken came from, and nobody traveling north had ever come back. The Upper Peninsula of Michigan was about three hundred miles to the southeast, and the city of Kalkaska only a few additional miles over land, but that would be a lot safer than trying to sneak past an underwater mutie larger than an ocean liner.

"Or rather," Ryan decided, thumbing loose rounds into an empty magazine for the Steyr longblaster, "we'll head south after first returning to the *Harrington* to get more brass and weapons. If we do encounter a bastard kraken, then I want some heavy iron on our side for at least a fighting chance at survival."

"Not matter how big, one implo gren ace anything," Jak declared confidently, stropping a leaf-shaped knife along a whetstone.

"Hopefully," Krysty added, adding some powdered

milk to her aluminum cup of coffee. "However, I do recall seeing some LAW rocket launchers in the hold. If they're still good, we should be able to blast through anything in our way."

"*Hopefully* being the key word," Mildred retorted, spreading hundred-year-old butter across a slice of nutcake.

Just then, there was the muffled boomed of an explosion, closely followed by a yowling scream of pain.

"They are here!" Doc bellowed from the darkness, and they heard a single boom from the LeMat. Then dead silence.

Chapter Eleven

Ryan charged out of the log cabin, the rest of the companions following close behind.

The night air grew cold fast away from the crackling flames, and now they could see the black silhouette of Doc standing on top of the sandbag nest. The scholar looked like he had gone insane, waving his arms as if assailed by a swarm of invisible hornets. Then there were several throaty growls, and something large jumped past Doc. The two silhouettes intertwined for a split second before the man fired both of his handcannons. The fiery light of the double muzzle-flash highlighted a cougar even as the furry body crumpled sideways from the point-blank impact of the two blasters.

"It's the cats!" Ryan shouted.

Swinging up the Uzi, J.B. took careful aim and put a long burst of 9 mm Parabellum rounds into the shadows below the scholar. An answering yowl of pain sounded, and then numerous dark shapes raced away from the man, spreading out in several directions.

"They strike from behind!" Doc shouted, triggering both the LeMat and the Ruger. The twin stilettos of flame stabbed downward to briefly engulf the head of a snarling cat before it exploded from the brutal arrival of the LeMat miniball and the .45 Magnum round.

Then a dozen shapes erupted from the overlapping shadows of the ruined ville, streaking low and fast across the weedy ground.

"Aim for the shoulders!" Liana shrieked, almost dropping the new blaster in her haste to thumb back the hammer. She fired at a shape in the gloom, but there was no response.

"Drive bone splinters into heart!" Jak yelled in agreement, shooting his Colt Python and the Para-Ordnance. "Skull too thick!"

The thundering discharge of the Magnum weapon completely overwhelmed the sharp report of the smaller revolver, but something yipped near a tilting wood pile and vanished inside a badly damaged log cabin.

Hefting his blasters, Jak snorted at the obvious ploy. Even if there had been only one of the cats, the albino youth knew better than to follow any night hunter into close confines where its agility, teeth and claws gave the beast a chilling advantage. Then inspiration hit, and Jak kicked at a loose rib cage on the ground, sending it flying through the sagging window. A split second later, Jak fired both weapons at the open doorway. There came the smack of lead hitting flesh, followed by a scream. But there was no death rattle, and Jak strongly doubted that the big cat was really aced.

"Frag the shoulders, go for the big three!" Ryan countered, firing steadily at the speedy animals. Hit smack in the open mouth, a cougar jerked aside, blood gushing from the terrible wound.

"Eyes, mouth, throat!" J.B. translated for the newcomer in their midst. As the monster cats crossed a pool of moonlight, the Armorer had spotted an odd discoloration across the shoulders of each cougar, and sagely guessed it was some sort of crude armor, probably just leather and wood, to protect their vulnerable spot. In spite of their unkempt appearance, J.B. knew that these weren't wild animals, but the main defense of Anchor ville. And it seemed that the local baron had traded some of their agility for a greater degree of resilience. Even as J.B. tried to track one of the cats down with the stuttering Uzi, he was forced to admit it had not been a triple-wise decision. He had hit one cat several times already, and the 9 mm rounds had scored only minor flesh wounds.

"Form a circle!" Mildred shouted, recalling a book she had once read about hunting lions in Africa. These mountain felines were not the legendary king of the jungle, but the same basic hunting instincts were probably driving them onward.

Quickly putting their backs to one another, the companions formed a circle and started firing into the darkness, aiming slightly ahead of any movements in the dense shadows. A cougar was aced, then another wounded, and the rest of the animals retreated slightly, then began to race around the companions, using the ruins as cover.

"Millie, on my right!" J.B. shouted, firing to the left.

Pivoting in that direction, Mildred cut loose with both of her blasters, and a cougar staggered from the small-caliber wounds. But it did not stop. Letting the empty Beretta fall away, Mildred assumed a two-handed grip on the Czech ZKR and held her breath, waiting patiently, listening to the sounds of the night as the deadly beast came ever closer to finally enter the reddish light of the dying campfire. Instantly, the ZKR spoke once, and the cat dropped in its tracks, its left eye gone, the neat hole oozing blood and brain fluids.

"How many of these fuckers are there?" J.B. demanded of nobody in particular after killing three more of the beasts.

"How in nuke-shitting hell should I know?" Ryan shot back angrily, triggering the Steyr directly into the face of a hidden cougar. The big head snapped back, and Ryan kicked it in the exposed throat, the bones audibly cracking from the powerful impact of the steel-tipped combat boot.

Unexpectedly, a cougar lunged for Jak from inside the burned-out ruin of a cabin just as he was dropping the magazine from the Para-Ordnance. Spinning, the teenager put his last round from the Colt Python into the animal, driving it back toward the sandbag nest, then he threw the empty Para-Ordnance.

Tumbling through the darkness, the albino teen unerringly hit the trip wire for the second pipe bomb, and the night came alive with a strident explosion. Blown apart, the bloody chunks of the cat flew away to wetly smack into the fieldstone wall and splash into the pool of water.

As if summoned by the blood offering, another cougar erupted from the pool and streaked toward the companions. Krysty, Mildred and Liana all tried to shoot the beast, but in spite of its huge size, the creature moved incredibly fast and proved almost impossible to track. Training the Uzi on the thing, J.B. hit it twice, but it only darted away, seemingly immune to the pain.

Trying to target the cat, Ryan noticed the odd demeanor of the soaked creature. The eyes were forced wide open, but the ears drooped, the tail lashed about insanely and white foam was dribbling from the black lips. Fireblast, the cougar had to have drunk some of the poisoned water! The cat was dying, but for the moment it was feeling no pain, not even bullet hits, and before it keeled over, the creature could easily take several of the companions along with it into the great abyss.

Working the bolt on the Steyr several times, Ryan jacked out the live rounds, then he pulled the trigger to make it click. As expected, the trained cougar immediately charged for the supposedly unarmed victim. For a single moment, Ryan considered going for the Desert Eagle, then realized he'd never get the blaster out in time.

Backing away as if frightened, Ryan waited until the very last second, then thrust the longblaster forward like a spear, the barrel punching into the chest of the beast like an awl. Snarling in frustration, the big cat clawed for the two-legs so temptingly out of reach, its sharp fangs snapping for the hands holding the weapon.

"Ace the fucker!" Ryan commanded, incredibly lifting the Steyr higher so that the cat hung suspended from the end of the longblaster like a fish on a spear. Confused for only a moment, the cat swung its hind legs forward and slashed bloody furrows across Ryan's shirt, red blood welling from the deep scratches.

In ragged unison, the rest of the companions tore the animal to pieces under a concentrated barrage of hot lead, until the tattered body finally went limp and slid from the barrel to the ground.

"T-tough b-b-bastard," Ryan slurred, hunching his shoulders. Then the big man went deathly pale and dropped to the ground, nearly lost among the tall weeds.

"Lover!" Krysty cried, rushing closer to kneel alongside the man. She rolled him over and inspected the scratches across his chest. It was as she had feared—some of the water from the fur had to have gotten into the cuts.

"Canteens!" Mildred barked, pouring the contents of her container across Ryan's muscular chest.

The water sluiced away the blood and sweat, revealing four straight lines, the puckered flesh already turning an angry yellow in color. The physician tried not to curse at the sight. Damn it, the mushrooms were mutations! Every treatment she had for a psilocybin overdose might cure Ryan, or kill him instantly. But with no other choice, she had to go with her best guess. If the mushrooms had mutated too much from the original strain, then they wouldn't have any effect on human beings, or cougars; they'd simply kill.

Running past the sizzling campfire, the rest of the companions dashed into the log cabin where they had made camp, and soon returned with their canteens.

Carefully, the precious water was poured over the cuts, while Mildred kneaded the flesh with her fingertips to try to force out every drop of the mushroom alkaloids that she could. When there was no more, Mildred added the small bottle of witch hazel from her med kit, just in case the dirty claws of the cougar had been carrying any infections. The witch hazel would also help neutralize the alkaloids of the mushrooms.

Studying the man, Mildred kept any expression from her face. Water and witch hazel—it wasn't much, but there was nothing else to do.

"Was it enough?" Krysty asked, her beautiful face pinched tight in worry.

"Maybe," Mildred said. "I don't know yet."

Around the companions, the night was still, even the ever-present cicadas were quiet. There was only the merry splashing of the poisoned water from the bamboo spill pipe.

Tugging on his sleeve, Liana pulled Doc aside and started to talk in a hurried whisper, the old man's dark expression becoming even more grim.

Peeling back an eyelid, Mildred checked the pupils of the supine man, and her frown told the others that she didn't like what she found.

"John, give me a grenade," Mildred demanded, holding out a hand.

"Sure," the Armorer replied, clearly puzzled. "But what do you want—"

"Now, John!" Mildred interrupted in a no-nonsense voice, snapping her fingers.

Rummaging in his munitions bag, J.B. unearthed the ferruled sphere of a gren and quickly passed it over. The physician looked at the deadly explosive charge for only a moment before working on the retaining ring around the neck and then carefully removing the detonator assembly on top. Setting that aside, Mildred dug inside the open sphere with a knife and extracted a small wad of gray clay. Using a handkerchief, the physician slipped it off the blade and rolled the material into a small pellet, then tucked it under the tongue of the unconscious man. Almost instantly, his face began to flush deep red, and his breathing quickened.

"What do?" Jak demanded, shocked by the bizarre action.

"Grens use C-4 plastic explosive as the main charge, and that is mostly made of nitroglycerine," Mildred replied, checking the pulse in Ryan's throat. "We got most of the poison off his skin, now we only have to deal with what got into his bloodstream. He'll have a monster of a headache, but the nitro should keep his heart pumping until the effects of these mutie mushrooms pass."

"Unfortunately, we have more trouble coming," Doc announced without any preamble. "It seems that these hunting cats are always accompanied by mounted sec men. They should be here any minute."

"No, we use pass," Jak reminded him, brushing back his snowy hair. "They go around mountain."

"That'll buy us an hour, or more," Krysty said, frowning. "But nowhere near enough time to run away on foot."

"Who said anything about running?" J.B. countered, pulling the clip from his rapidfire to double-check the brass. Fifteen rounds, and then he would be down to the scattergun and some pipe bombs. "How many can we expect?"

"Baron Griffin issues a hand of cats for each sec man," Liana replied, splaying her fingers.

It took a minute, before everybody understood that the former slave could not count. But then, there was no conceivable reason to teach a slave anything. Obedience was all that was required. An educated slave was only a time bomb waiting to go off in bloody revolution.

"Okay, five cats for each sec man means there are maybe six armed riders coming hard and fast," Krysty stated, looking toward the gap in the wall where the gate had once been located.

"Or more," Liana warned. "Sometimes they also send along the newbies to learn."

"Excellent!" Jak grinned without any trace of humor as he pulled out his sharpest knife. "Then start cutting!"

Working with a will, the companions got busy hacking and slashing at the dead cougars, blood and fur going everywhere.

Chapter Twelve

Ryan woke with a start, memories of the past few days flooding back. The last thing he clearly recalled was a cougar clawing at his chest, the pain fading into an oddly pleasant sensation, and then everything went triple-crazy, colors becoming tastes, sounds turning into colors, and then total chaos filled the world.

"Drugged," Ryan muttered softly, massaging his temples. That was the only possible answer. Some of that bastard poisoned water had to have gotten into the cuts and knocked him out. He could vaguely remember weird dreams. At least everything seemed back to normal again.

Thick furs and predark Army blankets lay under him as a crude bed. He was tucked into the corner of a large wooden room. There was a large Franklin stove in the middle of the room, jointed pipes on top carrying the smoke outside through a hole in the roof, and wonderful waves of heat were radiating outward from the cast-iron antique.

Soft light was streaming in through glass windows, and there was a large metal desk sitting kitty-corner across the room, a gooseneck lamp on top, as well as a small comp and piles of yellow paper. A wheeled chair sat partially behind the desk, the green leather cover badly ripped, tufts of yellow foam padding sticking out randomly. He grunted at the sight. Clearly, this was some sort of an office. But where were his companions? Through the window he could see a large campfire blazing, an aluminum pot that he recognized was suspended over the flames, the contents bubbling steadily, but there were no sign of the others.

Rising stiffly, Ryan checked for his weapons and found they were gone. Cold adrenaline flooded the man at the discovery, but then he saw his blasters and the panga lying on top of the desk, along with his backpack, coat and canteen. Okay, I'm not a prisoner. Good to know.

Shuffling across the room, Ryan suddenly noticed the awful taste in his mouth. He almost gagged, and his empty stomach rumbled unhappily.

Reaching the desk, the man quickly checked his weapons, finding everything clean, sharpened, oiled and fully loaded. Strapping on his gunbelt, Ryan then screwed the cap off the canteen and poured some of the contents into his palm. It looked and smelled like water, so he took a lick and was delighted to find that was exactly what it was. Taking a small mouthful, he sloshed the fluid for about a minute, then spit it out into the wastebasket, before taking an equally small sip. It deliciously eased down his dry throat and spread across his empty stomach like a healing balm.

Resisting the urge to drink more immediately, Ryan waited a minute to make sure his guts would keep the water down, then he started sipping and pausing, again and again, slowly letting his tissues absorb the water until the hunger pangs eased and the foul taste in his mouth noticeably lessened. Unfortunately there was also a distinct rancid aroma in the small room, and the one-eyed man was pretty sure it was coming from him.

Quickly opening the backpack, Ryan found some self-heats and yanked off the lid of one to drink cold soup straight from the can. Ryan was finished long before the container grew warm, and he tossed it into the wastebasket.

Feeling greatly refreshed, Ryan wiped his mouth on a sleeve and found a heavy beard on his face. His fingers checked the length and he guessed at least three days had passed since the fight at Hill ville.

"Nice to see you again, lover!" Krysty said from behind him.

Spinning in a gunfighter's crouch, Ryan eased the blaster back into the holster when he saw it actually was Krysty, her long hair moving constantly as if stirred by secret winds.

"About time you got up!" J.B. added heartily, stepping in through the open doorway with the rest of the companions. "For a while there, we were afraid that you were taking the last train west."

"Indeed, sir," Doc added in his deep rumble. "If the good doctor had not forced all of the blueberry juice down your throat, I do believe you may have never returned from the arms of Morpheus."

"Why…" Ryan was barely able to even get out the garble sound. He swallowed hard and tried again. "Why were you feeding me juice?"

"For the vitamin C," Mildred explained, going over to him and checking his pulse. "It helps counter the ravages of the hallucinogenic compounds." Ninety-five beats per minute, she observed. His blood pressure felt high, but that was understandable considering the circumstances.

"Liana showed us where to find the fruit," the physician continued, inspecting his eye for any dilation or discoloration. "The island is lousy with food, if you know where to look."

"Knowledge is power," Doc stated, looking fondly at the diminutive Liana, and she preened under the praise.

"I sang for you, trying to show the way home," Liana added, holding out a large leaf filled with bright orange strawberries. "But you were lost deep in the nightscape of the dreamworld."

"Got that right," Ryan replied, kindly dismissing the offer. He was starving, but not for fruit. "But thanks for trying."

Placing the leaf on the office desk, the woman seemed to pause, then blurted, "Kin helps kin."

"Kin helps kin," Ryan repeated formally in agreement, then gave a rare half-smile.

With that, Liana burst into a wide grin and hitched up her gunbelt. Half of the ammo they had originally given her was gone, and there were three small notches on the wooden grip of the blaster. The former slave had also put on a few pounds, all of it in the right places, and there were wildflowers tucked into her long hair, the bright yellow and blues reflected in the luxurious platinum waves.

"What is this place?" Ryan asked, glancing around the cabin.

"Museum," J.B. replied, crossing his arms. "There used to be a copper mine here, but it got nuked and now it's hotter than the Washington Hole, if you can believe it. The rad counters went crazy as we came out of the valley. But we're safe enough here."

"And it's triple-sure that no sec men or cats are going to coming after us through the pass," Krysty added. "They might go around, but according to Liana that will take them days on foot."

"Good to know," Ryan said, glancing around at the mostly bare office. "Was there anything here we could use?" Museums had always been a favorite of the Trader to loot. Lots of the old tech on display worked just fine.

"Just some pamphlets that'll serve as toilet paper, and a couple of oil lanterns, without any oil," Krysty replied. "Along with a med kit with only some bandages left, and some lead plumbing that we yanked out of the walls."

"The sec men were carrying exploding lances, sir," Doc explained. "According to Liana, they detonate when stabbed into a target. John Barrymore simply emptied out the powder, and filled several sections of the plumbing to make us a dozen new pipe bombs of frightening power."

"They'll do the trick," the Armorer said proudly, patting the munitions bag.

"Sounds good." Walking to the door, Ryan studied the rolling landscape. Nukescaping, without a doubt.

There were misty mountains rising to the clouds in every direction, and one big waterfall situated off toward the setting sun. "Where are we now?" he asked, brushing back his hair. "This isn't Hill ville, that's for sure."

"No, we left there right after the fight," Krysty stated, joining the man outside. "This is about fifty miles into the Crown Mountains, smack in the middle of Royal Island."

"You carried me through the mountains?" Ryan asked incredulously.

"Hell, no." J.B. chuckled. "We simply lashed your ass to a litter and dragged you along behind our new horses."

Horses? There was only one possible answer for that. "Sec men came after the cats arrived," Ryan guessed, turning toward the campfire. Whatever was cooking in the pot smelled wonderful, and he sauntered over for a better look. It was stew of some kind, but the meat was green.

"Yep, eight outriders," J.B. stated. "We skinned the cats and hid under the pelts, then placed some of our spare blasters near the bloody corpses to make them resemble us. Well, kind of, anyway. However, in the dark the stupes bought the ruse, and when they climbed down for the blasters, we aced them from behind, simple as opening a self-heat."

"Easier," Jak drawled contemptuously, a knife slipping out of his sleeve to land in the waiting palm of his hand. The teen flipped the blade in the air, then tucked it out of sight again.

"A couple of the horses died during the fight, so we only have six for the seven of us," Mildred said, going to the stew and stirring the contents with a green stick. "However, Doc was kind enough to offer to share with Liana, and she doesn't seem to mind too much."

"Is this horse?" Ryan asked, his stomach rumbling in anticipation. The smell was intoxicating.

"We butchered what we could carry, but we ate that already. This is hardbacks," Liana replied. "I tried to sing for snakes. They arrived instead."

"She sang at midnight, and the turtles arrived at dawn just as we were about to leave," Krysty explained with a rueful smile. "But better late than never."

At that news, Ryan grinned in delight. Hardbacks! That was some of his favorite eating.

"Rest horses out back," Jak said, jerking a thumb. "Lotta freshwater and grass."

"Along with a lovely little creek just perfect for bathing," Mildred said, wrinkling her nose as she laid aside the stick. "Now that you're awake, it'd be nice to be able to smell the stew instead of you."

"That is, unless you plan to conquer Northpoint by simply flapping your arms, my dear Ryan," Doc said, faking a cough.

Since it was blatantly true, Ryan accepted the rebuke. "Guess I do smell a little like a swampie," he admitted.

"Old aced swampie," Jak corrected with a grimace.

"Besides, it's almost dark, and we can't travel at night," J.B. added, watching the trees, a hand resting on the Uzi at his side. "There are too many flapjacks in the area, and the damn things are tough enough to see in broad daylight."

"Fair enough." Rummaging in his pockets, Ryan unearthed a plastic ziptop bag containing a small bar of used soap. It was military soap, without any perfumes or softeners, but it took the dirt off a person slicker than skimming pond scum.

"Take your time. The stew will be ready when you come back," Mildred called tactfully over a shoulder, her hands busy dicing wild carrots.

"Good to hear," Ryan stated, rubbing his unshaved chin. "Because I want everybody ready to leave at first light. Take only the weapons and food. I want to reach Northpoint by noon tomorrow, and get us some transportation off this fragging rad pit of an island."

"Steal boat?" Jak asked pointedly.

"Sure as shitfire not going to try to buy one again," Ryan declared gruffly, marching around the cabin and out of sight.

Chapter Thirteen

Taking a dirty cloth from a pocket, Baron Griffin wiped the sweat from his face. It had been over a day since he last slept, but in his dreams, the man constantly relived the events of that terrible day over and over. Sleep brought no rest, so he abandoned the thoughts of it and concentrated on something more tangible. Revenge.

By now, most of the destruction in the ville had been cleared away, the fires extinguished and the dead buried. Or rather, they had been until the kraken arrived. With the sec men almost too exhausted to fight, sec chief Donovan had devised a brutal new tactic and had the ville folk hurriedly dig up the corpses and throw them to the mutie. That hadn't been enough, so then he fed the thing the slaves, all of them, and then some of the ville folk. Finally sated, the kraken had returned to the depths of the sea, leaving the ville untouched. However, that was not a tactic the baron could ever use again. There was nobody else to sacrifice to the giant mutie.

Tucking away the rag, Griffin shuffled over to a worktable and assembled a sandwich from the assortment of dried meats and sliced breads. Without sitting, he consumed the crude meal in a few bites, then washed it down with scag-root tea. It tasted awful, even when sweetened with honey, but delivered a big kick.

"All right, let's try it again," the baron wheezed, returning to the construction site. "Light the fire!"

"You heard the baron!" Donovan bellowed, hobbling forward on his new crutch.

As most of the sec men backed away to a safe distance, a grim-faced man opened the iron door of the hearth and applied a piece of smoldering oakum to the pile of rags soaked in shine. Instantly, they ignited, and the fire quickly spread through the carefully arranged stack of dry wood filling the hearth to overflowing. Closing the door on the growing conflagration, the bare-chested man pulled on several levers and, studying the gauges, made sure that the fire had sufficient air.

As the temperature climbed, the needle on the repaired pressure gauge steadily rose higher and higher. Licking dry lips, the man muttered a soft prayer to the moon god. The previous ten people who tried this had been horribly aced, cooked alive by the escaping steam, the last one personally chilled by the baron to stop his agonized howling.

"We're at fifty percent, baron," the man called out, a tingle of hope in his spine. "Seventy percent... ninety...."

Suddenly a keening volcano of steam erupted from the valve on top of the machine, and the transmission lurched into action, wheels turning and rods shifting.

"Throw the switch!" the baron commanded, taking a step forward, hope giving his haggard face new life. "Throw it!"

Making a protective gesture, the man grabbed the big lever and pulled it all the way back.

There was a brief hammering from the machine, and then the rebuilt *Wendigo* rolled out of the repair cradle, smashing aside the wooden supports in an explosion of hemp rope and splinters.

Battered and bruised, the dirty repair crew cheered as the armored war wag rolled across the ville, huffing and puffing, but moving faster than ever before. The steam whistle keened again, the man at the controls beaming widely.

"It works," Donovan whispered, reaching out a hand as if to touch the chugging machine. "By the lost gods, we did it. The son-of-a-bitch thing works!"

Closing his eyes for a moment in silent thanks, the baron then pulled in a deep lungful of air and loudly bellowed, "All right, mount up! We roll right fragging now."

"To Northpoint!" Donovan added, brandishing his cane.

The sec men gave a ragged cheer. Dashing eagerly around, they grabbed their blasters and climbed into the saddles of their horses, every mind filled with savage thoughts of bloody revenge.

AT DAWN, the companions rose and had a breakfast of reheated stew and black coffee to fortify themselves for the long day ahead. Then they packed away everything useful and buried the campfire, first under dirt and rocks, then dry leaves, to try to disguise the fact that they had ever been here.

Checking the belly strap of the mare he had been given, Ryan heartily approved of the mount. Alvira wasn't the biggest horse of the bunch—Doc got the big stallion to support the double load of him and Liana—but the big mare was clearly bridle wise and had the look of a seasoned warhorse. This was not a horse that would buck and throw him off at the first sound of blasterfire. However, Ryan would have to be extremely careful of where the animal walked. With metal in such short supply on the island, there were no horseshoes. Unshod hooves had a tendency to bruise, and then the horse would be lame for a week. Which meant that one wrong move, and Ryan was on foot again.

Although seriously impatient to be under way, Ryan still spent several minutes stroking Alvira's muscular neck. As he checked the straps on the saddlebags, Ryan noticed his Desert Eagle was gone, then saw it tucked into Jak's gunbelt. He had seen the teen lose the Para-Ordnance in the fight with the cats and didn't mind the loan. Ryan already had two blasters, and that was enough for him. In the Deathlands, carrying too many blasters was almost as bad as not having enough.

Leaving the campsite, the companions crossed a misty field of grass at an easy lope, letting the animals warm to the work of the day. In a few hours, the companions encountered a wide field of wheat, the tufted stalks waving gently in the cool breeze. There were no rows or furrows anymore. No tractors, plows or silos. Any sign of cultivation was long gone. The grain grew random, choking itself in some areas, and painfully thin in others, the ever-present fog giving the landscape a faintly surreal appearance.

Grabbing handfuls of the stalks as they rode along, the companions wisely tucked the grain away to feed the horses later. There was plenty of grass, but wheat had more protein and the animals would need all of their strength soon enough.

Between Liana's directions, J.B.'s use of the sextant and map and Ryan's telescope, the companions found the dried river by noon. Several yards wide, it began at the base of a dead waterfall, the bare rock of the cliff tinged with green moss. Snaking away, the riverbed meandered through the rolling hills, forming a natural highway that disappeared into a mist-shrouded forest of elm and pine trees.

"The sec men say in the spring this is whitewater," Liana said, shifting her position on the leather saddle behind Doc. "Impossible to cross because of the mutie fish that swim upstream to breed at the falls."

"That's probably what the flapjacks normally feed upon," Krysty said, studying the scattered bones embedded into the desiccated mud.

Stopping to light torches made of wooden table legs wrapped in oil-soaked rope, the group proceeded down the sloping bank and onto the cracked mosaic of dried mud. Both banks grew steadily higher, the grassland giving way to thorny brambles and then a dense forest. Overhead, the branches reached out to almost touch, forming a cathedral effect, the dappled light sprinkling the ground with pinpoints of starlight in the middle of the day.

Keeping a tight hold on the reins of their nervous mounts, the companions rode slowly along, everybody holding a crackling torch as high as they could. The firelight banished the shadows, and the thick smoke wafted into the canopy of overlapping branches. There was no sign of the flapjacks, but there was constant movement in the treetops wherever the smoke touched. Staying sharp, the companions kept a close watch on the greenery, their hands never far from a loaded blaster, until the forest was far behind them, lost in the cottony fog bank.

Slow hours passed, and it was late afternoon when they crested a hill, and the companions slowed their mounts at the sight of farmland, rows of leashed slaves digging in the dark loam with their bare hands, while fat overseers smoked cigs and occasionally lashed out with a whip to make the men and women work faster. Only one guard was mounted, the gunboot of his saddle filled with a feathered lance. The sec men were dressed in warm furs and heavy boots, while the slaves were in rags, mud covering most of the skinny bodies as crude protection from the afternoon chill. Ratty canvas bags full of seeds were suspended from the wooden yokes around their throats, and they crawled along, kneading the earth to plant a single seed then moving forward a few inches to endlessly repeat the process.

"Look alive, ya gleebs," an overseer bellowed, snapping the bullwhip a few more times just to make the slaves jump with fright. "The winter snow will be here soon, and without the clover as ground cover there'll be no food in the spring!"

"Lessen we eat you!" A female overseer laughed heartily.

"Oh, don't bother talking to them," the corporal said from atop the chestnut gelding. Popping the cork from a canteen, he took a long drink, then returned the cork with a thump. "Slaves be too stupe to understand how—"

Tossing away the canteen, the fat overseer reeled in the saddle, the barbed point of an arrow sticking out the side of his head. Opening his mouth as if to speak, he only flapped his lips for a few seconds before slipping off the horse to fall facedown into the furrows.

Spinning fast, the other two guards gasped at the sight of the mounted companions. "Sound the alarm!" the sec woman shouted, then doubled over, clutching the arrow that protruded from her stomach.

Frantically clawing inside his jacket, the last overseer pulled out a whistle and raised it to his lips. Then there came a distant crack and his hand burst apart, fingers spraying across his face. Stumbling backward, the wounded guard tripped over a furrow and went sprawling. In a mad rush, the slaves swarmed over the norm, pounding him with rocks, their strong fingers ripping at his clothing. Trying to pull a wooden machete, the overseer disappeared within the howling mob, and soon warm red blood flowed along the cold ground.

Turning around in the saddle, Jak scowled fiercely. "Why do?" he demanded hotly. "Overseers disappear, ville get alert!"

"Kin helps kin," Liana said simply.

"Quite right, my dear," Doc agreed reluctantly, lowering the LeMat. "Freeing slaves is always laudable! However, you should have consulted with us first before acting. Now, we must continue on foot."

"Why?" Liana asked, clearly puzzled. "There are no more sec men in sight."

"That know of!" Jak retorted, furious over the newbie's mistake.

"The horses will help the slaves get away faster," J.B. growled. "And the more sec men that go after them, the less there'll be to protect the dockyard."

"This may actually make it easier to steal the boat," Mildred offered, trying to cover for the other woman. The physician applauded the intent, but the results could prove disastrous. Act in haste, repent in leisure, as her Baptist minister father always used to say.

"Maybe, or maybe not," Ryan growled, holstering the SIG-Sauer. "Only now we have no choice in the matter. We gotta help them, to help ourselves."

"Can't take them on a boat, anyway," Liana said in a rush, as if that had been her idea from the beginning. But the feeble defense fooled nobody.

"Depends on the size," Krysty countered, watching the slaves exact their gory revenge. Her voice and face were calm, but her animated hair revealed her true feelings.

Sliding off his horse, Ryan unslung the Steyr and worked the arming lever. "However, Liana, if you ever do something this stupe again…" He didn't finish the sentence, unsure of how far his temper would go.

The words so simply said sent a shiver through the woman. Having heard countless threats in her life, the former slave instinctively knew this one was real and dumbly nodded. She wanted to apologize, but Ryan and the others were already off their horses and pulling items from the saddlebags.

"Either with us, or not," Jak declared roughly, tucking a pipe bomb into a pocket. "Make choice!"

"Doc," Liana replied instantly, looking into his face. "I stand with Theophilus."

Trying not to smile, Doc reached out to gently touch her shoulder, speaking volumes without saying a word.

Cutting across a section of farmland, the companions tramped along the muddy furrows heading due north.

Chapter Fourteen

Darkness slowly descended, then the full moon rose, bathing the island with its clean, silvery illumination. The surface of the bay was calm, the gentle waves lapping listlessly against the thick wooden pylons of the dock. There were no cicadas to disturb the stillness, no owls, wolves or winged muties. After the kraken attack a few days earlier, everything had fled the area, leaving the ville by the bay in unaccustomed peace and quiet.

The docks were deserted that time of night, the fishing done for the day. A score of heavily patched nets hung from racks to dry, the barge poles and oars stashed safely away in wicker lockers, the ropes neatly coiled, hawsers and wooden pulleys swaying from raised hoists.

Extending along the entire waterfront of Northpoint, the dockyard was full of different size boats, each expertly moored to stone cleats with thick hemp ropes—small birch-bark canoes, rowboats covered with elaborate symbols of protection, a few crude barges used for hauling lumber across the wide bay and, of course, the *Warhammer.*

Several times the size of even a cargo barge, the

mighty *Warhammer* dominated the dockyard. The freshly scrubbed gunwale gleamed, and there were lovingly tended rows of predark car tires lashed to the painted hull to prevent it from becoming damaged by rubbing against the reinforced pylons.

Carved deep into the hull was the proud name of the vaunted warship, and the delicately carved female figurehead at the bow strongly resembled the local baron. Proudly bare-breasted, Brenda Wainwright defiantly faced outward, brandishing a lightning bolt and a blaster, as if ready to challenge the world. The sec men appreciated the likeness, but kept any and all comments to themselves. The baron could stroll stark naked through the ville if she wished, but anyone stupid enough to mention the event out loud was doomed.

The hull was studded with thick planks of dense wooden armor, the sides bristling with long spears. Even the mooring lines sparkled in the dim moonlight from the shards of glass woven into the tough fibers. Plus, strategically placed around the deck, were large canvas mounds, one at the front, and two at the back, the material lashed down tight as protection from even the fiercest storm. A large metal smokestack rose from the middle of the *Warhammer,* cutting through the end of a small wheelhouse. However, there was nobody inside to stand a turn at the circular helm at the moment, and the spacious glass windows looked across the shimmering waves of the bay with unseeing eyes.

Edging the dockyard, the wall of the nearby ville inadvertently blocked some of the moonlight at this hour, a thin slice of darkness masking the base of the massive barrier. Standing like black giants, the guard towers rose over the slumbering ville, the sec men inside huddling close to their only source of heat, a small oil lantern.

On the boardwalk of the dock, overlooking the *Warhammer,* a sec man was sitting on a small keg, puffing contentedly on a cig of dried seaweed, mixed with a little wolfweed smuggled in from the outer islands. The zoomer was strictly forbidden, but since the baron also smoked the stuff, the punishment was only having the cig confiscated, so he really didn't care. Besides, a man needed something to keep his mind sharp during the long and boring night.

Muffled voices could be heard from inside Northpoint: drunken laughter, a badly played piano, a woman crying and the low, monotonous work song of a trusted slave.

Sighing dejectedly at the music, the sec man concentrated on his smoking. Wearing a long coat of thick fur, he was armed with a crossbow, a half-arrow already notched into place, ready for instant use. Mostly, he aced the rats trying to climb the mooring line and get onboard the *Warhammer* to raid the stores of fish oil. The smell attracted them the way horse sweat did a flapjack. There was a small wicker basket near his furlined boots already partially filled with the little corpses, a testament to both his marksmanship and their unrelenting determination.

More important, there was a small whistle hanging from a cord around his left wrist. There hadn't been any trouble with the Hillies or outlanders for several months, which meant it was just about time for them to try to sneak into the ville to see what could be jacked. Just like the rats, the damn fools always got aced, but at least it gave the sec men something to do to pass the time.

Just then, there was a scratching noise near the mooring line, and the sec man instantly rose with the crossbow at the ready. But as he started forward, he heard a subdued cough from the darkness, and he gasped, the weapon falling from his limp fingers. A ghostly pale hand caught the crossbow before it hit the dock, and a pair of strong arms grabbed the dying man to haul him back to the keg. Sitting the corpse on top, Ryan lashed the warm body into place with some rope. Then slipped back into the night to join Jak in the gloom under the dock.

Creeping along the mossy beams supporting the boardwalk, the two companions approached the *Warhammer,* the slosh of the waves masking the sound of their combat boots. Ready and waiting, Doc already had a loose plank prepared, retrieved from a dry dock only a hundred paces away near the trees. Working together, the three men eased it upward from the blackness to rest on the gunwale of the warship. It settled into place with a thump, and they tensely waited for any reactions from additional guards onboard. No baron would ever trust a single sec man with a treasure like the *Warhammer.* Sure enough, a few minutes later they heard the sound of steps from inside the wheelhouse, and a door opened, exposing a grumpy sec man armed with a spear and carrying a lantern.

"Fragging rats," he muttered, shuffling along, the lantern held low and the spear raised high to strike.

Without a pause, Jak threw a leaf-bladed knife, which pierced the man's heart. Doc darted out to grab the spear and the lantern.

Sighing into eternity, the sec man seemed to deflate, easing slowly to the deck before becoming still. While Jak stood guard, Ryan took the body and lowered it over the gunwale. Krysty and J.B. took the corpse and dragged it under the dock and out of sight.

Moving stealthily, the rest of the companions gathered on the aft deck of the boat, then separated to start a fast recce. Several more sec men were found inside the craft, one of them asleep in a bunk, while another was making a pot of what smelled like fish stew in the small galley. Using his sword, Doc cut the throat of the sleeping man, and Jak dispatched the other.

Finished with the wheelhouse, the companions proceeded down the stairs and into the hold. This part of the vessel clearly belonged to the baron. Everything on the boat was elaborately carved, mostly scenes of the lady baron defeating giant muties, and standing triumphant on top of a mound of her fallen enemies. Mildred had to smile at the classic propaganda. Even in a land where nobody could read, the government still found a way to feed the people a steady diet of bullshit.

At the bow was a large room with a feather bed and a well-stocked liquor cabinet, plus a small assortment of crossbows and knives. Knowing that barons always kept a blaster nearby, J.B. searched the headboard of the bed, and sure enough found a sliding panel. Attached to the side was a predark rat trap that nearly took off his finger, but J.B. escaped intact, and nestled inside the hidey-hole were two loaded flintlock pistols and, wonders of wonders, a fully functional 9 mm MAC 10 machine blaster in excellent shape. There was even a spare magazine!

Warily inspecting the weapon, J.B. scowled in disgust. The stupe bitch had left both of the magazines fully loaded, and who knew how long they had been waiting here. Most likely, the springs in the magazines would be weak by now, and the rapidfire would jam after only a few rounds. However, the brass seemed in fine condition. Experimentally, J.B. cut open a round to make sure it was packed with gunpowder, and was delightfully surprised to find that it held predark propellant, the good stuff. Happily, the Armorer extracted all of the 9 mm rounds, and split the windfall with Ryan to use in his SIG-Sauer, while Doc got the black powder for his LeMat.

Going down to the engine room, the companions found the fuel bunkers fully stocked with dried wood, along with dozens of small kegs full of what smelled like rancid fish oil.

Easily filling half of the hold was a colossal steam engine, the boiler patently recovered from a factory, or apartment house, that still used steam heating radiators. Looking over the machinery, Ryan nodded in grudging approval. The conversion was actually very bastard clever. Junk parts from a hundred machines combined to make a functioning engine for the warship. Ryan's opinion of Baron Wainwright went up a few notches. Whatever else the woman might be, she was no fool.

Laying a hand on the iron side of the boiler, Krysty found it ice cold, and, checking the firebox underneath, she saw that it was spotlessly clean.

"This'll take hours to get hot and build up enough pressure," Krysty whispered.

"Then you better get busy," Ryan ordered, holstering his blaster. "Liana, get back to the galley and burn the stew, that should help disguise any smoke coming from the furnace."

With a nod, the woman turned and dashed up the stairs.

"I'll start chopping wood," Doc announced, tucking away the LeMat and pulling an ax from a chopping block. He was pleasantly surprised to find it was from before skydark, the head made of steel. Carefully testing the edge on a thumb, the scholar drew blood. Excellent, it was razor-sharp.

"Make pieces small," Jak suggested, rolling a keg of fish oil closer to the boiler. "That make burn faster."

Taking the kindling, Jak dipped it into the reeking oil, then tossed the damp pieces into the firebox.

Going to a porthole, Ryan swung back the louvered hatch and looked outside. There was no visible movement from the nearby ville, either along the top of the wall or in the guard towers. But he knew that could change at a moment's notice.

"How soon till we're mobile?" Mildred asked anxiously. She knew a fair amount of computers, but steam engines were from long before her day.

"Couple of hours at least," J.B. replied, running his hands over the complex array of levers and pressure gauges. "This is like no steam engine I've ever seen before."

At the news, Ryan tried not to scowl. Hours. He had hoped they could get under way a lot faster than that. Now, it was a race against time. Man versus machine.

"All right, we better get ready to defend this tub," the one-eyed man announced. "Mildred, help Doc and Jak get that boiler started. Krysty, stand guard by the porthole. If anybody comes this way, ace them with a crossbow, then let us know."

"No problem," she stated, holstering her blaster and swinging around the bulky weapon. She knew there had been a reason Ryan said to bring one along. Sniper duty.

Expertly, Krysty tested the drawstring before working the pump to notch a half-arrow. She knew the range wasn't very good, so she would have to let them get close before taking them out. Taking a position at the porthole, the woman remembered something about an ancient sec chief telling his troops not to shoot until they could see the white of the enemy's eyes. It was good advice.

"I'll go see if there are any maps of the bay in the tub," J.B. declared, tilting back his fedora. "It's a bastard maze out there, and if we hit a sandbar, we'll never live long enough to get free again."

"That right," Jak stated, sliding off his jacket and hanging it from a convenient wooden stud that seemed to have been made for just that purpose. The teenager flexed his arms, the hard muscles rippling under his alabaster skin.

"Will you be conducting a reconnaissance of the ville, my dear Ryan?" Doc asked, doing the same to his frock coat.

"Hell, no," Ryan said, looking upward as if he could see through the wooden planks to the main deck. "I'm going to see what's hidden under those canvas sheets."

DAWN WAS JUST STARTING to lighten the sky when a man-size door opened in the seawall of Northpoint ville and out walked a sec man wrapped in a heavy bearskin coat. There was a bamboo fishing pole resting on a shoulder, and he was carrying a wicker basket full of freshly baked bread, delicious wisps of steam rising from the small brown loafs.

Whistling an ancient tune, the sec man ambled toward the sleeping guard sitting on the barrel at the end of the dock.

"Hey, wake up, shithead!" he called out in a friendly manner. "Better not let the baron catch you snoozing on post, or she'll have your balls for breakfast."

But his voice faded away at the sight of the still man covered with dozens of the tiny blue crabs, their pinchers snipping at his clothing and pale skin. There was a large puddle of dried blood a few feet away on the boards, and a rope lashed around the throat of the sec man holding the corpse tightly to the wooden pylon.

Dropping everything, the sec man reached for the whistle lashed to his wrist and there was a blur of motion from the nearby *Warhammer.* Throwing back his head, the man clawed at the arrow in his throat, the shaft neatly pinning his mouth closed. Hot blood filled his mouth, dribbling from his lips and clogging his throat. Staggering from the pain, he tried to head for the ville, but tripped over the fishing pole and tumbled off the dock into the bay.

The cold revived him for a moment, and the sec man tried to reach the nearby ladder, when another arrow hit him in the back, the impact driving his face against a pylon. Vaguely, he heard a sharp crack of bone breaking, and then nothing more ever again.

Quickly rising into view on the warship, Doc and Jak appeared from behind the gunwale and released the mooring lines. Only seconds later, the low rumbling noises from the craft's engine room increased drastically, and the warship began to sluggishly move away from the dockyard.

Stepping out of the wheelhouse, Ryan went directly to the forward deck and yanked off the canvas sheet to reveal a honeycomb of bamboo pipes joined together with stout rope, and mounted on a platform atop a swivel post.

"Light it up, lover!" Ryan called, flicking a butane lighter into life and igniting a stubby fuse at the back of the weapon.

Already at the second launcher on the aft deck, Krysty did the same thing, and then the two companions impatiently waited for what seemed to be an inordinate length of time for the sputtering fuses to finally reach the cluster of bamboo pipes.

When the fuse vanished inside the honeycomb, there was a gush of smoke and a rocket flew away, streaking over the dockyard to slam into the wall of the ville and violently explode. The loud noise seemed to echo across the bay, disturbing a flock of birds in the distant trees on the far side. Then the first of Krysty's rockets launched to punch through the largest fishing boat moored at the dock. Spraying sparks and smoke, the rocket punched through the wooden hull and lanced into the water, hissing as it left behind a bubbling contrail.

Just then, a bearded face appeared on top of the ville wall, and Mildred triggered her ZKR blaster from the porthole. A split second later, the sec man vanished with a cry of pain.

Grabbing the heavy yoke of the honeycomb, Ryan moved the launcher into a new position just as the second rocket took off. However, it spiraled past the wall and missed the guard tower by a few feet. Exerting all of his strength, Ryan held the launcher still, and the third rocket flew true. With a thunderclap, the guard house detonated into flame and splinters, falling bodies arching down into the sleepy ville.

Gushing black smoke fumes from the smokestack, the *Warhammer* steadily chugged away from the shore and began slipping into a vaporous cloud of mist covering the middle of the bay. Knowing she had only a few moments of sight remaining, Krysty quickly swung her yoke around to aim rocket after rocket at anything that might be able to give pursuit. In short order, canoes, fishing boats and barges were blown to smithereens, the wreckage swiftly sinking to the bottom of the bay.

Meanwhile, Ryan took out the second guard tower, then the third.

Screaming and yelling were coming from inside the

ville, and suddenly they heard the steady gong of an alarm bell, closely followed by the shrill wails of a hundred whistles.

Inside the wheelhouse J.B. saw no reason to be covert anymore. Taking a hand off the wheel, he pulled on a dangling rope and a steam whistle loudly howled from atop the smokestack.

Out of sinkable targets, Krysty added the power of her honeycomb to Ryan's. The homemade rockets hammered the dock nonstop, blowing out pylons and crashing through the boardwalk. Then they ruthlessly aimed the weapons at the one door, catching a squad of armed sec men totally by surprise. The sec men were blasted into shrieking hamburger by the double salvo, the door itself blown off the hinges before the thickening fog masked the ville completely.

"Got more?" Jak asked, patting the smoking honeycomb fondly as if it were a well-trained hunting dog.

"No, this was it. They must keep most of the rockets inside the ville." Ryan smiled. "You know, just in case somebody jacks the boat."

"Do you think they will give pursuit?" Doc asked, his long hair riffling in the cloudy breeze.

"I would," Liana replied gruffly, just as something huge flashed past the warship to slam into the surface of the lake, throwing off a geyser of water.

"Arbalest!" Ryan shouted, leveling the Steyr. But it was impossible to see through the morning fog. That was why they had chosen this time to leave instead of at night. Only now, the fog that shielded them was doing the same for the ville sec men.

Opening her mouth, Mildred started to tell everybody to be quiet, the sec men were probably using the voice to aim the colossal crossbow. But then she realized that with the hammering steam engine, silence was impossible.

Several more of the giant arrows came out of the mist, slashing across the bay in different directions. Most of them only sliced into the water, but one hit a sandbar, violently exploding into a geyser of splitters and loose sand.

They know we're out here, but are as blind as we are, Ryan noted with some satisfaction. At least both sides were on equal footing.

However, unable to fight back or to hide, the companions could do nothing at the moment but tighten the grip on their blasters and wait for annihilation. If one of the giant arrows hit, the *Warhammer* would be cored like a ripe apple.

"Head for the western shore!" Krysty shouted, motioning in the opposite direction.

Nodding from behind the glass window of the wheelhouse, J.B. changed direction and started heading toward a small island covered with pine trees. It wouldn't offer much protection, but some was always better than none.

As the warship steamed behind the copse of trees, swarms of half-arrows arched down from the cloudy sky, sounding like rain as they vanished into the murky water.

Incredibly, there was the sharp report of a blaster from behind, the lolling boom telling it was a blackpowder weapon.

"It seems that we have awoken the beast," Krysty muttered, pulling out her own blaster.

Leaving the protection of the woody island, the *Warhammer* moved steadily along, trying to get as far away from the ville defenders as possible without approaching any of the countless sunken trees or small sandbars.

For several minutes the vessel steamed along, rapidly increasing speed until there was a jarring impact that threw everybody to the deck as the warship suddenly stopped. Loose items rolled across the trembling deck, and several went overboard to splash into the drink.

"Nuking hell, we ran aground!" J.B. cursed from the wheelhouse. Never letting go of the wheel, he grabbed a speaking tube made of joined sections of bamboo and shouted into the mouthpiece. "Jak! Reverse the engine! Give me dead slow!"

"Gotcha…" the teenager answered, the reply ghostly faint over the sound of the laboring machine.

Looking over the gunwale, Ryan saw only choppy water below the stern. Fireblast! Getting out of this passage was going to be a lot harder than he had ever imagined. The sunken log and larger sandbars they could see and easily avoid, but if there were many more of these hidden sandbars, they would still be fumbling about in the bay, looking for a way out, when the baron arrived with a hundred men in birch-bark canoes. That would be real trouble.

Slowly, the engine eased in tempo, and the trembling in the hull stopped. Mechanical clanks sounded from belowdecks, and the propellers spun for an inordinately long time before the *Warhammer* sluggishly pulled itself loose with a moist sucking sound. The water swirled darkly around the boat, then gradually cleared as it moved backward into deep water again.

"Liana, are there any man-eaters in the bay?" Krysty demanded, scowling at the muddy water. "Can we swim out ahead to check for more obstacles?"

"None," she replied quickly, eager to help. "Only the sea...I mean the lake, has killer fish."

"That won't help," Ryan growled, gripping the gunwale and staring at the wide bay ahead of them. "The bastard sandbar we just hit was too fragging far underwater to see. Swimming ahead of the boat would only slow us more!"

"Ah, but mayhap I can show us the way," Doc announced, holstering his blaster. "Keep us still for a moment, John Barrymore, while I find some string!"

"String?" J.B. demanded, looking over the rim of his glasses

"String!" the time traveler replied haughtily, disappearing down the stairwell. A few moments later Doc returned with a slim length of hemp rope coiled in his hands.

Going to the bow, he stretched the rope out to the length of his arm and tied off a knot. He kept doing that for the whole length of the rope, then he went back and added a larger knot between each of the arm's-length knots.

Looking for something to use as a plumb, Doc found nothing serviceable and reluctantly tied the Ruger to the end of the rope. At least it was waterproof and would not be damaged by a long immersion, unlike the precious LeMat.

"Clever, very clever, ya old coot," Mildred said, slapping the man on the back.

"My parents had a fool for a son, but that was my brother," Doc replied with a wry smile, tossing the rope overboard. The revolver splashed out of sight, and the man let the knotted rope run through his fingers until it stopped descending.

"John Barrymore, we have ten feet to the port side!" he bellowed over his shoulder. "Is that sufficient?"

"The what side?" J.B. replied from the wheelhouse, looking from behind the big wheel.

"Port has four letters, just like the word left."

"Ah, gotcha. Yeah, ten is fine," J.B. replied happily, snatching the speaking tube. "Jak! Move us forward at half speed! No, make that a third!"

"Third speed!" the teenager replied, and a few seconds later the vessel began to creep forward again.

Just then, in the far distance, there was a flurry of blasterfire, but it did not seem to be coming in their direction. At least, not yet.

Casting out the line again, Doc reeled it in quickly and read the depth. "Mark!" he called out. "Half twain to the starboard!"

"Dark night, speak English!" J.B. demanded from the wheelhouse.

"Full twain means clear sailing," Mildred answered from the forward deck. "Half twain means the water is getting shallow, quarter twain means danger, slow and back off!"

"Well, why doesn't he just say so!"

"Tradition, my friend!" Doc replied, casting out the rope once more.

With Doc leading the way, J.B. clumsily steered the bulky vessel through the sandy maze of the narrow channel. Progress was slow, and Ryan stayed a tense guard at the back of the boat, the Steyr clenched in both hands, straining to see into the wafting fog.

Slow hours passed, and the noon sun began to bake away the cool morning mist when the *Warhammer* finally entered a wide area of the bay, the clear blue water dotted with a series of small islands that strongly resembled the fjords of Norway.

"It should be clear sailing from here on," Doc called out in marked satisfaction, working the Ruger free of the wet rope. The blaster was streaked with mud and covered with kelp, but otherwise undamaged.

"About damn time," J.B. replied gruffly, turning to the speaking tube. "Okay, Jak, give me full speed!"

But the reply of the teenager was cut off when there came a dull boom from far behind the steamboat.

"Are those cannons?" Mildred asked nervously.

"Hope so," Ryan replied gruffly, the wind blowing his black hair forward to hide his expression.

Straining to hear over the hammering of the steam engine, the companions anxiously waited for the appearance of a cannonball from out of the fog, but nothing happened. There was only the sound of the steam engine and the lap of the waves against their wooden hull.

Then the boom came again, followed by another,

then more, slow and steady, the concussions coming in the pendulum beat of a human heart.

"That's a timing drum," Ryan stated, tightening his grip on the longblaster. "Fireblast, I thought we sank everything they had!"

"Guess we missed one," Krysty said furiously, her hair coiling and flexing. "There must have been a dry dock or a boatyard that Liana didn't know about."

Softly, the beat continued, regular and steady, slowly growing louder, a smooth counterpoint to the mechanical laboring of the steam engine.

"I saw a vid once about Roman galleys," Mildred said calmly, even though there was a tickle of fear in her stomach. "Mostly they used slaves, but during a war, sometimes sec men would crew the ships. Fifty, sixty, a hundred strong men rowing in perfect unison, the oars moving to the beat of a timing drum."

"How fast did they move?" Krysty asked, getting to the point.

"Very fast, too damn fast," Mildred replied honestly, her hands holding on to the gunwale. "With a properly trained crew, a galley could easily catch a windjammer near the shore and ram into it hard enough to crash through, completely through, coming out the other side." The physician shook her head. "The Romans didn't have to fire an arrow or draw a single sword. They just plowed the other ship down like roadkill and let the sea do the rest."

"How far did Liana say it was until we reach the open lake?" Krysty asked, pulling out her Glock to drop the magazine and check the load.

"Fifty more miles, just past a peninsula," Mildred answered, glancing ahead of the boat. Only smooth open water was in sight. "Think we'll make it before they arrive?"

Suddenly the beat of the timing drum changed, quickening slightly, the unseen enemy moving faster toward them.

"We'll find out soon enough," Ryan said, raising the Steyr.

Chapter Fifteen

Nothing could be seen moving through the thick fog covering the bay. There was only the dull beat of the timing drums, and the steady splash of oars slapping against the choppy water.

"Faster! Row faster!" Baron Wainwright commanded, leaning forward in the longboat as if she could hasten their progress through sheer willpower. "The mainlanders must not escape!"

Her velvet dress was blackened with soot and badly slashed, a plump breast almost fully exposed. But the leather bodice underneath had saved her life from a hail of flying debris. However, the baron had lost a lot of her beautiful hair in the fire that engulfed her ville when the guard towers collapsed, and the side of her face was horribly blistered. Her vaunted beauty was gone and her ville in ruins. Now, madness gleamed from her eyes, and the only thought pounding in her mind in tempo to the timing drum was the ever-repeating word: revenge…revenge…revenge…

Putting their backs into the job, the dozen sec men in the lead longboat obediently tried to move the oars faster, and stay in tempo to the beating drum. The tethered slave at the drum didn't care if the mainlanders were caught or not. But any slowing in the beat would result in a brutal whipping, so he tried his best to urge the sec men on to faster and faster speeds.

"Don't worry, cousin, they won't get away," Baron Griffin growled, working the bolt on his Marlin .444 longblaster. There were only four rounds for the titanic weapon, but he swore to make every fragging one of them draw blood.

That is, if I can shoot straight, the baron amended privately. In spite of a brief nap and several cups of strong tea, Griffin was still exhausted from the long trip to Northpoint, and yet exhilarated to be so near the hated mainlanders. There were two predark weapons in his gunbelt—the Ruger .38 his father had given him on his deathbed, and his wife's 12-gauge scattergun. When the one-eyed man fell to his feet to beg for his life, Baron Griffin would execute the coldheart with the sawed-off blaster. The sight of his head exploding would be a balm to his aching heart. It wouldn't be enough. Griffin wanted to torture the outlander for years as punishment for his cowardly attack, but a fast chilling would have to suffice. However, the slut would go into the gaudy house to serve his sec men until they rode her to death. And I'll be first to put rubies into that silk saddle, the baron savagely promised, feeling his manhood swell at the thought of the delicious agony he would inflict upon the stocky woman.

Grunting in reply, Baron Wainwright checked the load in her blasters. The coldhearts who attacked Northpoint and jacked her boat had made a critical mistake. They hadn't checked the warehouse located across the bay from the ville. The winter longboats had been stored there, undergoing their yearly repairs, along with a few birch-bark canoes she used to trade with the outer islands. The *Warhammer* was gone, but a hundred of the sec men from Anchor and Northpoint had been jammed into the hodgepodge of longboats, a good dozen more riding along in the small canoes. They had mounted the *Wendigo* on a barge, and Wainwright knew the outlanders didn't stand a chance against the war wag's big rapidfire blasters.

She grinned as she thought about the war wag, and the bulky arbalest filling a nearby longboat. The boat just behind it was stacked high with arrows for the deadly weapon, and the mixed crew of the two villes was carrying every working blaster the two barons possessed. Plus, hundreds of boomerangs, spears, bolos and grens. Baskets upon baskets of black-powder grens. More than enough to blow a hole through the world, if necessary. Cobbled together in less than an hour, this was more than a mere caravan, or a flotilla, it was a fragging armada!

Personally, Wainwright wished LeFontaine was here, but the sec chief had not returned from escorting that Hilly to some cave on the southern shore, near the Green Mountain. But such was life.

Just then a low breeze moved among the longboats and suddenly the sec men could see one another much more clearly.

"Must be about noon," Griffin said, awkwardly working the arming bolt of the Marlin. "The fog is almost gone."

"Good," Wainwright muttered. "That'll make it easier to chill them."

Suddenly, from ahead of them came the familiar noise of a badly tuned steam engine lumbering along. Without waiting to be told, the sec men in the center longboat started to work the windless of their arbalest, pulling back the ten-foot bow in preparation of loading a yard-long arrow.

"Just watch out for the one-eyed man," Griffin warned, hefting the heavy longblaster. "He's a crack shot with a blaster."

"Me, too," Wainwright whispered, drawing the S&W .44 Magnum blaster, and clicking back the hammer.

LEANING AGAINST the gunwale to steady himself, Ryan looked through the telescopic sights of the Steyr, but there was nothing to be seen across the bay but the damnable fog.

Softly muffled voices could be heard, along with the clatter of wood hitting wood, and a rhythmic splashing. Oars in the water. Lowering the longblaster, the one-eyed man strained to listen to the timing drum. Counting under his breath to get the beat, Ryan soon cursed at the realization that there were several drums. However, the bastard things were pounding in such perfect unison that it was impossible for him to even guess the exact number. There could be dozens, maybe even hundreds.

"Gaia, it sounds like the baron sent everything she had after us," Krysty muttered uneasily, swaying to the motion of the boat.

"Of course, madam," Doc rumbled, a blaster in each hand. "We have the speed, but they must intimately know this bay. It is the source of their livelihood. If our vessel becomes entangled with another sandbar, we shall most definitely become dead in the water."

Shifting the med kit to keep it out of the way, Mildred tried not to shiver at the phrase. Dead in the water. She had never truly understood the nautical term before. In a sea battle, standing still meant you died. End of discussion. Mentally, the physician made a note to add this incident to her growing codex. If we survive today, she added privately.

Suddenly there was the stomping from the stairwell, and everybody spun with their blasters at the ready as Jak came into view brandishing a stone ax.

"Could use hand," the sweat-drenched teenager stated simply, then turned and descended back into the engine room.

"I'll go," Krysty offered, holstering her blaster. "My snub-nose has the worst range."

"Fair enough," Ryan said, giving the redhead a meaningful glance. "I'll give a shout if anybody gets past us."

She patted her blaster. "If snakeskin boots appear on the stairs, the owner will never reach the bottom in one piece."

"Good. And if you hear me call you Amanda or Abigail…"

"We blow the engine and sink this tub." Reaching out, Krysty stroked his scarred cheek, speaking volumes, then she turned and headed off.

For a moment Ryan watched her go until she was out of sight, then concentrated on business. The best way to keep Krysty sucking air was to make sure that the baron and her sec men never got on this boat alive.

"Mildred, go see if J.B. can get any more speed out of this thing," Ryan growled, shouldering the long-blaster. "Then go load the arbalest."

Looking at the ungainly weapon, the physician nodded thoughtfully to herself, then strode into the wheelhouse. A split second later Liana came out, holding a handful of leather quivers filled with arrows.

"I found these in the armory," Liana announced, dropping the quivers onto the deck, a rapidfire cross-bow hung across her slim back. "With the wind at our backs they'll have much better range than anything coming this way."

"Our thanks, dear lady, but now you should seek refuge in the hold," Doc said in unaccustomed frankness. "Soon, we shall be in harm's way."

"Where you go, I follow," Liana said simply, feeding a half-arrow in the hopper of the elaborate weapon, then several more.

At the words, Doc took her small hand and gently squeezed. Then as if never seeing it before, Doc saw the wedding ring on his left hand. Emily.

"We need to talk," the time traveler said.

"Later," Ryan interrupted, pulling out the panga and testing the edge of a thumb. "Liana, know what a fire-brand is?"

"Sure."

"Go make some."

Immediately, Liana rushed off.

With Doc standing watching at the rear gunwale, Ryan went to the empty honeycomb and started hacking at the wooden pivot, alternating the angle of the strikes as if he was chopping down a tree. Soon, the support cracked and the spent rocket pod toppled and crashed onto the deck.

Leaving the gunwale, Doc started to drag the honeycomb aft, as Ryan hacked down the second launcher. Without any rockets, they were only good as shields. At least it gave them something better than the gunwale to stand behind. That was only waist high.

"This position will also make them easy to shove overboard," Doc added, dusting off his hands. "In case we need to lighten the boat."

"And a pipe bomb or two stuffed inside wouldn't hurt, either," Ryan agreed, dragging the launcher into position.

"Indeed not, sir!" Doc grinned. "It would be most appropriate for us to give the baron some small recompense for the use of her warship, and lead in the coin of the realm these days!"

"Bet your ass."

In the distance, the drums continued, growing ever louder.

Lashing the honeycombs into place with some rope, the men tested the knots to make sure they were secure. A few minutes later, Liana returned with a wicker basket full of rope, and a ceramic demijohn.

"Cooking oil," she announced, setting the items down behind the impromptive barricade. "I also told

J.B. the old poem on how to find the passage to the open lake."

"Poem?" Doc asked curiously, arching an eyebrow.

"'Two tall pines will show you the way,'" she recited, in a clear strong voice. "'One faces freedom, and the other looks away.'"

"How the frag does a tree look away?" Ryan demanded skeptically.

"Sir, trees have faces," Liana said patiently, as if explaining something to a small child.

"Faces," Ryan repeated.

She nodded vigorously.

After a moment Ryan shrugged in acceptance. Okay, the local trees had faces. Had to be muties. He just hoped that J.B. could figure out which way the fragging tree was looking when the time came. Ahead of the boat, the bay was starting to narrow, as if becoming an inlet, the water studded with an archipelago of tiny islands, most of them too small for even a newborn stingwing to safely land on, much less support a full grown tree.

"I brought air support," Mildred called, returning with the bulky munitions bag slung over a shoulder, the Uzi bumping into her backside with every step.

"Well done, madam!" Pulling out a knife, Doc began to cut the sounding line into several pieces of the exact same length.

As the companions started to lash the rope to pipe bombs, the drumming got noticeably louder, and a long narrow boat slipped out of the fog bank. At the front was a wooden shield more suitable for an ax fight, but

Ryan knew it would probably also serve well against blasters.

"There they be," a sec man shouted, pointing an accusing finger.

Instantly, Ryan dropped the pipe bomb, swung up the Steyr, aimed and fired.

The sec man flipped over backward from the arrival of a 7.62 mm hollowpoint round, his life spraying across the other sec men filling the boat. Several of them recoiled, dropping their oars, but most did not, and kept steadily rowing, their bloody faces full of murderous rage.

"And the whale beholds Captain Ahab," Doc whispered, drawing his two blasters, and thumbing back the hammers.

"Galley, my ass, that's a longboat," Mildred muttered, carefully cutting the fuse to each pipe bomb until it was less than an inch long. "It's much faster than a— Aw, crap!"

Exiting the mist came another longboat stuffed full of even more sec men armed with a wide variety of weapons. Then came a score of birch-bark canoes holding only a single occupant, closely followed by a dozen more longboats carrying at least a hundred sec men. One longboat was equipped with an arbalest and a stack of arrows, while another boasted the deadly bamboo honeycomb of a rocket launcher. And behind them all was a barge bearing *Wendigo*.

Instantly the four companions stopped what they were doing and unleashed a barrage of lead at the honeycomb, cutting down a sec woman trying to light the master fuse. With a strangled cry, she toppled over-board and disappeared below the choppy surface. A few moments later, the gasping woman resurfaced, only to have a longboat ram into her head. The skull cracked open with horrid results, and the corpse slipped below the keel of the vessel.

"Get that big bastard!" sec chief Donovan bellowed, fanning his blaster at the *Warhammer.* Incredibly, the lead hit the gunwale and honeycomb, sounding like somebody knocking on a door.

Kneeling behind the honeycomb, Ryan centered the crosshairs on the snarling face of the sec chief, adjusted for the wind and distance and gently squeezed the trigger. Spinning, Donovan fell, the longblaster flying from his bandaged hand to splash into the lake.

In reply, a swarm of boomerangs lashed out from the army of sec men, along with a flurry of half-arrows from their rapidfire crossbows.

The spinning boomerangs fell short, skipping along the surface of the lake to hit the hull of the *Warhammer* with a dull thud before splashing into the bay. But arch-ing high, the half-arrows came down like a rain of death, impacting everywhere on the warship, one of them pinning Mildred's med kit to the deck.

Lifting her crossbow, Liana sent off a single arrow, a piece of burning rope lashed to the shaft. For a long moment it hung in the air, almost seeming to stand still, then it arched down to hit the honeycomb.

Screaming in terror, a sec man yanked out the fire-brand, when a shot rang out and he doubled over, his belly gushing red life. Yelling obscenities, another sec man grabbed the smoking firebrand and used it to ignite the master fuse of the rocket launcher.

Lighting the fuse on a pipe bomb attached to the end of a rope, Doc spun it to near invisibility, then let go. The explosive charge sailed away, going much too high and lofting over the jeering armada before violently detonating.

The hail of shrapnel peppered the assorted crafts, the pieces of casing and bent nails shredding the exposed people, and ripping apart the longboat carrying the honeycomb. Listing at first, the craft slowed, then tilted sideways, just as the rockets started to launch. Skipping across the bay, they blew up two other longboats before the honeycomb went under the surface. The other longboats raced to get away as there was fierce bubbling, and then the launcher detonated, a watery geyser rising high into the afternoon sky, raining pieces of bamboo and human organs across the turbulent bay.

Spotting a busty woman who seemed to be shouting orders to the sec men, Ryan guessed that had to be Baron Wainwright, and centered his crosshairs on her when he saw Baron Griffin rise into view cradling a monstrously huge longblaster. Fireblast, that was a bastard Marlin!

Aiming quickly, the two men fired at the same moment.

The booming .444 Magnum Express round of the predark blaster hit nothing, the slug humming into the distance, but the 7.62 mm round from the Steyr slammed the baron smack in the chest, and he dropped, splinters exploding from under his clothing.

"More fragging armor," Ryan growled, trying again for the man's head. But the motion of the steamboat and that of the longboats was making marksmanship mostly a matter of luck. He wasted two rounds hitting nothing, then put two more into the hull. The lead slapped the wood, but the craft did not even slow, much less sink.

As the angry baron struggled to work the Marlin, Ryan coolly emptied an entire clip as fast as he could, the slugs hammering the baron backward, and finally hitting the longblaster. With an audible ricochet, the weapon was jerked from his startled grip and dropped into the bay. Instantly, a sec man dived for the weapon, but even if successful, he was soon left behind by the speeding armada.

Screaming wordlessly, Baron Griffin emptied his blaster at the companions. Holding his breath, Ryan got the man again in the chest. Staggering from the blow, Griffin merely reloaded and started banging away again, before sec chief Donovan pulled him down behind the wooden armor.

More half-arrows and boomerangs were released as several canoes darted ahead of the longboats, the sec men using both hands to paddle, stone knives held in their teeth like outlander pirates.

Peeking out from behind the honeycomb, Mildred kneeled at the gunwale and switched the Uzi to full-auto before hosing the nimble little crafts with a lethal stream of 9 mm Parabellum rounds. The copper-jacketed slugs tore through the sec men before sinking the canoes. Paddling furiously, the rest of the sec men in canoes tried to get away, and Ryan took out one with the Steyr, while Mildred aced the rest. Doc and Liana concentrated on the longboats.

Raising a protective shield, Wainwright shouted something the companions could not hear, and there immediately came the totally unexpected report of a big-bore blaster from a couple of longboats.

The companions ducked fast, and the gunwale of the *Warhammer* was pelted with incoming lead. One of the ropes holding a honeycomb into place snapped, and a window in the wheelhouse loudly shattered.

"No damage!" J.B. shouted.

As the companions stood to return fire, another salvo came, and Doc staggered backward, dropping his weapons as a dark red stain began to spread across his frilly shirt.

Chapter Sixteen

The ragged fusillade of blasterfire continued as a bleeding Doc slumped to the deck and the LeMat skittered across the slightly tilting boat, heading straight for the water. Diving forward, Liana caught the blaster just before it went over the edge.

Crouching behind the gunwale, Mildred shoved the Uzi over to Ryan. The one-eyed man checked the clip, then stood and burped the rapidfire at the sec men in short bursts.

"How bad is it?" Mildred demanded, checking the position of Doc's wound. The upper arm was usually a good place to get shot, if that was possible—lots of flesh, and only a single major artery to worry about. But that was not what she was worried about.

"Just a flesh wound," Doc said, straining against the pain. "Nothing serious."

"Glad to hear it," she remarked, setting down the med kit before pulling the man forward to check the back of the arm. There was no corresponding hole. Damn, she thought, the slug was still in him.

Blasterfire sounded from the longboats again, closer this time, and lead smacked into the wood along the hull. Then more arrows pelted down from the sky, feathering the deck and wheelhouse.

Slinging the Uzi, Ryan lit the fuse on a pipe bomb, then released it in an easy pitch. It was still airborne when he ducked, and the explosion rattled the *Warhammer*. Screams came from the sec men, along with a great deal of splashing.

"This is going to hurt, and you know these folks like poison," Mildred remarked, reaching into the kit to pull out a pair of needle-nose pliers recovered from a car shop, along with a bottle of shine. "So you know what's coming."

"D-do your worst, Hippocrates," the scholar growled, pulling out his old leather wallet and placing it between his teeth. "I am prepared."

Standing, Liana trigger the LeMat twice, the barrel jumping wildly with every shot. Stepping behind a honeycomb, she scowled at the weapon, then tucked it into her gunbelt. The recoil of the blaster was far beyond her ability to control.

Sloshing shine over the pliers, Mildred plunged them into the wound, causing a surge of fresh blood. Inhaling sharply at the contact, Doc went stiff, but said nothing, his free hand tightening into a fist until the knuckles audibly popped and cracked.

"Theo?" Liana said, the name a question.

"Tut-tut, dear girl, I am fine." Doc coughed, wiping his mouth on the back of a trembling hand. "The good doctor's administrations are sometimes medieval in nature, but always highly effective."

"Shut up, ya old coot," Mildred snorted, feeling the

contact of steel on the soft lead. As carefully as possible, she extracted the miniball, doing the minimum of damage to the surrounding tissue, and briefly inspected it in the wan sunlight. In spite of the red smears of blood, there seemed to also be some other color on the lead. Damnation, she thought, no choice then.

By now, small islands studded with scraggly trees were passing by the *Warhammer* on a regular basis, the craft constantly changing directions as J.B. tried to make the thick black smoke from the chimney flow toward the longboats to blind the enemy snipers.

"Liana, you better look away," Mildred ordered, tossing the lead overboard.

But instead, the woman offered the doctor a butane lighter.

Almost smiling at the act, Mildred poured some shine directly into the open wound, and Liana set it aflame.

Going terribly pale, Doc shuddered from the rush of fire, then collapsed, panting heavily. After a minute or so, the scholar removed the wallet. "I s-see you have been well tutored by Cort S-Strasser," he mumbled, referring to an enemy who had tortured the scholar on a daily basis before the companions eventually freed him.

"Sure, we're lodge brothers," Mildred retorted, quickly sewing the wound shut with an upholstery needle and lightweight fishing line.

"Of this, I have no d-doubt, madam," Doc said, grunting with every stitch.

"Shut up. I'm busy," she snapped, wondering who Strasser was as she put away the instruments and wrapped the arm in a fresh bandage.

Just then, the wind shifted, exposing the steamboat, and another swarm of arrows, lead and boomerangs pummeled the rear of the craft with savage intensity. Ryan replied with the Uzi, then moved to the other honeycomb before triggering two fast rounds from the Steyr, trying to pretend he was not the only defender.

Seeing that Doc would live, Liana rose to discharge her S&W revolver a fast three times, and changed weapons to launch an arrow before flopping onto the deck and crawling past the forest of arrows to reach the arbalest.

As Ryan maintained cover fire with the stuttering Uzi, Liana climbed up the weapon to crank the windless, notching an arrow into position. But then she paused and pulled out a pipe bomb. Lashing it to the yard-long shaft of the arrow, Liana swung the weapon around to face the armada of longboats, chose a target and fired.

Lancing between the two overturned honeycombs, the sizzling arrow streaked away to slam directly into the prow of a longboat, the barbed head coming out the other side and missing the drummer by a scant inch. Contemptuously, the drummer sneered at the companions, while the rest of the sec men laughed in an uproar at the failure, one particularly bold sec man loosening his gunbelt to actually drop his leather pants and moon the companions.

"The arrow!" Baron Wainwright shouted through cupped hands. "Get rid of the arrow, you feebs!"

But before the crew of the longboat could do anything, the small pipe bomb exploded, removing the front of the vessel. Spilled into the turgid lake, the mob of wounded men floundered helplessly as the rest of the armada rowed past them without even slowing.

Suddenly the steam whistle keened loudly and the boat angled sharply to starboard.

Dodging a hail of boomerangs, Ryan inserted a fresh magazine into the longblaster and glanced toward the bow. Just a little ways ahead of the craft was a tall pair of pine trees dominating a rocky escarpment. One of them was perfectly straight, while the other was badly windswept and bent like a dying oldster, the green bow pointing toward a break in the archipelago, a winding waterway that emptied into the vast body of the Great Lake. Safety was only minutes away.

The *Wendigo* suddenly was within range and opened fire, the stream of lead from its rapidfire churning the lake water, tracking after the steaming *Warhammer.*

Behind the safety of the bamboo honeycomb, Mildred twirled a pipe bomb to full speed and let it fly. The explosive charge flew true and hit the war wag, only to bounce off before detonating.

Swaying to the motion of the steamboat, Ryan leveled the Steyr and squeezed off five fast rounds. Sparks flew from the ricochets off the steel plating, then blood sprayed from the blasterport, and somebody inside the wag cursed, the rapidfire veering upward to waste precious ammo on the empty sky. Before the wounded gunner could recover, Ryan put five more rounds into the blasterport, and the rapidfire stopped working.

Angling into the channel, the *Warhammer* began to

move faster, leaving the combined armada behind in its wake.

Just then, a salvo of flaming arrows arched high into the sky from the longboats to streak back down and hit the steamboat, creating small puddles of fire everywhere.

Holstering their blasters, Mildred and Liana dashed around to beat at the spreading flames with their jackets before the wooden deck was set ablaze. There were buckets set into niches along the gunwale for just such an emergency, but the women knew that they would be cut down by the crossbows of the sec men the moment they tried to get a container free to dip into the lake. Surrounded by unlimited water, they were reduced to battling the conflagration with their bare hands.

Sending two booming rounds toward the barons in the distant longboats, Ryan then sent the next three shots at the war wag, trying again for the small target of the blasterport. It was down to just him now.

Pausing for a second, Mildred yanked open her med kit to yank out a plastic bottle of sterilized water she kept for washing deep wounds. Pouring half of the fluid over her jacket, she tossed the bottle to Liana, who did the same to her own garment, then the women returned to the fight, warily keeping watch on the sky as additional arrows arrived, setting new fires.

As Ryan hastily reloaded, he noticed more sec men in canoes paddling closer, those exploding lances lashed to their backs. Those could blow the honeycombs off the deck, leaving the companions exposed to the boomerangs and bolos of the armada. Not to mention the rapidfire of the war wag.

Making a fast decision, Ryan charged for the arbalest and dropped in a new arrow, then began hacking at the barbed head with his panga, wood chips flying everywhere. "Doc!" Ryan bellowed at the top of his lungs. "Get off your ass!"

Jerking awake, the scholar gazed around groggily, then lumbered erect and clumsily drew the Ruger. "I have your six, sir," Doc growled, glaring at the nearby canoes and alternately firing the massive Magnum handblaster.

Surprised, the sec men in the canoes tried desperately to get away, but the old man mercilessly cut them down, then turned his attention to the longboats. The range was much greater, but he hit living flesh with astonishing regularity. However, from the first discharge of the Ruger, the bandage on his arm became soaked through with fresh blood, and soon a rivulet of red was trickling down his arm to dribble onto the deck.

The *Wendigo*'s rapidfire went back into operation, and Ryan hastily cranked the windless. Hunching over the medieval weapon, the one-eyed man held his breath. He would probably only get a single chance at this, and better not miss.

The hail of lead from the *Wendigo* chewed a path of destruction along the starboard gunwale, throwing out a storm of chips and splinters. Swaying to the motion of the boat, Ryan did nothing, waiting and watching. Raising the angle of the weapon, the gunner of the *Wendigo* raked the wheelhouse next, shattering two more windows. Cursing vehemently, J.B. responded with the scattergun, even though the war wag was far outside the range, but it was all that he could do in retaliation.

Clearing his mind of any distractions, Ryan still did nothing, until the war wag turned slightly to get a better angle and he instantly pressed the release lever. Straight and true, the mutilated arrow flashed away from the arbalest and slammed into the front of the *Wendigo,* exploding into splinters directly on the driver's tiny ob port.

"My eyes!" the driver shrieked from inside. "My fragging eyes!" The war wag was no longer a threat.

A few minutes later the *Warhammer* steamed through a channel created by two small islands, and sailed into the limitless expanse of the Great Lake. Gradually, the angry shouts of the barons and their sec men faded into nothingness, and there was only the chugging of the steam engine and the gentle slap of the waves against the wooden hull.

High in the wheelhouse, J.B. yelled in triumph, then sounded the steam whistle. "Goodbye, Royal Island!" the man shouted happily.

Moving stiffly away from the arbalest, Ryan grunted at that. Not quite yet, old friend, he thought. Working the arming bolt of the Steyr, he withdrew a partially used magazine, and inserted a fresh one. There were no other steamboats on the island, and no matter how many sec men the barons put to the oars, or how hard they whipped the slaves, no longboat could ever catch the steamboat in calm water.

Now that the boat was out of the range of the sec men, Liana rushed to fill a bucket with water, and began to slosh it across the burned deck to extinguish any lingering embers. Retrieving her med kit, Mildred shuffled wearily over to Doc and forced the man to sit, so that she could tend his wounds once more. She sincerely wanted to admonish the scholar for ruining her fine needlework, however his actions may have just altered the outcome of the battle. For a man of peace, Doc Tanner was a bodacious fighter, a chilling machine when roused.

"Hurt much?" Mildred asked, tenderly removing the bloody bandage.

"Like the Dickens, madam," Doc muttered, slumping against the gunwale. "But then, after so many…I have…always…" Slowly, the man's head descended to his chest, and he began to softly snore.

Wisely deciding to let him sleep, Mildred passed on stitching the wound closed, and simply wrapped it in several layers of clean bandages, then rigged a crude sling with a length of leather she normally used as a tourniquet. The bleeding had slowed considerably, and right now the exhausted man needed sleep more than anything else.

Balling up the bloody cloth strip, she started to toss it overboard, when a small hand grabbed her wrist.

"Not out here," Liana said, anxiously looking over the vast waters. "Norm blood in a bay sometimes summons a kraken, but out here it always does."

"But—"

"Always."

"Fair enough," Mildred replied, tucking the gory wad into a ziptop bag and stuffing that into a pocket to be disposed of later.

Busily thumbing loose rounds into an empty clip, Ryan sharply whistled.

Leaning over sideways, the Armorer stuck his head out the smashed window, careful of the jagged glass edging the opening. "What's up?" he asked. There was a gash in his cheek from the earlier flying glass, and a new hole in the fedora, but the man still sported a wide grin.

"Keep going straight until we lose sight of the land," Ryan called back, working the bolt to tuck the clip into the breech of the Steyr. "Then circle back to the carrier."

"Already doing just that," J.B. replied, disappearing back inside the bedraggled wheelhouse.

"What are you... Where are we going?" Liana asked, emptying a bucket onto a smoldering firebrand. As the deluge hit, it hissed out of existence.

"Back to where we found you," Ryan replied, checking his pockets for any more loose rounds. But he found nothing. Three full magazines, fifteen rounds, and then he was down to the nine in the SIG-Sauer and his knife.

"For more supplies?" she asked, setting down the bucket.

While riding together, Doc had told her about the mountain of goods stored in the belly of the predark warship, enough brass to sink a barge, thousands of self-heats, clean clothing and a host of other things, each more amazing and miraculous than the next.

"Wish we could, but no," Ryan answered, grimly shouldering the longblaster. "But we weren't planning on fighting today, and it damn near used every brass we have. If there is even one functioning sec hunter droid onboard that huge carrier, we couldn't stop it. Nobody is setting foot on the bastard ship."

"Then why go back?" Liana asked, brushing the damp hair off her sweaty face. The woman saw the others make the simple gesture all the time, as if it meant nothing, but after a lifetime of hiding in the shadows, exposing her face to others felt wild and improper. Almost defiant.

"If the sec droids are still working, then maybe so are the repair robots," Mildred answered, easing her heavy bag to the deck and taking a seat on a coiled pile of wet rope. "And under no circumstances can we allow a functioning mat-trans unit to fall into the hands of the local barons."

Thoughtfully, Liana scowled. Yes, Theo had also mentioned those machines. "So, we're going back to smash them." She said it as a question.

"Better," Ryan said, proceeding to explain the plan.

As the day wore on, the steamboat chugged steadily due south, and the snowy tors of Royal Island sank below the horizon to disappear from sight. Immediately, J.B. altered their course to the west and started the long journey back.

Chapter Seventeen

Reaching the mouth of the bay, Baron Griffin raised a hand, commanding the armada to a stop. The drummers relayed the order, and the remaining sec men backpaddled furiously to ease the longboats to a gentle halt. Ahead of them was the vast sea.

"All right, is anybody bleeding?" Baron Wainwright demanded, looking over the assemblage of sec men and women. "Is there any blood on the outside of the hulls? Any on your oars or blasters?"

Fully aware of the danger that surrounded them on every side, the combined army studiously checked their possessions, and a ragged chorus answered in the negative.

"Well, check again!" Griffin snapped, rocking to the motion of the gentle waves. "Everybody inspect the person to your right! We're out of the bay, and a single drop can put us into a world of hurt!"

Knowing the baron was referring to a kraken, the sec men and women looked again, much more intently this time. While they were occupied, the two barons turned away from the others to hold a private conversation.

"Have you done a count?" Griffin asked softly, uncorking a canteen to take a small drink. Unlike those of the sec men, this container held a mixture of coffee sub, sugared milk and shine.

"No," Wainwright whispered, accepting the canteen to take a drink without wiping off the top first. That would have been a deadly insult between the cousins. "How many did we lose?" The brew slid down easy and put strength in her blood, clearing away the fatigue of her rudely interrupted sleep from the night before. She had barely escaped from the burning ville with the clothes on her back. All of her precious plastic jewelry was gone, including her irreplaceable necklace of mutie teeth from her childhood. Just another crime that the outlanders had to pay for with their screams.

"How many? Two longboats, fifty sec men and twenty canoes," Griffin answered, taking back the container and sealing it tight.

Absolutely stunned, Wainwright could just barely stop herself from turning to check the count. Shitfire, that was over half the armada! "Are you sure, cousin?"

"Unfortunately, yes," Griffin replied, slinging the canteen over his right shoulder so that the strap would not touch the bandaged wound on his left shoulder. "I was so damn sure they would be an easy chill. How the frag could anybody guess they had a working rapid-fire!"

"Several, plus grens," Wainwright muttered, hitching up her gunbelt. There came a tinkling sound from her hip.

Suspicious, the woman drew the knife to find the wooden handle ended in a small broken shard, the rest of the glass blade only tiny pieces rattling in the snakeskin sheath. Yanking it free, she tossed the whole thing away to splash into the sea.

"By the lost gods, I hate a fair fight!" Griffin said petulantly, resting a hand on his late wife's sawed-off scattergun as if somehow drawing strength from the blaster. "And now they've escaped. Gone south across the sea." He pointed. "Look there! You can still see faint traces of their smoke on the horizon."

"Nonsense. It's a trick," Wainwright retorted. "No-body could be feeb enough to leave our island paradise for the endless rad craters and acid rain of the mainland. That would be fragging suicide!"

"Maybe," Griffin countered. "I agree, due south is death, but between the Broken Thing, volcanoes, whirl-pools and krakens, so is every other direction. There's no nuking way off the world."

"Okay, if there's nowhere to run, then they're still on the world," Wainwright declared, looking along the rugged coastline in both directions. "So the question -becomes, which way did they go, east or west?"

Pulling out a well-maintained old Ruger, the baron spun the cylinder, finding solace in the sound of the oiled steel. "We could split the fleet," he said without much conviction. "But that's just as stupe as heading south."

"Agreed," Wainwright muttered, running stiff fingers through her tangled frenzy of hair. She still smelled of smoke, and longed to take a quick bath in the cold lake. But there was no time for such things now. Every sec-ond left the armada farther and farther behind the vile outlanders.

"Black dust, what I wouldn't give for a single falcon," Griffin said, rubbing a forearm where his beloved pet normally rested.

"Have faith, cousin, I might know where they are going," Wainwright said unexpectedly, thoughtfully touching the many blisters on her face. "A few days ago, I sent my sec chief to Green Mountain to check on a story of a Hilly about some outlanders supposedly armed with blasters. It must have been them."

"Green Mountain," the baron repeated. Wild muties supposedly lived in the ivy-covered hills, and nobody who ventured there ever returned. Still it was better than exhausting the sec men by rowing around aimlessly.

"All right, you gleebs, the rest break is over," Griffin shouted, facing the expectant crew. "Drummers, give me double time! We row west for Green Mountain!" Then he added, "And there's a bag of steel waiting for the person who brings me the head of the one-eyed outlander!"

"Five bags if he's still alive!" Wainwright continued, upping the ante to not lose control of her troops. "Plus, you get to keep any of the others as your personal slaves!"

Now the faces of the sec men brightened at the incredible offer, their weary expressions changing into greedy leers of raw avarice. Slaves, steel and revenge! Who could ask for better?

As the drummers started a beat, the eager sec men and women spit into their sore hands, and began rowing with renewed vigor, each making plans on how to capture the cowardly outlanders alive, and unharmed.

IT WAS LATE in the evening by the time the companions returned to the beached aircraft carrier. The huge green mountain of ivy was ridiculously easy to locate, standing out from the bare granite hills like an emerald sitting in a pile of fresh dung.

For the moment, everybody was on deck, the firebox of the engine packed full with dry wood, and the boiler filled with clean water from the lake. The balcony they had jumped off was now fully exposed from their blaster fight with the droids, the rusty metal jutting out like the hand of a beggar. Ryan mentally counted the steps they had climbed up, doing some rough calculations to try to figure out where the engine room should be located.

Strange enough, the plan had come to the one-eyed man when the *Warhammer* had gotten caught on the sandbar. The nose of the boat was mired in the muck, yet the back end was still deep in the water. It occurred to him that the *Harrington* was in the exact same position, albeit on a much larger scale. If he could just breach the hull of the aircraft carrier, then the lake would flood the engine room, drowning the sec droids, and destroying the ancient machinery of the power plants, removing any chance of a possible repair. Without electricity, the mat-trans unit was just an oddly shaped room.

Trying to imagine the metal hidden under the thick growth of plants, Ryan realized that the trick would be to correctly guess the location of the massive engines, without actually going inside the vessel.

"Gotta be near rear," Jak stated confidently, looking

away from the shore and toward the lake. "When we there, deck had tilt, so end must be deep."

"True, but we want to breach the hull," J.B. countered, removing his fedora to smooth down his hair, and then replace the hat. "Not just blow a hole in a bile pump, or into a room full of war comps."

"Those would be protected by watertight bulkheads," Krysty added, standing with her arms crossed.

Holding on to the gunwale tightly, Liana said nothing, intimidated by the sheer, staggering size of the predark warship. She had serious trouble wrapping her thoughts around the fact that Green Mountain was actually a machine. She had seen war wags, and steamships before, some of them as large as a log cabin, but this was mind-boggling. And it was made of metal. More metal than there was in the private treasure of every baron on the whole damn world!

"All right, head for the stern!" Ryan shouted, pulling out his panga. "That's our best chance."

"Aye, aye, skipper!" Doc called out from the wheelhouse, working the throttle and wheel.

Gently moving against the tide, the huffing boat eased around the imposing bulk of the carrier until reaching the far end. Reaching out with the panga, Ryan slashed at the vines and saw only darkness beyond. "Take her in," he shouted, sheathing the blade. "Dead slow!"

Throttling down the steam engine, Doc eased the boat through the hanging curtain of vines to slip into the thick gloom.

Lighting torches, the companions studied the rusty

hull curving above their heads, the metal sloping downward to form a sort of grotto. The water below them was choked with kelp, but dimly seen was a large plane of metal. It was mostly eaten through with corrosion, but still identifiable as a propeller blade.

Using that as his starting point, Ryan backtracked along the hull until reaching a relatively flat section. From his days with the Trader, building and repairing war wags, the man knew that any angle in armor would be the strongest point. His best bet would be a nice straight section like this. Having explored the wrecks of warships before, he knew the hull would be thicker than the reach of his arm, but the implo gren had a range of fifteen feet. More than enough. Hopefully.

Choosing a strong hanging vine, Ryan lashed the gren in place, so that it was dangling just above the choppy surface of the cold lake. Wrapping a fuse around the arming lever, Ryan made sure it was good and tight, then checked again before pulling out the ring and activating the device. When the fuse burned through, the lever would drop off and the gren would detonate.

"Get ready to leave," Ryan ordered, leaning far over the gunwale and extending the torch. With a sputter, the fuse ignited and sizzled away into the morass of damp vines, moving a lot faster than he had thought it could.

"Haul ass!" Ryan bellowed, tossing the torch.

Hearing the urgent tone in the man's voice, Doc gave no reply and simply shoved the throttle all the way forward. Sluggishly, the engine revved in power, and the steamboat began to chug faster as it moved away from the imposing bulk of the *Harrington*.

Charging through the hanging vines, the boat emerged into the pale moonlight. Heading straight into the waves, Doc held as steady a course as possible, their speed steadily building.

"I just hope this works," J.B. muttered as the boat crested a swell, to slam back down hard. "That was my only implo gren."

"It'll work," Ryan declared, cracking his knuckles. "And if not, we can always—"

Just then, light flashed from inside the hanging cascade of flowering vines, followed by a bizarre sucking noise that almost sounded like a recording of an explosion played in reverse. Instantly, a powerful wind grabbed the *Warhammer,* trying to haul the boat and companions backward, even as the entire lake seemed to rush toward the carrier.

Squinting through the wild spray, the companions saw that a large section of the vines was gone. The bare metal hull of the carrier was in plain sight, along with a fifteen-foot-wide hole in the hull, most of the wide gap situated under the surface. Swirling and gurgling, the lake rushed in through the breach. Success!

"Done and done." Mildred smiled in grim satisfaction, her beaded plaits whipping around. "I just hope the damn ship doesn't have any—"

A blinding flash of blue came from within the *Harrington* and what strongly resembled a lightning bolt began to crackle over the entire length of the warship. Thousands of flowery vines immediately withered and dropped away to reveal the great ship for the world to see.

"—electrical capacitors," the woman finished lamely as megavolts of raw power snapped and crackled over the warship, then expanded across the onrushing lake, leaping from wave to wave in a burning spiderweb.

At the terrible sight, the companions braced for death, but the static discharge faded into dancing sparks just before reaching their boat. Easing his stance, Ryan allowed himself a sigh of relief, when from deep within the *Harrington* there came a loud bang and a hard quiver shook the entire vessel, pieces of the hull breaking off to tumble into the shallows with countless small splashes.

Spinning, J.B. charged down the stairs into the engine room.

"Fireblast, we have cookoff!" Ryan cursed, dashing to the stern of the boat. Drawing his panga, the one-eyed man slashed at the ropes holding the two honeycombs into place. "Lighten the damn boat! Throw away everything we don't need!"

"Gaia, protect us all," Krysty said in a hoarse whisper as she sprinted for the heavy arbalest.

The withered vines remaining on the *Harrington* now burst into flames like a million fuses, the burning network of electrical sparks and fire racing across the carrier to expose a score of crumbled jet fighters on the buckled flight deck. Immediately, the smashed planes exploded into fireballs, then the defensive blasters along the sides of the carrier began to detonate, ripping away from the hull and still shooting as they tumbled through the turbulent night. A forward section of the hull erupted, throwing up a huge geyser of earth, stones and trees. As if in reply, a stuttering salvo of rockets from within the carrier streaked into the starry sky, spiraling randomly.

"Just wanted to flood the bastard ship, not remove it from the face of the Deathlands!" Ryan shouted. "If I'd know this was gonna happen—" Another explosion ripped apart the night, the blast sounding even louder than the others, and the boat was tossed about on the shaking lake, foaming waves crashing over the gunwale to soak the people. "I'd have used a longer fragging fuse," he finished in a bellow.

Just then, the megaton cargo of ammunition began snapping in a nonstop discharge.

"Ahoy, the engine room," Doc shouted into the speaking tube. "We've got cookoff! Give me everything you've got, my friend."

There was no reply from the other end of the tube, but a few moments later, the steam engine took on a more powerful tone, and the boat began to noticeably move faster.

"What's a cookoff?" Liana asked, clearly confused. Then she suddenly understood. The word had to mean exactly what it said. Theo had told her that the cargo bay of the carrier was full of live brass and grens, tons of the stuff, and now the metal hull was alive with a lightning bolt, hotter than the forge of any blacksmith, which obviously meant that at any second…

In a deafening explosion that brightened the night, the aircraft carrier violently detonated, spraying out a lambent halo of debris as it lifted from the shore in a thunderous column of smoke and roiling flame.

Dropping to the deck, the companions stayed as low as possible as a hail of shrapnel hammered the wooden hull like machine-gun rounds. Several times some metal object punched through the gunwale to slam into the deck, quivering and radiating waves of heat.

Holding on to the wheel for dear life, Doc glanced backward through the maelstrom to see the aircraft carrier fall back onto the shore in a triphammer crash that visibly shook the nearby foothills, starting an avalanche. Shattering into several large sections, the multilevel chunks of wreckage tumbled loosely across the landscape, smashing aside pine trees, and leaving behind a smoking contrail of buckled doors, twisted ladders, cookware, rifles, cables, tables and a host of severely smashed sec droids.

"Hallelujah," Doc muttered, maintaining his deathgrip on the wheel and forcing the boat to stay on course. With every passing tick of the clock, the companions got farther away from the crash site until it thankfully dropped below the horizon.

"All clear," Doc shouted, swaying to the motion of the rough waves.

Prying themselves off the littered deck, the battered companions painfully rose to inspect the damage to their stolen boat. The *Warhammer* had a dozen splintery holes in the gunwale and deck of various sizes, but the hull still seemed intact and relatively seaworthy.

Unexpectedly, an aced squid bobbed to the surface of the lake, tentacles flopping listlessly. Next came an assortment of various fish, then hundreds of them. In short order, the surface of the lake was packed solid with a sargasso of aced aquatic life of every description: fish, turtles, snakes, crabs, beavers, seals and a few things with multiple heads for which nobody had a name.

"After that, do you think the gateway is still working?" Krysty joked, trying not to smile. Every inch of her animated hair throbbed, and her stomach felt as though she had been rammed by a speeding Hummer.

"Not a chance," Ryan stated. "That ship is triple aced."

"Good."

Coming up the stairs, J.B. anxiously looked over the companions. "Everybody okay?" he asked, straightening his glasses, only to yank them off and dry the wet lenses on a handkerchief.

"We're fine, John," Mildred replied, massaging the back of her neck. "Although, I feel like I've spent a year inside a cement mixer."

"Okay, the break is over, back to work!" Ryan commanded, slapping his hands to get their attention. "J.B., join Doc in the wheelhouse and make sure we stay on the shortest course to Michigan. I'll be down in the engine room chopping wood. Liana, rustle up some hot food. The rest of you check the hull for any leaks. We've got a bastard long trip to Michigan, and there's no more land from here onward."

"Easy pie," Jak stated confidently, then frowned and turned with a hand tight on the butt of his blaster.

Softly in the distance, there came the muffled sounds of war drums.

Chapter Eighteen

Watching the craggy shoreline for any sign of the jacked steamboat, the barons and sec men heard the staggering array of explosions long before the longboats crested a rocky escarpment and saw that Green Mountain was gone.

In its place, thick gray smoke covered the shore like a wool blanket, and huge pieces of what looked like machinery were strewed around amid crushed trees and churned dirt, the irregular slabs of metal oddly steaming in the cool night air.

"By the lost gods, look at all that steel!" a sec man cried, pausing in his rowing. "There must be…be…" But the man had no word greater than pounds in his mind.

"All of it!" a sec woman shouted. "That is all of the fragging steel on the whole fragging world!"

"Metal! Unlimited metal!" a drummer whispered, lowering his stick, unable to believe the incredible sight.

Then the excited teenager recoiled in horror as a wave washed a score of limp fish onto the pebbled beach. The shore was covered with the shiny corpses, thousands of fish of every possible description lay on the shore for as far as could be seen in the moonlight. Several foxes and bears had already come out of the woods to start feasting on the incredible bounty. There was even a flapjack dangling from a broken tree branch, dipping a translucent limb down to the beach to snag creatures and haul them back into the recess of some dark arboreal lair.

Hesitantly, a sec woman started to reach for a fat salmon, but then quickly pulled her hand back. Strange deaths were always trouble. Tons of hot metal and waves of aced fish. Had the sea been nuked? Were they all now going to die of the Red Cough from rad poisoning?

"Baron, how is this possible?" a corporal asked, licking dry lips, the lucky talisman of dried human tongue clutched tight in a gloved hand.

"Them," Baron Wainwright answered, her hand white on the prow of the longboat. "I don't know how, much less why, but this was done by the outlanders. I can feel it in my bones."

"And there they are," Baron Griffin announced, pointing toward the south.

Quickly, everybody turned. On the horizon, a thin trickle of smoke rose into the silvery light of the moon. Then it faded and was gone.

"My steamboat…" Wainwright began plaintively, then abruptly changed her tone into a strident roar. "Drummer! Give me ramming speed!"

As the musicians promptly started beating out a new tempo, a monstrous shape broke the water between the armada and their quarry, the mound of mottled flesh and tentacles soon rising high enough to actually blot out the light of the moon.

"Dark night, a kraken," a sergeant gasped, dropping an oar to fumble for his new longblaster.

"Flee! Swim for your lives!" a sec man yelled, and dived out of the longboat to frantically head for the shore.

Standing in the prow, Baron Griffin leveled his blaster and waited until the traitor reached dry land before firing. The .38 Ruger hollowpoint round plowed into the back of the man's head, blowing his face across the weedy grass. Already aced, the body took a single step before collapsing, red blood pumping from the ghastly wound to pool around the twitching corpse before stopping.

Not a single drop of blood ever touched the water, but the noise echoed across the lake. Greedily feasting upon the multitude of aced fish, the kraken slowly turned toward the familiar sound and gazed stupidly for a moment at the flotilla of longboats. Then in growing comprehension, the gigantic mutie started toward the hated two-legs, howling loudly as it pushed the lake out of the way.

Instantly, every sec man began wildly shooting.

"Stop firing, you feebs!" Baron Wainwright commanded, rummaging inside a sack hanging from her belt. "Do nothing! Don't even breathe!"

As the ragged barrage slowed to a halt, Wainwright pulled a small gourd from the sack, and yanked out the cork with her teeth to pour the oily contents directly into the lake. For a long minute, nothing happened, and the kraken was almost upon them when the mutie incredibly slowed, then turned to quickly return to the deep waters.

The sec men from Northpoint ville cheered, while the ones from Anchor merely stared, dumbfounded. How was this possible?

"That was the blood of a dead kraken," Wainwright said proudly, corking the gourd once more. "We chilled one several days ago, and I saved the blood for just such an emergency. It's the only thing on the world that makes them flee."

"Got any more?" Griffin asked hopefully.

She smiled without humor. "Plenty."

"Enough to get us across the sea?"

"Oh, yes."

"Dust, too?"

"Of course."

"Excellent," the baron growled, hope renewed in his heart. "All right, you heard my cousin! We want ramming speed!"

"Follow the outlanders!" Wainwright shouted, brandishing the gourd. "To the end of the world, and beyond!"

With a will, the tired sec men returned to their arduous task, grimly intent upon making the outlanders pay for their misery with the only coin of the realm.

HIGH OVERHEAD, polluted clouds formed a solid roof across the world, rumbling sheet lightning flashing across the churning banks of orange and purple fumes in a never-ending barrage.

Baiting one of the upholstery needles from her med kit with a rancid piece of beef left over from an old MRE pack, Mildred found the atmospheric display oddly comforting. The closer the companions got to the mainland, the more the weather was returning to normal. The sky looked like hell, but it was familiar, and it had been well over a day since they last saw any fog, much less the aurora borealis.

Artfully casting out the makeshift fishing pole, Mildred immediately started pulling in the line by hand, jerking it occasionally to try to give the meat on the hook a semblance of life. So far, none of the companions had any luck fishing, and they were starting to get dangerously low on food. Liana had been unable to summon any snakes this far from land, and Jak had already cleaned out the bilge of rats, yielding far fewer than would have been expected on a craft this size. In another couple of days, the companions would not have anything to eat.

"Well, madam?" Doc shouted from the wheelhouse, both hands draped casually over the wheel.

"Still coming!" Mildred replied, casting again.

"Indeed. The bastards can probably hear our engine, the same way we do their drums!" Doc yelled back, checking the compass to keep them on course. "Most certainly, they can have no compass or sextant as a navigational aid."

"They're just following the smoke," J.B. stated, sitting cross-legged on the deck and tinkering with something inside his munitions bag.

Reeling in the soggy line, Mildred involuntarily

glanced at the thick column of black exhaust rising from the chimney and seeming to go all the way to the tumultuous sky. This far out on the open water, the smoke stood out like the finger of God, pointing straight down at the huffing boat.

Just then, something moved below the water, causing a low swell that rocked the boat slightly.

"Is that a kraken?" Mildred whispered, reaching for her blaster.

Rising, Liana took a look at the wake of bubbles. "No, just an elephant," she replied, sitting.

Everybody exchanged glances at the strange pronouncement, but since Liana did not seem concerned in the least, the companions returned to their tasks. Weapons and food were always a prime concern.

"Well, I want to know how they're keeping pace," Krysty demanded, trying her own luck over the side with a spear lashed to another spear to double the reach. "Gaia, we've got a bastard steam engine and they're always just over the horizon!"

"Agreed. They should have passed out from exhaustion after the first day or so," Mildred replied, casting once more and jiggling the line. For three long days, the *Warhammer* had steadily chugged across the vast expanse of the lake without sighting land or another vessel. It almost seemed as if the little craft was alone in the world, and the companions were the very last people alive. Then the wind would shift a little, and there came the muffled sound of those timing drums again. Forever just on the edge of disillusionment, but as unchanging as the beat of a human heart.

"Liana, do the barons have any more engines?" J.B. asked, holding up a U.S. Army chem fuse to visually check for any corrosion. "Or maybe some sort of a trained mutie that can pull a longboat, the way a horse does a cart?"

"No, those all died in the Black Fog long before I was born," Liana replied, fingering her flute. "These days, the barons use a white powder. Craz stuff. They give it to the slaves when they're out chopping through the winter ice. It makes them trip strong, and they can't feel any pain anymore. They don't sleep, or even want to eat, or nothing. They just work away, laughing."

"Laughing?" Mildred demanded with a scowl, pulling in the line by hand to inspect the hook. The untouched beef was still there. "You sure about that?"

Blowing a single clear note on the flute, Liana nodded in reply. "Oh, yes, I've seen a slave accidentally chop off his own leg and keep on breaking ice, still singing a happy work song until he toppled over."

"That sounds like some form of PCP," the physician guessed. "Probably mixed with jolt or wolfweed."

Having no answer for that, Liana merely shrugged and went back to playing her instrument, concentrating on calling in snakes to the baited hooks on the fishing lines. However, there was no answering tug inside her mind, aside from a faint sensation coming from the direction of Krysty. Liana glanced that way to see the redhead looking back. The two woman shared a secret smile, then went back to their work.

Angrily casting again, Mildred tried to recall the lessons she'd learned at summer camp to make the wind carry her line farther away from the boat than she could possibly throw. Wonder of wonders, it actually worked, and the baited hook hit with a plop, then sank out of sight. Wonderful, we're being chased by a small army of murdering lunatics cranked on animal tranquilizers, Mildred raged internally, moving the pole back and forth. In her time, Angel Dust had been the scourge of the civilized world. That was, until the arrival of crack, and then crystal meth. Often, it seemed to the physician that humanity had always been trying to destroy itself in some manner or other, with skydark merely being the inevitable, and terrible, success.

Stomping sounds from the stairwell heralded Ryan's arrival from belowdecks. Dripping sweat, the one-eyed man was stripped to his shorts and combat boots, a rag holding back his long curly hair. Taking a bucket from a niche, he filled it from over the side and poured the contents over his head, sluicing his body clean.

"Hi, lover, how's the fuel?" Krysty asked with a smile.

Without replying, Ryan smashed the bucket over a raised knee and tucked the pieces under his arm before wearily stomping back down the stairs. A few moments later, Jak appeared holding an ax. Wordlessly, the half-naked teenager hacked apart the door to the stairwell, then made a bundle of the slats and returned to the engine room.

"My guess would be that we are out, dear lady," Doc said loudly from the wheelhouse, looking at where the speaking tube had been only a few hours ago. That had been the first thing deemed as unnecessary, and taken to burn in the firebox of the engine. "How far do we have yet to travel, John Barrymore?"

J.B. took out the minisextant and scanned the stormy clouds until getting a brief glimpse of the sun. Quickly, he did a few mental calculations, then checked a plastic map of North America. "According to this, we're already fifty miles inland," he snarled. "So I have no idea where we are at the moment."

"Unless this is—" She stopped talking at the sight of Liana sitting bolt upright then spinning around to stare at the front of the boat.

"Trouble?" J.B. asked, reaching for the Uzi machine pistol. "Did the barons somehow get ahead of us?"

"No, it's snakes," Liana cried happily. "I can feel them in my mind. Hundreds and hundreds of snakes."

"Food." Mildred sighed in obvious relief.

"Better," Liana stated, rushing to the gunwale and leaning dangerously over the side. "These snakes hate the water. Any type of water."

That took a full second to process. "They're on dry land?" Mildred asked softly, the words pregnant with hope.

"And there it is!" Krysty shouted, squinting into the distance. Far ahead of the boat was a rising swell of green that rapidly extended along the horizon as snow-capped mountains gradually began to ascend toward the heavens. Then the ruins of a metropolis came into focus, a ragged array of windowless skyscrapers and crumbling office buildings, and some kind of a dome.

This city was in just about the worst state of anything Krysty had ever seen. Most of the masonry had crumbled back into the soil from which it came, leaving only the bare metal skeleton jutting like the bones of a decaying corpse.

"Yeah, we're not gonna find anything useful there," J.B. announced glumly, adjusting his glasses. "Aside from rust and dust and a zillion cockroaches."

Stashing away her fishing tackle, Mildred grunted at that. In high school she had been taught that the common roach was as resistant to hard radiation as any living creature could be without mutating. Her teacher had theorized that after a nuclear war the lone survivor on the planet would most likely be the lowly roach. And he hadn't been half wrong.

Just hadn't given humanity enough credit to muddle through the holocaust anyway, Mildred added privately, feeling an odd sense of pride over the matter. The quintessential definition of the human race had always been as survivors.

"Better steer clear of the dockyards," Krysty advised, watching the pattern of the waves. There seemed to be a lot of wreckage under the water. "At this speed, if we hit a submerged bridge, or railroad, it'll rip off our keel as clean as opening a self-heat."

"Too true, madam!" Doc said in agreement. "However, observe! There is a pristine beach just to the west of the city. That should serve us well as an impromptu dry dock."

"Then we're gonna land?" Liana asked excitedly, looking across the new world.

"Immediately, my dear. A bird in the hand, and all that."

Was worth two in the bush. Yes, she knew that old saying from her father. "Okay, I'll go tell Ryan and Jak!" Liana said, dashing down the stairs, her boots barely touching the steps.

In only moments she returned with the two sweaty men. They went directly to the bow to study the fallen metropolis, and bathe in the cool, clean air.

"Looks good," Ryan announced, almost smiling. "Between the ruins and the mountains, we can lose the barons easy in this sort of terrain."

"On our world now," Jak agreed, hunching his shoulders to work out a few kinks. The muscles under his pale skin moved like bundles of steel cables.

"However, those sec men still outnumber us ten to one," Ryan replied without enthusiasm. "So, everybody get ready to run as soon as we hit the fragging beach."

Quickly, the companions raced around the boat, reclaiming their meager possessions and stuffing them into their backpacks.

Less than an hour later, Doc eased the boat through the cresting waves washing onto the smooth beach, the glistening sand grinding under their wooden hull until the boat came to a complete stop, only slightly tilting sideways. Then Doc pulled back the throttle to turn off the engine. The clatter from belowdecks immediately lessened, but the engine kept working for a few minutes before finally expiring with a long exhalation of compressed steam.

"What now, Captain, oh my Captain?" Doc asked, awkwardly climbing down from the wheelhouse. The wound was healing quickly, but his left arm was still rather weak. As he reached the deck, Liana stepped alongside the scholar, never offering assistance, but staying close in case it was needed.

"We head for the valley between those two big mountains," Ryan stated, pointing the Steyr in that direction. "Hopefully, they waste time checking the ruins. If for nothing else than sheer curiosity. There's nothing like this on Royal Island."

"Nothing," Liana agreed wholeheartedly. "But do not count too much on their curiosity."

"Well, the only thing we can be sure that they'll recce is the *Warhammer*," J.B. said, dusting off his hands. "And when they do, we should be able to see the blast from the other side of the continent."

"Groovy," Mildred said with a curt nod, hefting her med kit. "Let's blow this pop stand!"

"Madam?" Doc asked with a quizzical expression.

"Time to leave," Krysty said in translation, kicking out the hinged section of the gunwale and jumping to the sand.

The fall was only a yard, and the woman landed on her boots, the S&W blaster out and ready in case of any surprises among the sand. Ryan went next, and the rest of the companions soon followed.

Spreading out, they walked swiftly along the pristine expanse of the silvery beach, leaving behind a clear trail of their footprints. Unfortunately, there was nothing to be done about that. The nearest branches were more than five hundred yards away, and they weren't going to waste time going back. This was now a race to the nearest redoubt. Until the companions were safely locked inside, they could not allow anything to get in the way, or slow them.

Slowly, the sand merged with dirt and got firmer, allowing them to walk faster. However, the companions were only yards from the trees when they heard a familiar sound from the direction of the ruins. They turned to see a group of people on saddled horses galloping their way. Large men with long ponytails, they wore a mixture of predark clothing and badly tanned hides, the vests edged with fringe. More important, each rider was sporting a longblaster and a handblaster. Then one of them smiled, and Ryan saw that his teeth were filed to needle-sharp points as an aid to ripping meat from bone.

"Cannies!" Ryan growled, feeling a surge of cold adrenaline at the knowledge. There would be no palaver or negotiation with these barbs. This was a hunting trip for them, nothing more. Knowing how low the group was on brass, the one-eyed man debated trying to run and hide in the forest, then he decided on a different plan and quickly relayed brief instructions to the others.

"Hold it right there, outlanders!" the lead rider shouted, and then fired a longblaster in their general direction.

If the intimidation tactic had ever worked, it failed miserably this day. While most of the companions raised their hands in surrender, J.B. quickly lit the stubby fuse on a pipe bomb and let it fly. As the high-explosive charge soared over the cannies, the companions dived for the sand and covered their ears. A split second later, a powerful detonation hammered the beach, the startled screams of the cannies and their horses lost in the deadly concussion.

As the shock wave of the blast faded, Ryan charged forward, his panga slashing at anything that moved. The others were right behind his attack, and soon they were alone on the beach, surrounded by corpses.

"There!" Liana shouted, pointing toward the ruins.

Spinning, Ryan cursed at the sight of a lone cannie, bent low over his horse and riding like a madman toward the crumbling city. But as he worked the bolt on the Steyr, Mildred raised the Czech ZKR and stroked the trigger. A hundred yards away, the horse flipped over, trapping the cannie underneath. As the frantic man flailed helplessly, Ryan centered the crosshairs of the scope on the cannie and blew off his head with a single well-placed shot.

"A running horse with no rider would have told any other cannies in the ruins far too much," Mildred stated, holstering the blaster. The act had been a simple matter of survival.

"How did the baron send these men after us?" Liana asked, looking in the cloudy sky for any messenger falcons. "Or have they gotten here before us?"

"Didn't," Jak replied, retrieving one of his throwing knives. He cleansed the gory blade on the clothing of the corpse. "Just local boys. Cannies."

"Cannies!" Liana gasped. "But…but those are only legends. They don't really exist."

"Not on your island, no," Doc rumbled. "But alas, they most certainly do exist here."

"Are there many more like these?" Liana asked in a worried voice, her blaster out, the hammer cocked.

"Some," Krysty admitted honestly, opening a leather bag. "But not many." Inside, she found only dried meat. Closing the bag, she tossed it aside and continued looking for brass.

"Is food short on this island?" Liana asked, suddenly suspicious that she had been brought along purely for the sake of her flesh. But then, she dismissed the nonsense.

"No, my dear, food is plentiful," Doc said, cracking a revolver to empty out the brass. Three live rounds. Better than naught, he supposed. "These are simply men who…have lost their way."

Slowly holstering her piece, Liana could hear the sadness in his voice. Theo aced cannies on sight, then nearly wept over the loss of life. A new emotion welled from within her breast, but the woman could not find the correct words. Was this love? She had no idea.

When the arduous task of looting the bodies was completed, the companions headed straight back into the forest. Never stopping for a moment, they tore some branches loose and lashed them to their gunbelts to drag along behind and muddle the trail. Separating around a pond, they joined again on the far side, then started for the mountains. The trick to throw off hunters wasn't new, but it was the best they could manage under the circumstances. Hopefully, it would be enough.

Finding a dry riverbed, the companions broke into a full run, trying to get as much distance as possible between them and the army of the two barons.

"So where in Kalkaska is the redoubt located?" Krysty asked in artificial indifference. Attempting to force information out of Doc's damaged mind was like trying to squeeze a song out of a bird by crushing it in your fist. If you got any results at all, they would only be incomprehensible noise. Guile and misdirection were the only paths to success.

"City hall," Doc replied without thinking, stepping past a gopher hole. Then he looked around in confusion for a minute, before returning to the uphill walk.

Ryan and Krysty shared nods at that, filing away the location.

"Is it on the map?" Mildred asked.

"Should be," J.B. replied, pausing to unfold the map and check the key. Then he began to curse.

"What's wrong?" Liana asked nervously, pulling her blaster.

"Remember that crumbling drek hole on the coast?" J.B. said. "The sagging ruin that looks like it burned down after getting nuked?"

"Kalkaska?" Jak asked with a pronounced frown.

"Yeah!" J.B. fumed. "Dark night, I thought fifty miles inland had a familiar ring."

"No choice then," Ryan grumbled, turning and heading toward the desiccated river once more. "Back we go."

Once more, the companions did an abrupt about-face and kept going.

"But what about the cannies?" Liana asked.

With a grim expression, J.B. said, "We'll just have to reason with them."

Moving quickly, the companions had barely crested the top of a low hillock when a sprinkling of black shapes appeared on the horizon of the lake heading steadily for the white sand shore.

Chapter Nineteen

Frothy waves crested over the sandy beach, and the forces of Royal Island sloshed onto a bizarre shoreline. Constantly looking around in unfettered fear, the barons and their sec men pulled the longboats onto the shore until the crafts were completely out of the water.

Less than a hundred paces away, the *Warhammer* lay tilted on her side, without a sign of life on board. But then, the outlanders would have to be feebs to stay on the craft once they reached land.

"Trapped?" Baron Wainwright asked, looking over the vessel.

"Trapped," Baron Griffin agreed. "We're gonna have to disassemble the engine before we dare put a stick of wood in the boiler."

Clearly annoyed, she grunted. Yeah, it made sense. After all, it would be exactly what she and her cousin would have done. "All right, nobody go near the *Warhammer*," she stated loudly. "That is, unless you're fond of seeing your own innards fly!"

The mob of sec men chuckled at the witticism, and took more sips from their canteens of brew. Whatever the stuff was, it put a fine buzz in a man's head, and made him feel stronger than a bull moose during mat-ing season. They had been rowing steady for three days, and still felt ready to continue the chase on foot, or start rowing back home, if necessary.

Hesitantly bending, sec chief Donovan took a handful of the weird material covering the beach, curiously running the strange dirt through his fingers. "This be some sort of rock," Donovan told the others in amazement. "No. No, its crystal!" Crystal dirt. What sort of stupe-ass island was this? What kind of plants could grow in crystal?

"Sand," Baron Wainwright muttered, extracting the word from a childhood memory. Her grandfather had talked about white sandy beaches, instead of the pebble beaches that the world had. But those could only be found on the mainland.

"Sandy beaches," Baron Griffin whispered, clearly thinking along the same lines. There was a forest up ahead, and he recognized most of the trees—pine, elm, oak and maple, but not the others. "Could those be palm trees and coconut trees?"

"Guess so," Wainwright lied, not willing to demonstrate any ignorance in front of the troops.

Pulling out half of a broken binocular, Donovan swept the area for any dangers and found none in sight. Then he settled the optical device on the ruins to their south.

"Are they building a ville, or taking one down?" the sec chief demanded gruffly. There did not seem to be any outer defensive wall around the ville, which was beyond strange. However, all of the buildings seemed to be made of brick or concrete. All of them. There wasn't a sign of any logs, wood shingles or even a fragging thatched roof in the whole damn place.

Even more outrageous, lying smack in the middle of the ville was a bridge apparently going nowhere. It was a perfectly ordinary bridge of the type they used in Northpoint to cross rough ravines or deep water. But this one was obviously made entirely of metal, not pine boards bounded with rope and reinforced with glue boiled from old bones. But actually forged from metal and bound with metal. The entire place seemed to be made of metal in a thousand different shapes, sizes and types. Sheets, rods, beams, it dwarfed the treasure trove of Green Mountain into insignificance. Whatever else this voyage might accomplish, their shortage of steel was over with, now and forever.

"Don't know, don't care," Griffin replied, spotting the line of footprints leading from the *Warhammer*. Then he saw that the marks ended at what had to be the blast zone of a gren, the churned sand dotted with the corpses of man and horses. A thick cloud of flies buzzed over the still forms.

Shitfire, had the outlanders already been aced by some local baron? "Double time!" Wainwright bellowed, pulling her blaster. "The bastards went this way."

Shouting a rally cry, the barons and their mixed troops surged forward, only to stop halfway as a feral dog looked up from amid the piles of flesh and bared its teeth to loudly snarl, laying claim to the bounty of food.

"What in the nuking hell is that?" a sec man screamed at the bizarre creature.

"Mutie," a sergeant bellowed, and everybody cut loose with their flintlock longblasters.

The barrage of miniballs tore the dog apart, and as it fell, several more dogs rose from their ghastly feasting only to turn and scamper away, yipping in fear from the hated two-legs.

Sneering in contempt, a sec woman lashed out with a boomerang, and the spinning length of hardwood crushed the skull of a dog in a spray of blood and teeth. The death only made the other dogs spread out to head in every direction, then crisscrossing the paths of one another, making the pack nigh impossible to track.

As a grinning sec man spun a bolo to killing speed, Griffin waved aside the attack.

"Let them go," the baron commanded. "They can't hurt us, and we've got plenty of meat right here already chilled."

"Haven't had me some horse since the last Solstice," an older sec man said, smacking his lips in delight. They had feasted on fresh fish the whole way here, but without any fire, the sec man had soon grown tired of eating the pale flesh raw. Some nice cooked horse sounded utterly delicious.

"Watch for traps," Baron Wainwright commanded, a blaster tight in her fist, the hammer already pulled back. There were only two live rounds in the cylinder, but only she knew that.

Carefully investigating the bodies, the sec men did not find any booby traps, only an unlimited amount of metal knives, belt buckles, even buttons! They also did not find any of the outlanders strewed among the carnage, which was more good news as it meant that the bastards were still alive.

However, from the pattern of the blood splatter, most of the chilling seemed to have been done after the explosion with blades, which might mean the outlanders were low on brass. That would have been even better news, except that the horseback riders had been heavily armed with blasters, metal blasters. Every damn one of them. The weapons were still here; only the brass was gone.

"The cowards aced some friendly locals just to get their brass," Griffin snarled, kicking aside a longblaster, the arming bolt pulled back to reveal the empty breech.

"Which makes the local baron an ally," Wainwright said thoughtfully, studying the tracks of the animals. They led straight back to the half-built ville down the coast.

Discovering a set of saddlebags, a sec man checked inside and found that it was packed with an unknown meat. Dried, and salted, the dark meat was rich with the smell of hickory smoke. Stealing a piece, the sec man found it delicious, and filled his pockets before passing the bag around to the others. Greedily, everybody took a handful and marveled over the fine texture and succulent flavor.

"Gotta get us more of this," a sec woman mumbled, tearing off another long strip.

"All right, stop stuffing your faces," Baron Griffin barked, cracking open his scattergun to check the load. "I want a full combat formation, just as if we were going after some Hillies."

"You there," Donovan snapped, pointing at a group

from Northpoint. "Take the lead position. You five, cover the rear."

"Just keep your damn hands off the damn blasters," Wainwright commanded. "We're going to talk to the baron of the ville, not invade."

"But, Baron, the outlanders plainly went into the trees," a young sec man stated, gesturing at the footprints in the sand.

"And with their lead we'll never catch up again on foot," Baron Griffin retorted, annoyed over having to explain his commands. "But with horses we can ride them down in a day, easy as chilling a newborn!"

There was some shoving and scuffling as the sec men from the two villes awkwardly formed marching columns, but finally sec chief Donovan and the corporals got them into a rough formation.

"Forward…" Griffin began, but paused before finishing the command.

Shuffling out of the nearby trees came a man wearing only ragged clothing, most of it hanging loosely in dirty strips. His skin was a ghastly pallor and covered with circular spots, or marks, that kind of looked like the suckers on the tentacles of a kraken. As the stranger staggered for the pile of corpses, more of the diseased people appeared from the forest, only to stop and stare at the orderly ranks of armed sec men with blank expressions.

"Are…are those muties?" a sec man asked nervously.

"Don't be ridiculous. No norm ever mutated that badly," Wainwright snapped in reply. "Those are probably just tattoos."

"Sure look real to me," Donovan muttered softly

under his breath, gently clicking back the hammer on his Colt .45 blaster.

"Greetings," Baron Griffin shouted, unsure of what else to do. "We no harm. You savvy talk-talk?"

As if in reply, the mob of stickies charged forward, waving their boneless arms and insanely hooting in savage bloodlust.

MOVING LOW AND FAST through the bushes covering a long hill, the companions paused to look down upon the remains of the city below. Loose leaves were sticking out of their clothing as crude camou, and each had dirt streaked across his or her face. The light-haired people in the group, Doc, Liana and Jak, also had dark cloths wrapped around their heads.

This close, they could see there were sections of the ruins that were still in livable condition, but not many. Entire neighborhoods were only piles of loose rubble studded with assorted plant life. Most of the streets were only a wild mosaic of cracked asphalt, and bushes grew on slanted rooftops.

Whatever disaster had struck Kalkaska down had nearly removed it from existence. However, a couple of office buildings survived relatively intact. Reaching only ten stories, the structures stood like giants among the field of desolation, their decorative outer marble cracked to show the solid concrete underneath, and the plastic windows still intact, although all of the lower ones were boarded over.

"What in the name of the Elders are these?" Liana asked in a shocked whisper.

"Ruins," Ryan replied stoically. "Nothing special."

"But they're gigantic," she said, looking down upon the office buildings in wonder. "Hot rain, they reach to the clouds!"

"Near enough," Jak said politely, remembering the first time he had seen a building over two stories tall. That had been one of his best days, and his worst day, combined. The albino teen had thought the colossal structures were a dream, until the hooting stickies boiled out of the doorways.

"Still, all this metal," Liana whispered, reaching out a hand, then quickly pulling it back to hug herself. Ever since the attack on the cliff, her world had been changing faster than an arrow in flight. It was always for the better, but she desperately longed for just a little peace and quiet to try to absorb this deluge of startling information and new ways of thinking.

Lying on his stomach, Ryan crawled under a laurel bush to sweep the ruins with the Navy longeye. "There it is," he muttered, adjusting the focus.

"City hall?" Mildred asked hopefully, hidden behind a flowering shrub.

"The ville for the cannies," Krysty corrected her, squinting through some tall weeds in that direction.

The home of the cannies was one of the office buildings, the block surrounded by a high wall of sidewalk slabs, topped with what looked like barbed wire. There was no sign of the horses, so the locals had to corral the animals inside the building for safekeeping. The roof was covered with plastic sheeting, probably to protect the building from the acid rains and to collect the polluted water to extract the sulfur for making into black powder. Smoke rose from the ventilation shafts set among the sheets, and the wind carried the faint smell of roasting meat.

At the first sniff, Liana started to gag.

"Chicken," Mildred said quickly. "That's just chicken, not people."

"Really?"

"Really."

With a deep sigh, the woman relaxed.

Turning his head, J.B. arched a questioning eyebrow, and Mildred shrugged in reply. Ignorance was bliss.

Locating the gate in the wall, Ryan saw that it was an impressive hodgepodge of sheet metal in every color and size imaginable, all welded together into a rather formidable piece of armor. Studded with spikes on the outside, the gate hung from a massive pair of hinges, and was reinforced on the inside with railroad ties used as locking bolts.

"Nobody is getting through that baby without a lot of explosives," J.B. stated, studying the layout. "Sure hope that's not city hall."

"Quite so, John Barrymore," Doc growled in dark harmony. For some reason he felt morally offended that cannies were not particularly stupid, as if their demonic hunger for human flesh was merely a peccadillo and not the aberration of a twisted soul.

"No prob," Jak drawled, gesturing a pale finger toward the left. "There it be."

Swinging the longeye that way, it took Ryan a few

moments to spot what the teen had discovered. Then he saw the fallen marble columns and traced them back to a smashed building that once had possessed a domed roof.

"Thank goodness the U.S. government loved Roman architecture," Mildred muttered in wry amusement.

Doc muttered something in Latin, and the physician nodded in agreement. In everything, be mighty. That Cicero really knew his stuff.

"Not going to be easy getting there in broad daylight," Krysty said, thoughtfully stroking her animated hair, the filaments coiling around her fingers. "That office building has a direct view of city hall."

"Even then, we don't even exactly know where the damn entrance to the redoubt is hidden," Mildred added. "If it's located under those heavy columns, or worse, the dome, we'll need dozens of pipe bombs to blow our way inside."

"No need for that," Ryan said calmly, still intently studying the ruins. "We'll use the sewer."

The sewer? But before the physician could comment, a crunching explosion erupted from the ruins below.

In the middle of the fallen metropolis, smoke was expanding from the only remaining bridge, the flaming pieces tumbling down into a white-water river rushing to the lake. On the far side stood a large group of stickies, angrily waving their arms and most hooting like crazy.

Across the river stood the triumphant barons and a good thirty sec men. A few of them started to shoot arrows and blasters at the muties, but the two barons soon put a stop to that waste, and the small army turned to head deeper into the sprawling ruins.

"They head straight for cannies," Jak said with a wide grin. "When meet, nobody gonna notice us slip into redoubt."

"Sewer," Ryan corrected him, compacting the Navy longeye. "All right, follow me."

Easing out of the bushes, the one-eyed man started down the sloping side of the grassy hill with the others close behind.

Chapter Twenty

Moving swiftly down the side of the hill, the companions kept low as they skirted along the ruins. The pavement was long gone, scavenged by the cannies, so the companions kept to the streets. Potholes were everywhere, some of them deep enough to have small trees growing inside, and one held the fiberglass chassis of a car. Insects had consumed the rubber tires, but the rest of the vehicle seemed to be in fine shape, with a grinning skeleton behind the steering wheel wearing the tattered remains of a three-piece suit, a PDA poking from the breast pocket of his suitcoat.

Mildred snorted at the AAA sticker on the window, but said nothing. There was too much death here, and her normal defiance of the Grim Reaper was weakening. In her opinion, the sooner the companions left Michigan, the better.

The weed-filled outlines of where houses had once stood lined the broken streets, along with some charred holes that were always situated on a corner.

"Gas station," J.B. said, recognizing the pattern of the explosion.

Cutting through a tangle of weeds and trees, Ryan found a small bridge going nowhere. Bypassing the oddity, he could only guess it was something for the tourists. Maybe a playground, or miniature golf. In spite of his long association with Mildred and Doc, that was still a concept he found difficult to understand. Tourism. Truly, the past was a different world.

As the companions got closer to the city center, the destruction steadily lessened, and soon pieces of walls were standing around them, then a few telephone poles, and finally the huge mounds of broken masonry, pipes, cables, cars, mailboxes, billboards and skeletons. Mostly people and what looked like dogs, but the piles were uncountable, and the companions hurried past the unnerving remains of the former inhabitants.

Moving through a strip mall now covered with a thick growth of ivy and numerous apple trees, the companions paused as they heard raised voices in the distance. Then there came the boom of a black-powder blaster, followed by shouting voices and a crackle of blasterfire, mixed with screams and dull explosions.

"Sounds found each other," Jak said in dark satisfaction.

"Indeed, my young friend," Doc rumbled, shielding his face with a hand to look at the office building. "And may the sole winner of their conflict be the emperor worm!"

All conversation stopped as Ryan raised a clenched fist. Studying the ground, he began kicking at clumps of weeds until he was rewarded by a hard metallic sound. Drawing his panga, the man slashed away the plants to reveal a circular manhole cover.

Working together, it took three of them to move the

heavy iron disk. But underneath was a dark tunnel. As always, Ryan took the lead, carefully climbing down the rusty ladder with the SIG-Sauer in his hand.

As the sounds of battle faded away, he dropped the last few feet and landed in a crouch, his blaster sweeping for any targets. But there was nothing in sight, aside from a dark, brick-lined tunnel heading in opposite directions. The ceiling was slightly cracked, most likely from the nuke quakes that had reformed the Upper Peninsula of Michigan, and countless pale roots dangled from the curved ceiling like jungle vines.

Whistling sharply, Ryan stood guard while the others joined him in the sewer. As Mildred pumped her old flashlight into operation, everybody else lit candles and the companions started off in the rough tunnel heading toward city hall. However, the roots hung so thickly that after only a short distance Ryan was forced to pull out his panga and start hacking a path. It would leave a clear trail for the others to follow, but there was no helping that at the moment.

Reaching an intersection of tunnels, J.B. checked his compass and they went in a new direction. Twice more they changed tunnels, then Ryan called for a halt. There was a side tunnel branching off the main passageway, but unlike all of the others, this one was sealed off with a steel gate and large padlock. Going to the lock, J.B. pulled out his probes and worked diligently for several minutes before he was rewarded with a click and the gate swung away, squealing loudly.

Moving to take the lead, Krysty abruptly stopped before crossing the threshold, her hair flexing wildly. Just then, something moved in the flickering shadows and a large snake came toward the woman, rattling its tail and baring long fangs. The thing was a monster, almost a foot thick and more than twenty feet long.

As the companions raised their blasters, Liana bent and reached for the deadly killer, softly singing a wordless tune. The snake paused in confusion, then began to move in tempo to the telepath music. Ready to shoot, the others said nothing, afraid of breaking the spell. This was clearly not just a mutie; the snake was some bastard mixture of rattlesnake and cobra.

Smiling at the deadly killer as if it were a kitten, Liana tilted her head, and the snake finally slithered past the companions, moving down the tunnel and out of sight.

"A present for the barons in case they follow," Liana said, rising to dust off her knees.

"Well done, girl." Doc smiled, slapping her on the back. "Very well done, indeed."

However, Ryan shrugged and felt a new worry grow inside his gut. Fireblast, what couldn't this woman do if she ever learned how to master her special talents? Maybe she could figure out a way to order all of the stickies to go jump off a cliff. That sounded wonderful, a world without stickies. But then, what would stop her from learning how to sing to norms, making them her slaves? The one-eyed man did not think that was likely to happen, but had learned from bitter experience to always plan for the worst. Nine rounds out of ten, it came true. Liana could be the greatest blessing to ever grace the Deathlands, or the harbinger of a brand-new type of hell on Earth. However, Mildred often used the phrase "innocent until proved guilty" and Ryan could find no fault with that line of thinking. He would do nothing for the moment. But at the first sign of her controlling one of them, he'd blow her head off on the spot, in spite of what it would do to Doc.

If anybody else noticed the conflicting emotions on his face, no comments were voiced out loud.

Moving along the side tunnel, Krysty noted that there were no stains in the concrete between the bricks from this ever being used. Better and better. So, this was either a brand-new tunnel when skydark hit, or it was a fake.

Reaching the end of the tunnel, Krysty smiled at the sight of a blank wall, the plaster smooth and undamaged. Plaster in a sewage tunnel?

Kicking the wall with a boot, she made several large pieces of plaster crack off to expose wooden planks underneath. Now, the rest of the companions joined her, ripping off the plaster with their bare hands, then hacking into the planks with their knives. Weakened with age, the boards soon splintered apart, and out poured a small avalanche of clean white pebbles. Shoving those aside, at last was revealed a seamless steel door. There was no keypad, lock or even a handle.

"Escape tunnel," Jak explained as J.B. got to work again. "In case trapped in bomb shelter, barons could still get out this way."

"So we're going in backward," Liana said slowly, chewing over the morsel of information.

"Back door never guarded as well as front," the teenager stated as if it was a rule of the universe.

With a sigh, the steel door swung aside to show a toilet seat and small stall. Ryan actually gave a half-smile at that. The pencil pushers had hidden the escape route inside the lav. Smart.

Holstering the SIG-Sauer, Ryan dripped some wax on the end of the barrel of the Steyr, stuck in a lit candle, then extended it forward as far as he could reach. He could see the place was a single huge room with rows of cots, workbenches and shelves stacked with cartons marked with the symbol of the U.S. government.

"Jackpot," he whispered, easing into the bomb shelter.

Spreading out, the companions set down a ring of candles to brighten the darkness.

Heading for the workbench, J.B. fumbled with some wires for a moment. The overhead lights flickered into life, then brightened to full strength. Two of them immediately blew, but the rest stayed shining brightly.

"Nuke batteries?" Jak asked hopefully.

"Not quite," the Armorer replied, clearly annoyed. "Car batteries." He waved at the row of batteries and waiting bottles of acid. "Just pour some acid into the batteries, and after a few ticks, the lead plates start making current."

"Old tech." Jak scowled in disappointment.

"From before skydark," J.B. agreed, tilting back his fedora. "Don't add the acid, and the batteries last forever."

"How long will they last now?" Krysty demanded.

J.B. shrugged. "Can't say for sure. Couple of weeks, maybe more."

Briefly checking the medical cabinet, Mildred muttered unhappily at the poor condition of the supplies. Mice had gotten inside and nibbled almost everything, puncturing the protective envelopes, and then abandoning the pungent chems. Broke the seals then left, allowing the medicine to slowly dry into the consistency of a brick. There were some hypodermic needles still in good shape, but that was all. Still, better than nothing.

Unexpectedly a soft breeze came from a wall vent, blowing out a cloud of bitter dust. But soon that was cycled away and the air began clean, tinged with a smell of chems. Then warmth began to pour from another vent and a radio crackled to life on a small table in the corner, then sputtered and died.

Going to a cardboard box on a shelf, Krysty quickly checked the expiration date listed on the canned goods. "Oh, for the love of Gaia, this is from 1950!" she exclaimed. "We're not going find anything usable among this junk."

"But hold, what have we here!" Doc exclaimed, opening a metal cabinet. Stacked neatly inside was a small arsenal of revolvers and shotguns.

Eagerly opening a box of .45 rounds, Doc extracted a cartridge and used his knife to separate the lead from the brass. Pouring out the contents, his hopes sank at the sight of the dull gray gunpowder. Applying the flame of his butane lighter to the stuff, it merely sizzled a little, but that was all.

"Dead as Descartes." Doc sighed, brushing off the residue on his pants. "This ammunition must be from excess stores they had left over. The brass is loaded with actual gunpowder, not cordite, or that silvery stuff modern blasters use."

"Nitro cellulose," J.B. supplied. "Too bad. If the fools had used cordite, we might have found something still in working condition."

"Forget it, we're just here for the exit," Ryan replied, walking toward the front of the bomb shelter. There was a slab of lead standing kitty-corner in the room, and sure enough, there was a large door set into the wall behind, truncating the corner. The inside of that was also thickly lined with lead.

Opening the door, Ryan found the way blocked by a large pile of skeletons, most of them with broken bones or bullet holes in their heads. On the floor was a dusty collection of blasters and knives. The damn fools fought one another to get inside, and so nobody had. What a bunch of feebs, he thought.

Pushing aside the dead, the companions moved into the basement of city hall. Rubble was everywhere, along with dozens more skeletons.

"You better be right about this, Doc," Krysty said, trying not to step on the old bones.

"Right about what, my dear lady?" Doc asked, obviously confused. Then a wave of panic swept over the man. "Have…have I been here before?"

"She meant about the brass, ya old coot," Mildred lied hastily.

As the worried face of the time traveler eased, Liana

looked hard at Krysty, and the redhead shrugged in response. Sooner, or later, she would have to learn about the lapses in his scrambled memory.

As the companions probed the darkness, every step raised a small cloud of dust, and soon they were forced to tie cloths around their mouths to be able to breathe. Searching for the least damaged section of the building, they soon located a corridor ending in the furnace room. Some of the bricks in the wall of the corridor had come loose over the decades and fallen away to reveal the armaglass slabs reinforcing the walls. The sight renewed their hope. The mat-trans units of the redoubts were made of armaglass.

Inside the furnace room, they separated for a recce and easily located a small keypad set into a concrete wall. Almost holding his breath, Ryan tapped the entry code for a redoubt into the alphanumeric pad. There was only a brief pause before a section of the concrete wall broke away from the rest and slid aside to reveal a long ferro-concrete corridor extending far out of sight.

Sluggishly at first, panels set along the ceiling flickered into life, illuminating the corridor for a hundred yards. But then, just as quickly, they died away, leaving it in total darkness.

"Never saw that happen before," J.B. muttered.

"Yeah, I know," Ryan answered with a grimace.

With no other choice in the matter, the companions entered the corridor and grimly started forward with a growing sense of unease.

Chapter Twenty-One

Once, the theater on the fifth floor of the office building had shown movies, or people had performed live plays, even the occasional radio play had been acted out on the elevated stage to record the laughter of a live audience. But now the electrical equipment had been removed, the wires used to rig snares, the heavier cables made into crossbow strings.

A dozen lanterns shone bright with fish oil, extracted from the denizens of the nearby lake, and two large torches crackled on either side of the Skull Throne. Piled on the stage were blasters, knives, spears, machetes and even a couple of swords, recovered from pre-dark museums. On the throne sat an angry woman, her face streaked with blood, her clothing ripped and torn until her leather bodice was all that kept her from being completely naked. But her blistered face shone with victorious contempt, and a loaded military longblaster lay across her lap.

"Kneel! Kneel before your baron!" Brenda Wainwright bellowed, sitting in the throne of bones.

Openly bleeding, the last of the cannies kowtowed before the woman, splaying their hands on the carpeting to show their complete and utter subservience. The plump outlander had won the battle against the stickies, and had then taken on the cannies. Now they were her property, to do with as she pleased. That was the ancient law.

Proudly holding their weapons, the twenty surviving sec men from Royal Island walked around the cowering mainlanders. The poor stupe bastards had never seen a boomerang before, and laughed as the first salvo went sailing by them. Then they were aced in droves as the 'rangs came curling back to smash open their heads from behind. After that, chilling the rest had been easy, and now their massive collection of blasters belonged to the barons. Wheelguns, scatterguns and more different types of rapidfires than anybody had ever dreamed. Some of the sec men had already taken to calling the mainlander ville by the new name of Blaster Haven.

"At least they know how to bow, if not fight," Baron Griffin said with a sneer, dangling a leg off the stage.

"Good thing, as I do not plan on leaving," Wainwright stated, shifting to a more comfortable position on the Skull Throne. "These gleebs have the wealth of the predark world just lying around them, and they choose to live in one cabin?" She dismissed that nonsense with a wave. "Ten stories tall is nice, damn impressive, but this could be the ville of all villes!"

"Agreed." Griffin shrugged in acceptance, then he worked the pump action of his newly acquired remade Neostad scattergun. "But first, we have some more chilling to do."

"Not me," Wainwright declared bluntly. "I'm done

with that. They took my ville, but now I have a better one! Forget the one-eyed fool, and rule with me, cousin. Side by side!" She lowered her voice to a lusty growl. "In everything.

"We can be lovers here, Nolan," she purred. "That is allowed here as there is no Book of Blood. I asked, and they've never even heard of such a thing. Which means all the sex partners, and children, that we want. Two, three, ten. There is no limit."

So I could have her at last, as more than a secret ride, but as my new wife for life. More than tempted, Griffin massaged a broken rib, and considered the proposal. Aside from the limitless sex, more important the ville had unlimited land, unlimited metal, and these feeb man-eaters knew how to make black powder, while he knew how to convert it into the much more powerful gunpowder. Side by side, the two barons could make this a truly formidable fortress, perhaps even take over another ville, then a third, a fourth, ten! They could create an empire unseen since the glory days of North America!

Then Griffin recalled the face of his wife as she lay on the cold ground, and the glorious dream faded away. He could never rest, never stop, until the man called Finnigan was chilled, and hopefully in as painful a way as possible. His heart ached from the loss of his wife, and his rage was reborn at the thought of abandoning the quest for vengeance to a life of luxury.

"Keep it. You can have the ville," Griffin stated. "It's yours, all of it. I will lay no claim, aside for asking a single price."

"Name it," Wainwright said cautiously, ready for betrayal.

"Half of the sec men, horses and blasters and brass."

"Hot pipe, are you still…" But she paused at seeing the determined look in his face. He would never give up the hunt for revenge. "Most of the horses were aced in the battle, you can have half of those that survived, and enough sec men to ride them." She smiled now, sweetly, but with no warmth. "You'll need speed, dear cousin, if you're to catch up with Finnigan."

"Exactly how many horses are we talking?" Griffin demanded, rising from the stage.

"Ten."

Only five horses were to be his? He started to argue, then realized that most of the survivors from Royal Island were from Northpoint, not Anchor. He could push only so hard before she would have the cannies put him in the pot for stew. "The best five horses," he countered, "saddlebags of smoked fish, no meat, blasters, grens, brass, and the best two island sec men, plus the best local tracker, and the very best torturer."

Wainwright was impressed. By the lost gods, he did think ahead.

"Everybody, but me," sec chief Donovan stated, moving closer to rest a bandaged arm across the back of the throne. The tall man was covered with blasters, a bandolier of live shells draped across his chest.

During the takeover of the ville, the sec chief had aced a cannie about to gut the baron. Afterward, she had informed him what the reward would be, in detail. Blasters, brass and her bed forever. What man could want more?

"Accepted," Griffin growled, furious over the betrayal, but knowing full well there was nothing he could do about it at the moment.

"Done and done," Wainwright said, pulling a knife and slashing her palm.

Walking closer, Griffin did the same and they sealed the deal in blood.

At the sight, the islanders shouted a war cry, while the cannies only moaned in submission, still not exactly sure what was to become of them now that the lunatics had seized control of their ville.

THE SMALL SUPPLY of candles burned out after a few hours and the companions had to continue through the darkness using only Mildred's old flashlight. The pale yellow beam did little to brighten the gloom inside the corridor, but it was just enough for them to dimly see a few feet ahead. There were no branching corridors, gates, twists or even turns. The passageway ran straight and true like the barrel of a blaster.

In the lead, Mildred said nothing, carefully watching the floor ahead of them for any sudden drops as she kept gently pumping the handle on the survivalist flashlight, trying to get as much illumination from the ancient device without risking an overload.

"At least we'll know which direction to go if the flashlight dies," Ryan growled, one hand tight on her shoulder as a guide, the other filled with the primed SIG-Sauer.

"Like drek through goose," Jak quipped, his hand on the big man's shoulder.

"Thank you for that lovely image," Doc muttered, the LeMat held ready in his good hand.

Walking between Doc and Krysty, Liana kept mum, and tightened her grip on the tall scholar's gunbelt, as his shoulder was a little too far out of her reach.

Moving single file, the companions walked for what seemed like hours, stopping only once for a lav break, Liana mortified by the casual acceptance of the biological need by the others. There were no bushes in the corridor.

As their words gave a slight echo effect in the corridor, the companions stopped talking and concentrated on simply walking, when far ahead of them a faint glow seemed to infuse the blackness. Forcing herself not to hurry, Mildred maintained an even pace as ghostly pearlescence steadily increased until they could plainly see the interior of the corridor and the flashlight was no longer needed.

"Aw, shit," Mildred snarled, releasing the pump to click off the device.

Less than a hundred paces ahead of the companions the corridor abruptly ended in a wooden glen, slanting beams of morning sunlight coming through the leafy trees to dapple the smooth armaglass floor. Softly, they could hear the sound of a babbling brook and birds singing sweetly.

"Fireblast," Ryan drawled, letting go of the physician. "I had been afraid of something like this."

"Must have been a nuke storm," Krysty added, surveying the damage. The ragged end of the corridor was dotted with hard lumps where the material had been melted through, only to congeal later. "Probably the same bomb that rearranged some of Michigan."

"Well, there are no rads," J.B. announced, checking the counter on his lapel as he stepped into the sunlight. Blinking a few times, the Armorer let his vision adjust, then checked again, but he had heard no telltale clicks. Whatever force had sliced through the passageway was long gone, and fully dissipated.

"Been going straight for almost day," Jak drawled, checking the trees for any muties. "Might as well keep going."

"How long do you think it is to the next redoubt?" Liana asked, stumbling over the unfamiliar word.

"Only one way to find out," Ryan declared, starting forward again at an easy stride. Normally, the companions never openly discussed the redoubts. But Liana had proved herself numerous times over their brief association, and Doc seemed happy enough. In fact, Ryan had noticed that ever since Liana had joined the group, Doc hadn't slipped away into the past even once. Maybe all the man had needed was the attention and care of a good woman.

It was noon when they found the rest of the corridor. Smashed and broken into countless pieces, tiny shards of armaglass lay scattered across a wide grassland, the material reflecting the bright sunlight like partially buried diamonds.

A low hill rose just ahead of the companions, the sloping sides covered with thick tufts of green grass, and set flat into the truncated curve was a large black door.

"By the lost gods," Liana whispered, going pale. "Is…is that the door?"

"Oh, this is nothing," Mildred said, patting her on the back. "Wait until you see inside."

"Hot showers," Jak added in a heartfelt drawl, brushing back his greasy hair.

Advancing warily to the blast doors, Ryan and Krysty checked the ground for any sign that the cannies or anybody had ever tried to get inside. But the area appeared clean, and Ryan went directly to the small keypad set into the black metal frame on the titanic entrance.

Tapping in the entry code, Ryan instantly heard a deep vibration come from below the ground, and the black door rumbled aside to the sound of a controlled thunder.

Liana could say nothing as the pristine armaglass corridor became revealed on the other side, rows of electric lights shining brightly from the clean ceiling.

"Come on, my dear." Doc smiled, offering her a hand. "This way to a new world."

Biting a lip, she hesitated only a second, then joined the others as they walked over the threshold and out of the natural world. Feeling the sterilized air from the vents wash over their faces, the companions smiled in relief and did not react as the blast doors closed with a boom.

Startled, Liana jumped at the loud noise, then grinned sheepishly. "Sorry," she murmured.

"Don't worry about it. Gaia knows I did more than jump the first time I heard the blast doors seal," Krysty lied diplomatically.

Following the zigzag path of the antiradiation tunnel, the companions entered the huge garage of the redoubt.

While the others strolled around, checking for evidence of previous visitors, Liana could only marvel at the spotlessly clean floor, the neatly painted lines showing where wags should be parked, long workbenches lining the walls covered with tools. There was even a thing in the corner that Theo had called a gas pump. It was exactly as he had described it to her on the long boat trip. At the time, Liana had merely assumed he was joking to pass the time, but now saw that the man had told the absolute truth. Could it all be true? Mat-trans units, comps, droids? A moment of irrational fear swept through the woman, then she banished it with a sheer force of will. Tech was tech, how did a door differ from a blaster or a self-heat? Besides, she trusted Theo completely, and she would follow where he walked. End of discussion.

"All right, you two stay here and watch the entrance while we do a fast recce of the place," Ryan commanded.

"Do you think anybody could get through that huge door?" Liana asked quizzically.

"The wise never plan for what an enemy might do," Doc rumbled, "but for what they might do."

Chewing over that morsel of military advice, Liana found the flavor to her liking. "Check," she stated, hefting her blaster.

Unfortunately the rest of the companions returned in less than an hour with glum faces.

"Clean," Jak snarled in annoyance. "Not can beans or pack salt in galley."

"And the armory is emptier than a stickie's pockets," J.B. added.

"Just another dead redoubt," Mildred said. "Hell, we found more supplies at that bomb shelter."

"Well, at least the showers must work," Ryan said, rubbing his unshaved jaw. "We'll get clean and grab some sack time before making a jump. Maybe we'll do better at the next redoubt."

"Can't do much worse," Krysty retorted, fighting back a yawn.

Summoning the elevator, the tired companions shuffled inside and descended to the barracks of the redoubt, the noise of the cables and motors completely masking the sound of the blast doors opening again, then closing.

Chapter Twenty-Two

Hidden behind rocks and fallen logs, Baron Griffin and his sec men waited for the outlanders to appear from behind the big black doors. The second they showed, a trip wire would lash across the doorway at knee level, crippling their prey and making them easy pickings.

But long minutes passed and nothing happened.

"You sure they went in there, Baron?" a sec man asked, awkwardly tightening his grip on his rapidfire.

"Yes, I saw them enter only an hour ago," Baron Griffin replied gruffly, awkwardly cradling the Neostad scattergun. There were a pair of ammo tubes on top of the blaster, one packed with steel slivers that could cut a griz bear in two, and the other loaded with homemade cartridges packed with rock salt to blind an opponent. If Finnigan didn't lose his knees to the trip wire, then the baron would take his eyes…eye, he mentally corrected, and the result would be the same.

"What is?" a muscular cannie asked, holding a brace of boxy blasters. "Some kind a bomb shelter?"

"Shut up, feeb," Baron Griffin growled, clearly annoyed. What were they doing inside the shelter?

Incredibly, Wainwright had dealt fair, and the cannie tracker was exceptionally gifted. He easily found the path of the outlanders in the forest and followed them through the ruins and into the sewers, where the torturer got aced by a mutie snake that took a gren to chill. The blast destroyed any sign of footprints in the dust, and took down the hanging roots for several yards, but the cannie found the tracks again behind an iron gate, and followed them through a bomb shelter filled with wonders, only to lose Finnigan once more at a locked metal door situated in a basement.

With no other choice, the baron and his men circled around to the outside and searched through the night, never stopping for sleep, until finally pausing for some much-needed food on top of a low hillock. Checking through binocs, Griffin almost choked at the sight of Finnigan and his coldhearts crossing a field in the next valley.

Unfortunately the outlanders were much too far away to even try a longblaster shot, so Griffin watched them closely to mark their trail, only to see them open a huge metal door after touching some buttons in a little box. Griffin had no idea what the thing was, but marked down the pattern of the buttons, and the order in which they were touched. The baron had some vague knowledge of reading, and knew the squiggles were letters and numbers, but which was which he had no idea, and could not care less. He was a baron of the blood, not a fragging whitecoat.

Rushing to the hill, Griffin had his men rig traps while he studied the little box, and when all was ready he tapped in the sequence. Sure enough the massive slab of metal rumbled aside. But that was it. Nothing else happened. When he tapped in the numbers again, the door closed.

"Should we go in after them?" another sec man asked, holding on to the reins of their horses. Shuffling their hooves on the ground, the animals nickered softly, sensing the tension.

Pensive, Griffin said nothing for a moment, juggling hundreds of possibilities in his mind. "No, not just yet," he said carefully, as if the words were rotten wooden boards under his feet. "Let them sweat for a bit. Make them realize they're trapped like rats in a shitter, and starting to fight each other. Then we go in with our blasters blazing."

"What if there's another way out?" a sec man growled, his throat badly scarred from a poorly healed wound.

"With that door?" Griffin snarled incredulously. "Without the secret of the buttons, there's not enough black powder in the world to blow a breach in that fragging thing."

Preparing for battle, the baron hunched his shoulders. "No, they're in there," he whispered, as if trying to convince himself. "Trapped in an iron box."

A chilling box, the baron thought, his mind filled with savage images of knives and screaming. So, my dear, you will be avenged. Very soon now....

EVENTUALLY ALL the companions had finished taking showers, reclaimed their blasters and donned fresh clothing from their backpacks.

While getting dressed, Mildred and Krysty had both

given Liana a few personal items, along with a new shirt.

"This is wonderful!" Liana marveled to Doc later, running her fingertips along the soft cotton material. "I've never felt animal skin like this before in my life." Then her empty stomach rumbled loudly.

"Alas, I feel the same, my dear," Doc agreed, rubbing his stomach. "My dear Ryan, water has eased our pangs, but might we consider jumping immediately. Food is quickly becoming a requisite."

"Been thinking the same thing," Ryan admitted, lacing tight a combat boot. "Anybody object?"

"Fuck no," Jak said, rubbing his gut.

"I'm a little peevish myself," Krysty admitted honestly.

"Ditto," Mildred stated.

"Could eat a bear," J.B. said, trying to appear casual.

The Deathlands warrior smiled at the boast. "Fair enough," he said, resting the Steyr on a shoulder. "Let's leave."

Returning to the elevators, the companions rode down to the middle level and proceeded directly to the control room. Trying not to react, Liana gasped anyway at the humming banks of machines completely spanning the wall, the monitors scrolling incomprehensible data, and the controls twinkling with multicolored lights as if the night sky had been imprisoned behind plastic.

Ryan walked through a doorway into the small anteroom, then proceeded to another door set into an armaglass wall.

"And that is the trans-mat unit," Liana said hesitantly.

"Mat-trans," Mildred corrected her. "A matter transmitter."

The woman appeared skeptical. "And this will really take us to another redoubt, somewhere else on the planet?"

"In less than a heartbeat," Krysty said gently. "Although the experience is not very pleasant."

"Most time arrive puking out guts," Jak stated bluntly. "But can't lose what don't got." His stomach roiled in empty harmony.

"Fair enough," Liana said resolutely, then clumsily added, "Okay, let's leave this pop stand, Chief."

Chief? Mildred openly burst into laughter, while everybody else merely grinned widely. Even Ryan nearly smiled. "Get your ass in the box, Singer," he commanded in a friendly manner.

Startled for only a moment, Liana grinned widely in response, feeling accepted by the others at last.

The companions entered the unit, and Ryan turned to close the door to initiate a jump.

Suddenly the oval door to the control room swung open and in stepped Baron Griffin flanked by several armed sec men.

"There they be, Baron!" a cannie shouted, displaying rows of pointed teeth.

Cursing, Ryan started to draw the SIG-Sauer.

"Surrender, murderer!" Baron Griffin bellowed, aiming his scattergun.

"Never!" Liana shouted, stepping in front of Doc,

her blaster leveled. Too late. She fell to the chamber floor, riddled with bullets as Ryan pushed the door closed to cycle a jump. The floor dropped away beneath the companions and they plummeted into the swirling void of controlled subatomic chaos.

Searing pain filled their twisting universe, and bizarre visions of the past filled their beleaguered minds. Then the mists thankfully vanished as quickly as they had appeared.

The gasping companions fought to keep from retching, their stomachs heaving in wild rebellion. Forcing his vision to focus, Ryan grunted at the sight of the now empty antechamber, the walls a deep blue in color, with maroon highlights. Then icy cold adrenaline flooded the man, banning the usual sickness as he saw Liana on the hard plastic floor, her blaster nearby.

"Liana," Doc whispered, the word a prayer and a plea combined. The old man could not believe what he was seeing. The woman lay on the floor, bleeding from a dozen wounds.

"What now?" Krysty asked, panting in exhaustion, her hair hanging limply as if soaking wet.

"We go back," Doc said quietly. "We must stop the madman."

"Can't, too weak when arrive," Jak warned. "Get aced!"

"This won't arrive puking," J.B. snarled, pulling out his last pipe bomb.

The companions reverently moved Liana's riddled remains into the anteroom.

"How long do we give them?" Mildred asked, taking a long pull from her canteen.

"The Last Destination button is only good for thirty minutes," Ryan said, leaning against the wall to save his strength. "We'll wait as long as we can before going back."

"Doc, I am so sorry," Krysty began, but the old man turned away, his face a study in anger.

As their wrist chrons registered twenty-five minutes, the companions grimly got back into the chamber and sat with blasters in their hands. A double jump was always bad, and already weak with hunger, they knew this might very well end in disaster.

Waiting until the very last moment to give the companions as much recovery time as possible, Ryan hit the LD button, and once more the mists descended.

In what seemed like only a heartbeat later, the sparkling mists faded. The companions feebly managed to stand as Ryan slightly opened the chamber door. Incredibly, several of the baron's men had remained in the control room, ransacking drawers and collecting bits of metal. When the gateway cycled down, they stood transfixed, not knowing what to expect. Without a word, J.B. tossed the pipe bomb into their midst. The startled men had no time to react, cut to pieces by the pipe bomb's shrap. Jak made sure no one was possum.

Doc lurched from the mat-trans chamber.

"He escaped!" the old man roared after checking the corpses.

Running into the corridor, Doc paused at the sound of footsteps on the stairs, and went straight for the ele-

vator. Banging on the call button never seemed to bring
the car any faster, but Doc did it anyway. If nothing else
it served as a very small vent of his towering fury. First
Emily, then Lori and now Liana... What did the universe want, his very soul to break? Would that be
enough payment for his crime of being the first time
traveler to ever survive the hideous experiments? De-
mons tugged at his mind, but the ding of the car doors
opening brought him back to sanity, and he stumbled
inside only a split second before Ryan and Krysty.

"Do not get in my way," Doc said as the doors closed
and the cage began to slowly ascend.

"Whatever you say," Krysty answered. She could
only dimly imagine what would be her reaction to the
person who aced Ryan, and it frightened her greatly.

Checking the load in his weapon, the one-eyed man
said nothing.

When the doors opened, Doc dashed across the garage and reached the door to the stairwell just as it
opened and a panting Baron Griffin came into view.
Ruthlessly, Doc fired the LeMat and took off the
baron's blaster hand. Shrieking in pain, the man staggered backward and tumbled down the stairs to crash
in a heap on the next landing. Standing above the baron,
Doc aimed and fired again, blowing off a boot, the tattered end of the leg gushing a torrent of blood.

"Please," Griffin begged, pitifully raising his good
hand.

His face a rictus of madness, Doc shot the hand
through the palm.

Screaming, Baron Griffin soiled the floor as he

struggled to get down the concrete stairs, bleeding and crying.

"Doc, that's enough," Ryan stated forcibly. But when the old man did not respond, he grabbed him by the shoulder. "I said enough!"

For one single moment Krysty thought Doc was going to turn the LeMat on Ryan, and started to bring up her own blaster. Then the life seemed to drain from Doc, and he pointed the massive handblaster at the wretched man on the floor and put a gaping hole in his forehead.

"No, my friend, it will never be enough," Doc said simply. "But it will do for now."

Epilogue

"Catch baron?" Jak asked as the companions entered the control room.

"Yes," Krysty replied, helping a weary Doc past the albino teen and into the jump chamber. For the first time since they met, the man actually appeared to be old; his eyes were full of sadness, but no tears had come yet. Anger was keeping him going. Nothing else. Soon, he would mourn. But not here, and not yet.

"There were five horses outside," Ryan said, radically changing the subject. "How many got aced here?"

"Four," Mildred said hesitantly.

"What now?" Jak asked.

"Now?" Doc repeated as if never hearing the word before. "Now, my young friend, we get the fuck out of Michigan."

Exchanging startled glances over the old man's use of the word, the rest of the companions joined him on the floor, waiting as Ryan shut the gateway door then hurried to join Krysty. The electronic mists swirled and enveloped them once more.

TAKE 'EM FREE

2 action-packed novels plus a mystery bonus

NO RISK

NO OBLIGATION TO BUY